The Prime Minister's Wife

The Prime Minister's Wife

Susan Crosland

 Robson Books

First published in Great Britain in 2001
by Robson Books, 10 Blenheim Court,
Brewery Road, London N7 9NT

A member of the Chrysalis Group plc

British Library Cataloguing in Publication Data
A catalogue record for this title is available from the British
Library

ISBN 1 86105 386 X

Typeset by FiSH Books, London
Printed and bound in Great Britain by
Creative Print & Design (Wales), Ebbw Vale

For Bron

Chapter One

AFTER Jakie's death, Blanche Winslow wondered whether to take her own life. She was the youngest of two extended families – her mother's from the South, her father's from New England. This cousin she loved passionately was on her mother's side of the family: his father and Blanche's mother were brother and sister. Blanche liked to pretend Jakie was her brother. He was five years older, strong, with nearly black hair and pale blue eyes. His mother died when he was a small boy; after that two stern, unmarried aunts lived in his house in Richmond, Virginia, to help bring him up.

Blanche's father, Nathan Winslow, had come from New England to join the *Richmond Herald* as a journalist. There he fell in love with a young reporter. When he married her he made Richmond his home.

Jakie's house was known as 'the other house'. On evenings when Blanche's parents went out, her mother ritually told the child-minder: 'If anything happens, just call the other house.' Blanche was rooted in the security of an extended family.

Her Southern grandmother lived with the Winslows. For much of the day she stayed in her bedroom. On Saturdays, before meeting friends for lunch, Blanche and Mavis, her older sister, took turns going to the grandmother's room to keep her company. She told them stories she had heard from her own grandmother.

Most of these concerned the aftermath of the Civil War, that four-year slaughter which wiped out more young men than perished in all other American fighting. More than a hundred years later, Northerners would say Vietnam was America's first experience of defeat. They were wrong. Half the United States had already learned its traumatic lessons. For Southerners, the shadows of defeat stretched from generation to generation.

Although Blanche didn't tell anyone, she did not really like her grandmother, who was cast in the mould of the grande dame, intolerant and capricious. Slowly shaking her head in disgust, no matter that the terrible event had occurred over a century ago, the old lady vilified Abraham Lincoln for the summary hanging of Mrs Surratt, the Virginian who sheltered John Wilkes Booth the night after he assassinated Lincoln.

With the logic of a child, Blanche asked: 'Why do you blame Lincoln for what was done to Mrs Surratt after he died?'

'Lincoln didn't die like the rest of us. Lincoln was the Devil,' the grandmother explained.

Blanche never tired of hearing about the long-ago Uncle Robert and Aunt Eliza and their emancipated slaves. 'When the War ended,' said the grandmother, 'Uncle Robert called all his slaves together. "All right," he said. "You're free now to leave me. But any of you who do so and then change your minds will not be taken back by me." Six months later Black Robert and his family came up the road.' The prefix was necessitated by the black families' custom, a nightmare for the census-man, of taking the names of the white family. There might be six or seven souls with the same name on the place.

'They'd been up north to Pennsylvania and found it wasn't the way they thought it would be. Uncle Robert said he wouldn't have them back. Black Robert's wife threw herself down on her knees at Aunt Eliza's feet and begged her to make Uncle Robert relent. Aunt Eliza went down on her knees before her husband, these two women crying and begging him to let the family come back. He said no.'

'But *why?*' Blanche asked, anguished anew each time the grandmother told this ghastly story.

'I guess his pride was hurt,' she said.

On fine days Blanche and Mavis would take their grandmother for a stroll. She dressed in white. Even her shoes were white. These walks began slowly, as invariably one of the girls had to go back for the grandmother's lawn handkerchief. It always smelled of Yardley's Lavender, which Blanche liked to sniff before handing it to the old lady. Inevitably a neighbourhood dog appeared and barked at the grandmother, who rapped her cane on the sidewalk and stamped her foot, calling out: 'Go way! Go way!' This made the dog, now barking hysterically, race round and round her while the two girls tried to stifle their amusement.

All of Blanche's visits to the other house were thrilling. This was in part because physically it was so glamorous. On the first landing was a window-seat with bookshelves soaring to the ceiling, and a polished rod with a hook to reach the books high up. In the sitting room was a periwinkle blue velvet sofa, and the grand piano made quite different sounds from the upright one in Blanche's house. A dark-panelled library smelled of leather armchairs and her uncle's rich tobacco. That's where he read and reflected when he got back from the independent publishing firm he built up and edited. Being a small firm, it could publish books far more quickly than the conglomerates. When Nathan returned from his second assignment to Vietnam as a war correspondent, he advised his brother-in-law to rush out a manuscript urging the Pentagon to admit defeat in Vietnam.

In her uncle's absence from his library, Blanche would open

its door and step in to smell the room. When she examined some of the books on the shelves, she found history amid philosophy and politics too densely written for her. Once she opened *John Brown's Body* in the hope it would be a gruesome story about a murder, but it turned out to be a long prose poem about the Civil War, and looked much less exciting than her grandmother's stories.

The greatest attraction of the other house was that Jakie lived there. Each time one of the aunts opened the front door to Blanche, she asked: 'Can I go play in Jakie's room?' Her body got tingly when she climbed the back stairs and opened his bedroom door. He was often sitting at his desk, with his back to her. She would touch his straight hair, dark as her father's. After a minute he stopped his homework, turned and said something which made them both laugh. Then he took a ball of twine from his desk and tied her to a bedpost, after which he resumed his physics. She struggled silently to free herself, all the time feeling peculiar and strangely excited.

On his visits to her house, they went upstairs to her bedroom where he used her skipping rope to tie her up. When she managed to free herself, he pulled each of her fingers until the knuckles gave a loud crack. Then she got him to tie her up again.

Sometimes as she climbed the back stairs in the other house, she heard one of his classical tapes. Best of all she liked the triumphal march in *Aida* and the march from *Die Meistersingers* which Jakie taught her how to pronounce. He often played his tapes while he did his homework, Blanche sitting on the floor near his chair, beating time on the floorboards with her fist.

When she was eleven her mother said: 'We must have a talk.' These words always meant that Blanche would be told something she didn't want to hear. Her mother said that the grandmother believed Blanche was too big a girl to play with Jakie in each other's bedroom.

'Why not?'

Her mother was vague. 'Well, dear, your grandmother is an old lady, and we must consider her feelings.'

'I hate her,' Blanche said and burst into tears. She cried bitterly for days. She hated her mother too.

Most of the time Blanche loved her mother dearly. Kitty Winslow was imaginative, amusing, hospitable. Apart from Christmas and Thanksgiving, the biggest family events were Nathan Winslow's homecomings. As a foreign correspondent for the *Richmond Herald*, he was usually posted wherever a war was being fought. When he walked in the front door on his returns, it was as if a charge of electricity ran through the house.

Blanche had known forever that her parents loved each other. Seeing love given and received simultaneously gave her a deep security. Anything that seemed to threaten it filled her with alarm. Once in her father's absence, she had found her mother crying. 'You are too young to understand what it's like for me without him,' Kitty said.

Some evenings when Nathan returned from his newspaper office, and the girls were in their night clothes, Kitty said: 'Your father is tired and going to lie down before dinner. I think it would relax him if you brushed his hair.' Blanche, excited, tentatively applied his hairbrush. On growing more confident, she silently brushed the short dark hair harder and harder. Mavis got the other brush and took a turn. After that, Nathan opened his eyes and washed his face and went downstairs for dinner with Kitty and the grandmother.

Other evenings when he came home and stretched out on the bed, he told them Indian stories. Mavis had first choice and always asked for a good Indian story. Blanche invariably asked for a bad Indian story. While Mavis stopped her ears, Blanche listened, rapt with horror, to an account of a Massachusetts captain who left his garrison to go on a scouting foray in Indian territory. On his way back three days later, he and his men encountered a small party of Indian warriors. Hanging from the belt of one brave was a scalp with long golden hair. The captain recognised it as his wife's. Often when Blanche was in bed at night, she adapted the story so that the captain was Jakie, and she was the girl he saved from an Indian who had carried her away and was about to scalp her.

Soon after Blanche's twelfth birthday, the grandmother died. She was laid out on her bed, a Victorian monstrosity with an immensely high headboard. Blanche was taken solemnly into the darkened bedroom. Awed, she saw a statue lying there. When her uncle and Jakie arrived, her uncle went in alone to see his mother laid out. In the hallway, Blanche and Jakie whispered. At seventeen, he was self-conscious about the rituals that attended death. Then his turn came to go in to see the grandmother.

When he came out, Blanche beckoned him into her bedroom across the hall, hoping her mother wouldn't catch them there.

'With Mama unhappy,' she told him, 'it makes me feel sort of uncomfortable that I don't feel sad. You're meant to love all your family and miss them when they die.'

'Well, I won't miss Grandma,' Jakie replied. 'I never really liked her.'

'Me neither.' Blanche looked over her shoulder as she said this, lest her mother pass the open door and hear them.

'Why should we feel guilty just because she's dead?' said Jakie defiantly.

In his last year at school, Jakie was middle-weight wrestling champion of the state. A long and popular tradition of wrestling continued in a number of East Coast prep schools. This loner went in for it rather than football because he liked the one-to-one testing of strength. Blanche watched his matches with a mixture of worship and fear. The slow motion of wrestling gave the sport a creepiness. When Jakie's opponent got him in a neck-and-arm-lock, she sat motionless in the stands, willing Jakie to break the hold. One time she shouted at the top of her voice: 'You can do it, Jakie!' Over dinner that evening, he told his aunts that he'd been on the point of capitulation when he heard Blanche's shout and made one final effort, which brought him victory.

In the South, doors were normally left open to provide a cross-current of air during the dreadful humid months. One Sunday afternoon Blanche's parents' bedroom door was shut, and she could hear low angry voices within. As she had never heard them angry with one another before, she could not know that it wasn't sinister. Outside the door she sat on the hall stairs, anxious and dismayed at the thought that her parents were going to be divorced. Half the girls at school had divorced parents. Only when the door opened and Kitty came out looking strained but otherwise as if nothing untoward had occurred did tears of relief start down Blanche's face. Quickly she brushed them aside and went downstairs, jumping over the last six steps, to visit Queenie in the kitchen.

Queenie was the mainstay of the household. Each afternoon when Blanche came home from school, the front door was opened by Queenie.

'Is anybody home?' Blanche always asked.

'Why you say "Is anybody home"?' Queenie replied indignantly. 'Ain't I anybody?'

This made Blanche laugh, as did most of Queenie's admonitions. At times she thought she loved Queenie better than anyone else except Jakie. When Blanche was younger, she used to get bronchitis, and Queenie would sit by her bed and read to her. Both of them liked the *Uncle Remus* stories which had been published before political correctness prevailed. Each time Queenie got to the part about the palms of Uncle Remus's hands and the soles of his feet being white, Blanche would take

Queenie's hand and turn it over tenderly, so she could study its palm and check that it was the same colour as her own.

'Show me the soles of your feet, Queenie,' she used to implore.

'I ain't going to take off my shoes and stockings jes so you can see the bottoms of my feet,' said Queenie fiercely.

'Please, Queenie, *please*,' begged Blanche.

At which point her mother might walk in. 'Blanche, don't keep asking Queenie that. How would you like it if somebody kept asking to see the soles of your feet?'

Queenie was the only person in whom Blanche sometimes confided her feelings for Jakie: 'If I get married when I grow up, I want my husband to be exactly like Jakie or Daddy.'

'You don' know nothin' 'bout marriage,' said Queenie. 'You think it gwine be like yo' parents' marriage. Ain't no other two people live together like Mister-Miz Winslow. You in for a big surprise.'

When Jakie went away to college, Blanche missed him terribly. But in a year or so, with a fourteen-year-old's hormones charging around, she started dating boys of her own age and was soon in that heightened sense of bliss which characterises young love. Kitty Winslow was strict with her daughters. Only at the weekend could Blanche have a date, and even then she had to be home earlier than the other girls she knew.

She was not a natural liar. On the whole, Blanche was disarmingly open. Should circumstance lead her to fabricate some tale, all too often she made a hash of it. This was because she tried to make the lie believable by adding more and more details, each of which increased the risk she would be found out.

When she got back from her evening date, she always went to her mother's bedroom to say goodnight. 'Did you have a nice time, dear?' asked that fresh-faced, pretty woman, putting aside the *Richmond Herald*. She was propped against pillows in the four-poster bed shared by Nathan when he was home from his travels.

Blanche was not about to tell her mother that she'd spent the evening being groped in the back seat of her boyfriend's car.

'Oh, we went to Fraling's and rode the rollercoaster. And the other scary rides. We ate hot dogs and had one of those really thick chocolate milkshakes that you can only get at Fraling's. Then some more wild rides. The Tornado. The Parachute Jump. Everything.'

She saw a flush spreading over her mother's face.

'I've just seen in the paper, Blanche, that old Mr Fraling has died. The amusement park is closed for two days out of respect.'

Awful, awful. What could Blanche say? She'd only told the lie because she didn't want to upset her mother, who was bound to disapprove of her young daughter spending three hours embracing her boyfriend.

'You'd better get ready for bed now, Blanche,' her mother said in that horrible cold voice she used when you had let her down.

In bed Blanche thought of her father. She wished he would come back. When he was home, her mother's angry moods evaporated rapidly. When he was away, the heavy pall of her disapproval could hang over the house for days. Blanche's thoughts switched to Jakie.

Even though she was madly in love with a boy still at prep school, better than anything else were holidays when Jakie was home from college. Best of all was sitting astride his shoulders, pressing her bare thighs tight around his neck when he dived into a water-filled quarry.

Next best was target-shooting, she with the German Mauser he had given her, he with his revolver, a Smith & Wesson 38 like those used by police. Blanche thought the revolver ugly. When she picked it up, even on hot days it felt cold.

She knew he played Russian roulette with the revolver. 'Show me how,' she said.

'Don't be silly,' he replied.

They laughed in almost everything they did together, as if no melancholy existed.

As she grew up, the semi-sibling adoration of Jakie grew complicated: deep love, taboo and sexual attraction mixed. He was away even more than her father – first at Harvard, where this brooding loner was not happy. When he was home he took Blanche to Monticello to see the house built by Thomas Jefferson. As he drove, he told her sardonically about life at college. 'Its club system sums up the smugness of the place,' he said, putting his foot down hard on the accelerator as he overtook a truck and cut in front of it while an oncoming van blared its horn. 'It's even more self-satisfied than Richmond.'

One weekend he turned up at the Winslows' house in the middle of the night. Blanche didn't see him until the next morning. She had put breakfast on a tray which she carried to what had been the grandmother's bedroom, trembling with excitement as she went through the doorway. His dark hair looked black against the white pillowcase. She set the tray on a bedside table and put out her hand tentatively to touch his face. He opened his eyes and gave a low laugh of delight.

Largely to oblige his father, who had wanted as a young man to study law but had been unable to afford it, Jakie went on to the state law school. Few professions could have been worse chosen for someone struggling against cynicism. He told Blanche that one day he would draw the revolver in court and shoot all the lawyers there.

When the time came for Blanche to go to college, mostly she chose Vassar for its glamour and left-wing reputation. Politics were regularly discussed over dinner in her home and at the other house. But apart from her general empathy with the underdog, Blanche was as interested in the method of arguing as in the substance. One evening at the dinner table, the complacent cynicism of a guest led Nathan suddenly to lose his temper. It was the visitor's self-satisfaction which made his cynicism different from Jakie's. Jakie's had an edge of despair.

From the start she was at ease at Vassar, even though few of the freshmen were from the South. In her house, she roomed with another girl, Harriet. She was glad that Vassar didn't have the club system which Jakie had so disliked at Harvard. Except to her mother, she wrote no letters. She and Jakie had never written to one another. It wasn't necessary. She could lie on her bed day-dreaming while she listened to the Love Music from *Tristan und Isolde*.

She went home for her mid-term break, and when it was time to go back to college, Jakie drove her to the railway station. As he kissed her goodbye on her mouth, she had that delicious warm feeling between her legs.

Gazing out the train window, listening to the *kuchup-kuchup* of the wheels, all at once Blanche was certain that Jakie was going to kill someone. She'd never seen him really drunk, but she knew he got like that to blot out despair, and now she sensed he was going to kill someone, perhaps accidentally, when he got in a fight. He was excessively strong from his wrestling.

Then her fantasies took over: she would save Jakie from arrest. Lying on her bed in her dorm, she fantasised how they would run away together in his car. She would buy their food and travel tickets, while keeping him out of sight. She imagined a dozen different ways she would save him.

Towards the end of term, she and her roommate were listening to Brahms's *Tragic Overture*, Harriet having muttered, as she always did, 'I do wish some musicologist would discover who was in his thoughts when he wrote that.'

A student knocked on the door: 'Long-distance call for Blanche.'

The telephone boxes stood along one side of the main hall. From within the glass door she could see a meeting of students taking place across the hall. Then the voice of one of Jakie's aunts was on the line. 'Something has happened,' she said.

Blanche went cold with fear. 'What has he done?'

In all her fantasies, she'd never thought about the person Jakie would kill. Alone in his room he'd put the revolver in his mouth. Had he been playing Russian roulette? He left no note.

Chapter Two

*I*N the period ushered in by that telephone call, the family in
Richmond took turns giving one another support. When
Blanche was home from college, she moved into the other
house to be with Jakie's father. But when away at college, she
was determinedly irresponsible. She had scant regard for hurts
she inflicted on young males, falling in love until, a week or two
later, she was physically attracted to another male. At once she
threw over the previous one without a qualm. Some risk-taking
was what you might expect of an eighteen-year-old – driving her
friends' cars, they sometimes hapless passengers, with a
recklessness that was disagreeable to recall. Other times it was a
more considered teasing of death, catch-me-if-you-can.

In the mountains not far from her college, half-hidden by a
grove of maples, was a famous whirlpool, believed to be a
favourite spot for resolute suicides. Twice Blanche climbed over
the security fence to sit at the pool's edge, looking down into
the swirling water ten feet below, calculating how a strong
swimmer could escape the vortex by somehow getting hold of a
trailing shrub which hung above the whirlpool. On her third
visit she took off her clothes and jumped in. As the current
swept her in its contracting circle, she managed to grasp the
longest piece of the shrub and hold on against the force. It took

her time to pull herself slowly up the shrub, but its roots held fast and she finally scrambled on to the ground above. Lying on her back, panting, she gazed at a ragged patch of china blue sky between the full-leaved maples and muttered: 'I *knew* its reputation was exaggerated.'

Obsessively she played with the neat Mauser pistol Jakie had given her. She involved herself in a violent affair with the most unsuitable man whose path crossed hers. These things, of course, she kept from her family, though faint glimmerings must have made their way South. 'I sometimes worry, dear,' her mother wrote, 'that you are rather highly strung.'

What armoured her against self-destruction was family love. She had learned the legacy of suicide too well. She didn't want to do that to her family. Yet her taunts to death continued.

In the spring of her final year, the debating society at her college played host to the team from Cambridge University that was touring the States. The proposition was to be 'Suicide Is The Coward's Way Out.' Blanche knew from her roommate, who was on the college team, that the Americans would argue in favour of the motion, the English visitors against.

'I wish our team was taking the against position,' Harriet said, uneasy about Blanche's feelings, 'but we drew the long straw.'

Blanche answered acidly: 'Why don't you rehearse your argument to me? I'd be curious to hear how you defend such an asinine proposition.'

Uncomfortably Harriet said: 'If I over-rehearse, I'll lose any semblance of spontaneity. We're supposed to sound as if we half-way believe what we're saying, even though everyone on the planet knows it's all hot air and we could just as well argue the opposite. Thank God you won't be attending all this total bullshit.'

'I wish people wouldn't make assumptions,' Blanche replied irritably.

That night she had a new variation on the recurrent

nightmares in which Jakie tried to commit suicide in different ways and she always tried to save him and failed. She was sitting in her uncle's library in the other house. He was smoking a cigar which had no smell. Salvos of rain hit the windows in great whacks. In another part of the house the doorbell rang. She wondered if one of the aunts would answer it. It rang again, persistently now. Blanche suddenly knew it had to do with Jakie. He was driving home tonight. She ran to the front door and flung it open. Torrential downpour made the night grey. A man with a blue face stood on the step. 'Something has happened,' he said. And she knew.

The following evening she walked alone to the college hall where the debate was to be held. Taking an aisle seat towards the front, she glanced along the rows behind her and saw two students from her house looking at her and whispering. Blanche resented being regarded as an emotional cripple. She felt her face harden in defiance. When she looked up at the stage where the American team sat on the left, Harriet was watching her, and gave a little flutter of her fingers. Blanche glanced at the English team on the right, her eyes resting for a moment on a strongly built young man with straight black hair.

The American team leader opened with the case for suicide being cowardly. Though Blanche made a conscious effort to distance herself, several times she felt her face flush with anger. It was a relief when the Cambridge team's turn came. As its leader stepped forward to take the microphone, she saw it was the man with straight black hair. When he turned to the audience, she felt a stab as she saw his eyes were pale blue. His accent was not one of those caricature English accents. She looked down at the programme and saw his name was Luke Dalton.

He began with rhetorical questions:

'How many of you in this building tonight would risk jumping down the stairwell from the seventh floor, knowing the risk of failing to kill yourself and ending up paralysed instead?

'How many of you would be able to leap in front of the approaching train knowing you might survive with severed legs?

'How many would trust your finger on the trigger not to flinch and cause you permanent brain damage amongst the living rather than the oblivion that you sought?'

He went on from there, rebutting the American leader's assertion that the brave always faced life's problems rather than chicken out. Different situations required different arguments. The soldier who stepped on a mine and lost all his limbs. The cancerous woman in terminal terrible pain. The severe stroke victim, blind, immobile, who survived in a speechless hell. The depressive who could not cope with life. What about responsibility to your loved ones? Would they suffer more or less in the long run if suicide occurred? However close Blanche's attention, her mind wandered to Jakie. Which of the illustrations applied to him?

With a start she leant forward. Luke Dalton was saying:

'We are talking about the most isolated action a human being can perform: obliteration of self. Is there any way to soften the survivor's shock and pain? In an ideal world, we would discuss our intention with the family, with the loved one, and make our farewells. Yet in the real world this is hazardous, for with rare exceptions, those who love us will try to talk us out of our intention.

'The surer way allows no argument: write a letter of explanation and farewell to be found after death. Some individuals find that too difficult. Personally I would write the letter, however difficult. It would mitigate the survivor's haunting need to know *why*.'

He argued with reason rather than anger – except for one or two moments when his voice was icy with contempt for the self-righteous bigots who claimed that all suicides were cowardly.

It was once again the turn of the American team. Despite Blanche's efforts to disengage her emotions, more than once she shifted in her seat sullenly, especially when Harriet was making the charge of cowardice. Mostly she listened coldly, reminding herself that she'd heard all these ignorant, morally superior arguments before. She looked forward to the final rebuttals which would be made by the two team leaders. Both argued well, and when the Englishman was winding up the debate she sat even more intent and intense than she had throughout.

The vote was taken. The English team won. While Blanche joined in conversation with other students as they all filed out, her thoughts kept reverting to points made by the speaker with the straight black hair.

'Blanche! Blanche!'

Harriet was waving her arms at the back of the auditorium, and when Blanche reached her she said: 'We're all going to dinner at the Plough Inn. The English are coming too. Join us.'

Over pre-dinner drinks, Blanche looked around the room. There were about twenty students and a few faculty chattering, a number of them continuing the debate. The winners were amiable, the losers somewhat less so, all of them still wound up. She joined the knot around Luke Dalton. He had loosened his tie and undone the top button of his shirt.

'You deserved to win,' she said.

He studied her face for a moment and said: 'Why people want to stand around when a perfectly good sofa is in sight beats me. Let's sit down.'

They had just made themselves comfortable when someone shouted that dinner was served. To Blanche's distinct regret, she and Luke Dalton were seated about as far apart as was possible. After a convivial hour or two of toasts, speeches and endless wine, coffee was served at the table. Blanche used that moment to slip out of her chair and walk around the long table to where Luke sat.

'Do you want to talk?' she asked.

'Let's go,' he said, getting up.

Ten minutes later they were walking down the middle of a nearly deserted street, heading for the town's public gardens. Blanche had drunk quite a bit. Her earlier tension, angry and defiant, had turned into uncontained excitement. Swinging her arms, she strode beside him, neither of them speaking until a car's headlights drew near, a third light over its windscreen, and she shouted 'Taxi!' She looked at Luke and laughed: 'I'll show you something beautiful.'

'Do you always make snap decisions?' he asked drily, as she settled in the corner of the cab.

'It's not far,' she replied, ignoring his question. A few miles later she told the driver to stop. 'We'll walk the rest of the way,' she told him, adding to Luke who had taken out his wallet: 'It's just as well you're a rich English guy. I've only got five bucks.'

'Most Americans complain that the English always expect them to pick up the tab,' he remarked, chuckling.

Taking his hand, she led the way through maple trees made blue by a three-quarters moon. She climbed over the security fence and he followed.

'It's in there.'

She pointed to a large dark circle on the ground ahead. 'Careful.' She took his hand again.

'There,' she said, stopping several feet from what he saw was dark space amidst the moon-paled grass and shrubs. 'Don't fall in.'

Drawing nearer, both looked down into the concentric surging of the whirlpool. At its widest, the water gleamed black and satiny. Where the circle reduced to its narrowest, white froth fringed the sucking vortex.

'Would you like to sit at the edge?' asked Blanche.

'Not specially,' Luke answered in a slight drawl, undecided whether this girl was mad or just eccentric.

'Not for long,' she said, carefully sitting on the ground with her legs dangling above the whirlpool.

As he gingerly seated himself he said: 'Don't take it personally if I sit a few feet apart lest one of us spontaneously decide to push the other one in.'

This struck Blanche as wildly funny, and her laughter sounded loudly in the spooky enclave. She used her hands to push herself back from the edge and scrambled to her feet. He did the same. Together they returned on the path through the maples.

'We may have a long walk back unless we're lucky,' she said.

'Why were you so interested in that debate?'

'My cousin didn't write a letter.'

Neither spoke further until they neared the moonlit opening of the copse. They stopped. He took her shoulders and turned her towards him. 'I've wanted to do this since you first came up and spoke to me. Do you always affect people this way?'

He leant over to kiss her, light short kisses on her mouth. 'Just getting acquainted,' he said and continued until she lifted her arms and wrapped them round his neck, pressing herself hard against him, like someone whose life depended on physical closeness. 'Now we're acquainted,' he said, kissing her this time long, deeply. He drew back to look into her hungry eyes. 'Where do we go from here?' he asked, not expecting an answer. She resumed kissing him.

He pulled them together to the ground. 'I hope you have another pair of pants,' she said, laughing. 'These will be covered in mud.' She reached a hand to them, then faltered. 'So will my dress,' she added, 'and I've got to look decent for the guard on the campus gate.'

'Why not give him a miss and come back to my hotel with me? How many miles do we have to walk? Ten? Twenty?'

They got to their feet and set off, hand in hand.

Blanche gave a low shout of joy. 'I feel so good,' she cried. 'As if a great prison wall has crumbled.'

They heard a car approaching from behind them. Both stepped aside from the centre of the road and turned with their thumbs held up. 'My mama done tol' me never a hitchhiker be,' said Blanche.

The car slowed to a halt. 'Come on,' said Luke.

He stood by the car while he and the driver surveyed one another.

'We're heading downtown,' Luke said, using the local idiom. 'Get in.'

The driver dropped them near the Mitre Hotel. Blanche went first through the narrow revolving door, Luke following. But instead of stepping inside the hotel, she kept going around until she was back on the sidewalk again. Luke did the same, scowling. They faced each other on the sidewalk.

'I've changed my mind,' said Blanche.

'Don't be a kid,' he replied.

She shrugged. It was the first time he had seen her petulance. 'Thanks for coming with me to the pool,' she said. 'Goodnight.'

'I'll walk you back to campus,' he replied unenthusiastically.

'I'm not a kid, whatever you may think. I'll walk alone.'

'Come on,' he said impatiently. He fell into step beside her. 'Has anyone ever called you a cocktease?' he asked.

'All the time,' she replied.

She knew she was being gratuitously unpleasant, and she couldn't stop herself.

At the campus gate she said: 'I was so happy earlier. With you, I mean. You remind me of somebody.'

'You're not the easiest person to figure,' he said.

'Goodnight, Luke.'

He gave a sardonic smile. 'Goodnight, Blanche.'

Chapter Three

*T*EN days later, Blanche and Harriet were sprawled in two battered, overstuffed armchairs listening to Menuhin play Brahms' Second Violin Sonata when a loud knock came on their bedroom door. 'Long-distance call for Blanche.'

Harriet saw Blanche's face drain as she left the room.

When a long-distance call was from one of her family, she went to pieces, babbling: 'What's happened? What's happened?' And the caller had to reply: 'Nothing has happened. Everything's all right,' before Blanche could calm down and listen to what the person had phoned to say. Today it was not one of her family.

'It's Luke Dalton.'

'Where are you?'

'New Haven. It's our last port-of-call before we return to England. We have tomorrow free before flying out of Kennedy. Any chance of you coming to New York tomorrow? We're staying at the Biltmore. If you get here for lunch, we could eat Eggs Benedict and then go strolling on the sidewalks of New York.'

'I've forgotten how the old song goes.'

Luke sang its closing lines. He had a pleasant baritone.

Boys and girls together,
Me and Mamie O'Rourke,
We trip the light fantastic on
The sidewalks of New York

'That was very pretty,' said Blanche. 'If I cut some classes, I could catch the eleven-thirty train. It gets in Grand Central just before one. Shall we meet under the clock?'

'What clock?'

'The Biltmore clock. It's a famous clock in the lobby.'

He was standing beneath it, reading the *New York Times*, when she arrived. He looked up before she reached him and they both gave a big smile.

'Shall we find somewhere to catch a bite?' she asked. 'I'm about to pass out.'

'I found a good place. You don't have to eat Eggs Benedict if you'd rather have something else.'

Over their Bloody Marys, she asked him about the cities the debating team had visited. During a pause she said: 'I wouldn't have liked you if your team had been putting the opposite argument.'

'Good thing we met when we did then. In Baltimore our team took the cowardice stand.'

Her face fell.

He gave a sympathetic smile. 'I'm sorry to disillusion you. But if we made the same argument a million times, we'd get stale. In Philadelphia and Syracuse, we debated both sides of an entirely different subject.'

'How can you argue completely opposite positions with equal conviction?' she asked, suddenly intense.

Again the condolent half-smile. 'I've got to get into practice. Next autumn I begin studying for the Bar.'

'I knew someone who found law school unbearably cynical,' she said. 'It made him want to shoot all the lawyers dead.'

'Is he practising law even so?'

'No.'

'What's he doing instead?'

She turned her attention to the Eggs Benedict that had been placed before her. 'The first time I had this, I thought it was two piles of frozen custard. Till I cut into them.'

Luke didn't comment on her evasion.

She had polished off one egg when she said: 'You called me a cocktease.'

'That wasn't very courteous.'

Blanche laughed. 'Where shall we go this afternoon?' she asked.

'I have one idea, but tell me yours first,' he answered.

'Have you ever been to the Metropolitan or the Museum of Modern Art?'

'This is my first time in the States,' he said.

They opted for the Metropolitan. When they reached the room with Poussin's *The Rape of the Sabine Women*, she stood for a long time in front of the huge canvas. He crossed the room to join her there.

'This always excites me,' she said. 'Sexually, I mean. It's that violent tangle of brilliant-coloured gowns and gleaming swords, the women's smooth bare arms contrasted with the men's muscles, fear against appetite. I'm sure all our senses are linked to our sexuality. I get the same feeling when I listen to the Love Music from *Tristan und Isolde*.'

He gave a short laugh. 'You're doing it again,' he said, making a slight adjustment to his trousers. Her eyes followed his movement and she gave a wry smile.

When they came out into daylight, the late afternoon sun cast a warm light on concrete skyscrapers, the Trump Tower's black walls reflecting blindly like sunglasses.

'Shall I tell you my idea?' he asked.

'Okay. Let's hear it.'

'During the tour we were introduced to what you Americans call English muffins, even though they don't exist in England. Like vichyssoise in France.'

'Or Swiss cheese on the moon.'

'Shall we return to the Biltmore and go up to my room where the windows overlook East 43rd with all those taxis blaring below? We could have room service bring us a tray of hot buttered English muffins and eat them sitting in the window.'

Throughout this proposition, her eyes looked into his. After a moment's silence she said: 'With Oxford coarse-cut marmalade?'

'Naturally.'

Another long pause as she went on meeting his eyes. 'Okay,' she finally said, quietly.

A light seemed to flicker across the pale blue eyes. 'Shall we take a taxi back or walk?' he asked.

'Let's walk.'

They strolled side by side without talking. After a few blocks he took her hand. 'We have all the time in the world,' he said.

'Do you like champagne with your English muffins?' he asked.

'Sure. But what's this with the muffins? Some kind of muffin obsession?'

'Okay. Lobster and salad and muffins then.'

While he telephoned room service, she stood with her back to the room, gazing down on the street with its discordant din of horns. When she turned, he had taken off his jacket and tie. She watched him undo the top buttons of his shirt.

He made no effort to touch her. They sat down in two chairs by the window, exchanging a quizzical smile as they looked at one another. 'We have all the time in the world,' he said a second time.

The room-service boy wheeled in a table covered with a white linen cloth on which stood an ice-bucket with champagne, along with the food. He uncorked the bottle and poured them each a glass. It looked so luxurious that Blanche smiled with delight and could hardly wait for the waiter to leave before she tucked in.

When most of the food was gone, Luke said: 'Let's save the rest of the muffins for later.'

'Okay.'

She craved intimacy.

He put his hands beneath her arms and raised her to her feet. Smiling to himself as much as to her, he unbuttoned her shirt and tossed it on to the nearby chaise longue. He looked at her pretty bra and she turned to make it easier for him to undo it. She turned back and he pressed his face to her, watching the nipples stand erect. Still kissing her, he removed her skirt. He knelt to take off her shoes and skimpy panties and tights. When he stood again facing her, he stripped off his own clothes and tossed them after hers. He put out a hand to stroke her. 'You're so beautiful,' he said. She didn't answer, instead pressing her mouth into the curve where his jawbone met his neck.

Daylight was fading when they lay side by side, taking turns sketching in their lives before their meeting, as new lovers do. She told him about her extended family, though she didn't mention Jakie. Then she asked about his family.

'Almost the opposite to yours,' he said. 'My parents were from Yorkshire. That's where I was born. My father worked for an export-import company which sent him to Singapore when I was two. I had an Indian amah as my nurse, and one of my earliest memories is of her getting me to go to sleep by masturbating me.'

Blanche smiled. 'I was six when my best friend and I discovered the joys of tickling, as we called it, each other. Where did you go to school?'

'I was sent back to England when I was five to live with my mother's two unmarried sisters. In York. To start with I went to a day school. Then when I was eight I went off to boarding school. They do that in England, you know.'

'You must have missed your parents terribly.'

'Desperately.'

She lifted one of his hands and held its palm to her face.

'They came home once a year – at Christmas. When my mother said goodbye I wept. In China they both caught some exotic disease. My mother died first, I believe. I was nine.'

Blanche kept his palm on her cheek, rocking a little from side to side as she held it. 'Do you remember your sadness?' she asked.

'It's blurred. I had good friends at school, and I liked team sports. I captained a couple of them. The two aunts did the best they could, but it was always a relief to spend school breaks with one of my friends in a normal family home. Then I won a scholarship to Cambridge, and in my final year, I went with the debating team to America and met Blanche Winslow. Now you know the complete unabridged story of my life.'

He had retrieved his hand, but she took it again and pressed it to her breast.

When once more they lay quiet and were filling in a little more of their lives, Luke said: 'The last time we said goodbye, you told me I reminded you of someone.'

'I meant physically.'

'Someone you like, I hope.'

'I loved him. I'll always love him.'

They fell silent.

After a time she said: 'Shall we finish the English muffins? I should check the train times back.'

'What about taking a train tomorrow morning instead?'

They decided not to go out for dinner. 'I've become rather fond of this room,' he said, dialling room service.

Over their supper by the window, looking out on New York at night, he told her about his dream of trying to improve the lives of some of those less lucky than himself.

'Lawyers don't *have* to be quite as cynical as your friend found them. True, the "cab rank" principle requires barristers to represent some unappetising clients. Solicitors aren't under the same obligation. They can pick and choose. But if a barrister is available and financial arrangements are satisfactory, one is not allowed to say: "You're a no-good piece of scum and I'm not going to represent you." However, at a vastly reduced fee you can also take on someone you believe is a victim of injustice.'

Blanche sipped her wine thoughtfully.

'My ambition is to win a seat in the House of Commons – to start with. Politicians don't *have* to be slaves of the party system. They can truly serve their country if they want to – and if they have the power to get their way.'

'I like talking to someone who has ideals,' said Blanche. 'Cynics bore me. They imagine they're so superior, when in fact they're just plain megalomaniacs.'

They were still at the table finishing their wine when she told him about Jakie. Once she began, she couldn't stop, as if long dammed-up emotions were suddenly free to flow. Luke made no attempt to interrupt her, to ask questions or offer a consoling thought. He knew that any comfort he might give would be illusory.

When they went to bed and fell into sleep, Blanche's familiar nightmare began. This time she had just arrived home from college to find her parents having a family party, and she saw that Jakie wasn't there. She knew at once that he was killing himself and that she must find him in time. She ran through the pantry and kitchen and out of the back door. The garage doors were closed. She pulled them apart and flung them wide to the fresh air, then tugged the length of hose from the exhaust. Slipping along the passenger's side, she opened the car door to reach in and turn off the engine. He was lying across the front seat. She climbed in beside him, lifting his head tenderly to hold it against her breasts. He was not yet cold. The miracle happened. The faintest flush returned to the grey face. She had saved him. She woke to utter joy. She had saved Jakie. Realising where she was – in a hotel bed with Luke Dalton – she put out a hand to feel his warmth.

She couldn't know it at the time, but she would never have the nightmare again.

Chapter Four

NOT long after Luke returned to London, he crossed the Atlantic again, this time flying to Baltimore airport to catch a flight to Virginia. Blanche had gone back to Richmond for the occasion, and she met him at the airport. The first time he walked in the Winslows' dining room, his face lit up: the starched white linen placemats, candles winking above silver, Queenie's apron ironed so stiff that it stood out around her hips. Best of all, Nathan Winslow was not away covering a war. When he was home, a perpetual frisson was in the air. With all the people Blanche loved most coming together, and her certainty that they would like each other – how could they not? – she was at a level of elation which almost made a sound in her head.

Without being a smoothie, Luke had a chameleon-like ability to get on with people, whoever they might be. Later that night, Nathan said to his wife: 'Blanche tells me that Luke wants to make the world a better place. He's an idealist, she says.'

'I know. She's very proud of him,' Kitty replied. Glancing at her husband, she added: 'I don't need to ask what you're thinking. You've written about it enough times in your dispatches – that idealists can cause as much damage as villains.'

They went on undressing for bed. 'He's clearly intelligent as well as exceptionally personable,' Nathan said. 'I suppose if his ambition was simply to make money as a lawyer, I'd have more reservations.'

It was an expensive courtship. Young as they both were, Luke was determined to advance towards his destiny. What had begun as sexual passion was soon joined to the belief that Blanche would be the ideal partner to help him reach his goal.

On the next visit to Richmond, Blanche's sister Mavis and her husband came to family dinner, along with Jakie's father who tucked a twenty-dollar bill in Queenie's starched white apron pocket while she was serving him. After dinner when Kitty sent Luke to the kitchen to get another liqueur glass, he felt pleased at being treated as a friend of the family, if not yet a son-in-law. On the windowsill above the sink stood a tumbler more than half filled with amber brown liquid. Queenie saw his gaze.

'After dinner,' she said, 'Mister Winslow he always bring me my glass of whisky. When I's finished washing up, I puts it in a jar and takes it home. Once I's in bed an' cain't fall down, I drinks it.'

That summer, Blanche used a mid-term holiday to take Luke north to meet her father's side of the family, all those rugged cousins whom she perpetually found exciting, stripped to the waist on their farms. Luke gave a miss to the horse-riding, but joined in the swimming and boating on Lake Champlain and the barbecue suppers for twenty. The skewered lamb turning over the coals, spitting little fireworks of fat, had been trotting around the farm a few days before, and corn and tomatoes and cucumbers were picked earlier in the day. Blanche's extended family was the antithesis to Luke's upbringing.

'Your family work and play together,' he told her. 'They're like a team. It's very unEnglish. My only experience of being part of a team was at school.'

She went to England to meet his two aunts in Yorkshire. They had a brisk restraint which reminded her of the aunts who brought up Jakie. Blanche asked one of them if Luke had any uncles or cousins.

The aunt replied: 'Oh yes, there are several scattered across the county. One cousin is the Canon of York Minster. But except at funerals, we seldom meet. We are not a "family" family,' she added with a sniff.

Blanche caught Luke's eye. Something in the sniff suggested that being a 'family' family was slightly common.

At Vassar Blanche majored in both English and history of art. After graduation, she joined the *Philadelphia Inquirer* as a feature writer. She hadn't attempted to get a job on the *Richmond Herald* lest her father's position influence the situation. She and her old roommate Harriet rented an apartment together in Philadelphia.

Blanche quickly carved out a niche for herself on the newspaper as a shrewd and witty interviewer of artists and museum directors and rich art patrons, whom she managed to tease while also treating them as significant individuals. Part of this balancing act was effected by sending up herself.

Hot weather had returned when Luke flew to America's eastern seaboard to put a formal marriage request to Nathan. The prospect carried more ramifications for Blanche than for Luke. She was the one who would be transplanted across the ocean. It would mean giving up her job in Philadelphia. At least as important was the fact that she would be leaving her family on one side of the ocean while she moved to the other. Of course she would be returning for regular visits. Even so.

Much later on the same evening that Nathan gave his blessing ('before your air tickets bankrupt you'), Blanche and Luke returned from Mavis's house and started to go out on the screened veranda for some air. But they checked themselves, for the swinging couch was creaking rhythmically, and in the dark they could make out Nathan in his shirt sleeves lying with his head in Kitty's lap as she pushed the swing with her foot.

The wedding took place in the Presbyterian Church of Richmond two and a half years after the college debate on suicide. The honeymoon was in Scotland, and though all honeymoons are fraught with risk, only once did the bride weep in the night.

In London they rented a furnished flat while Blanche looked for a home for two. This turned out to be a terraced house in Lamont Road, not far from the World's End pub which gave the area its name. World's End marked where Chelsea ended and Fulham began. Blanche furnished the house largely from auctions and street markets. As a wedding present, Kitty and Nathan had given them four eighteenth-century New England Windsor chairs, their backs made of spindles carved like bamboo. Once the rudimentaries were in place and the curtains hung, she and Luke moved in.

Meanwhile she had written to the editor of the *Evening Mail* to ask for an interview: 'As an American journalist living in England, I believe I can offer a fresh slant on Britain. Of all the newspapers, the one I want most to work for is the *Evening Mail*.' She signed it 'Blanche Winslow'.

The editor was notoriously idiosyncratic in hiring staff. He had set his face against political correctness, and it was widely understood that a female applicant had a better chance if she was pretty (although the latter preference could hardly be called idiosyncratic). When she was shown into his office, he looked her up and down, beaming, gestured for her to sit on the sofa and almost at once asked if she was married.

'Yes. To an Englishman. It means I don't have any of that hassle about work permits.'

'What does he do?'

Inwardly Blanche bristled. You'd think it was Luke applying for the job. 'He's a law student. Called Luke Dalton,' she said without expression. 'I hope you don't have a thing against wives of aspiring barristers.'

'Not this time,' he said heartily, his already flushed face growing more so. She suspected that this editor, known for his ferocious right-wing opinions and his bullying, was slightly shy with women.

'Will you try me out?' she asked, resisting the unworthy idea of exaggerating her light Southern accent.

'You'll be hearing from the features editor. He'll ask you to write a piece as a trial.'

He got up and walked to his door with her, saying to his secretary in the next room: 'Will you take Mrs/Miss/*Ms* Winslow' – he grinned at Blanche – 'to meet the features editor? Tell him I'll be speaking to him later.'

The telephone was ringing when she got back to Lamont Road. It was the features editor of the *Evening Mail.* Would she write an eighteen-hundred-word piece on the horrors of honeymoons?

'It's odd,' she said to Luke a few weeks after she'd written her trial article and been taken on the *Evening Mail* features staff. 'When we first came to England, I imagined I would be homesick for my family. Instead, I found this unexpected sense of freedom. It was the first time I realised that being loved so much by the family carried with it a responsibility to them. Not wanting to let them down. Trying to conceal from them my behaviour that would dismay them. And then I arrived in London and found myself anonymous, without any responsibility to anyone except you and now my editor. It was like a weight being lifted off me, a weight I hadn't even known was there. Now I find I like the camaraderie of a newspaper office – the teasing, lunches together, being shown how to fiddle my expenses.' Like all journalists, she had not the slightest compunction about submitting the biggest claim she could get away with. 'The office has a camaraderie I associate with family. I must have been missing that after all.'

She also liked being able to spend money on something that was not necessary. After some months she was able to buy Charles Eames's classic black leather armchair and ottoman for Luke. 'As well as being the most elegant piece of furniture in the world, it's the most comfortable,' she said confidently, watching his pleasure as he lay back in the chair and propped his feet on the ottoman.

Fairly quickly she began to make a name for herself. Her editor had limited interest in the arts, but she used the same technique she had developed on the *Philadelphia Inquirer*, whether she was interviewing actors, politicians, controversial bishops, whomsoever – sending them up at the same time as taking them seriously, and always mocking herself as well. If you could make the subject laugh, she had discovered, you could get away with murder.

She found that not being English was an advantage in a country where the moment an English person spoke, all the others could place them socially, and individual class prejudice immediately came into play. This was crystallised for Blanche when her editor told her to try to get an interview with the 17th Baron Mallory, whose wife had tried to have him sent to prison. Blanche phoned him at his castle in Derbyshire and was astonished when he told her to come there. She signed out the library's cuttings file on him – like many journalists she preferred working from hard copy – and read the cuttings on the train, taking notes. She had left her tape recorder behind, a sixth sense telling her it would make him ill at ease. On at last reaching his splendid seat in the depths of Derbyshire, she was met by the 17th Baron in old tattered tweeds. He appeared to be the only living soul in this vast heap.

In his clamp-jawed noble accent he said in greeting: 'I haven't changed for you. I hope you don't mind.'

They went into a spectacular, lavish Perpendicular hall at least eighty-five feet high, where he poured them each a whisky.

'You must forgive me if I take only this. I still have a great deal of work to do tonight. After my supper I must make the stew for tomorrow's shoot.'

They settled themselves on a brocaded sofa in the elegant salon. 'My daughter has been to see me only once since I gave her tea in the housekeeper's room – which I always myself use now. I'm only using the salon out of courtesy to you.' While Blanche scribbled non-stop on a large lined pad, Lord Mallory discussed the painful litigation between him and his estranged wife.

'Do you really think it would be for the good of the country that I should be put in prison for the loss of several articles including her grandfather's wig? When you consider how I have tried to serve my country over such a very long term of years, what a comedown to myself to be in court with a tipstaff blowing down my neck, ready to seize my person in the event of the judge sending me down. I think it's shocking. I say, I must look after you a tiny bit.'

He leant forward with a quick graceful movement and handed Blanche the whisky which she had put on the floor beside the sofa.

'Do you want me to give you some food? I'm going to have a herring, which I shall split and grill myself. And I shall have a bit of toast with it. And I'll tell you something: I bought a second herring in case you would have it with me.'

As the 17th Baron cooked their two herrings he told a still scribbling Blanche: 'Just before you phoned, some chap from the *Daily Mail* rang to ask for an interview. I said no. Couldn't stand his accent.'

Her host had no way, Blanche realised, to place her own accent.

When Luke completed his finals, he joined the chambers of an eminent barrister he had long admired, Thaddeus Spearman QC. Spearman was immensely clever, short-tempered, arrogant to the powerful and kind to the downtrodden – though when he was in a bad mood he was arrogant to everyone. That was one reason why his wife had divorced him. From the outset Thaddeus took a special interest in young Dalton, as he called him, sensing Luke's self-image of a leader who knows the way forward and is only waiting to be called. Spearman couldn't put his finger on what it was in Luke's manner that conveyed this sense that he had been touched by Providence.

There was twenty years' difference between them. Luke soon looked up to Spearman as a father figure. Blanche found him extremely attractive. One night on their way home from dinner with Spearman, she said: 'You didn't have a father, so perhaps you're looking for one. And I have a father whom I love dearly but do not often see, so perhaps I'm looking for another of him. With opposite upbringings, we both want the same thing. Maybe.'

'Maybe,' said Luke.

Chapter Five

*L*UKE had been practising at the Bar for two years when he first stood for Parliament, urged on by his close friend Robert Oakes, not much older and already an MP. Luke knew he was contesting an unwinnable seat in a Conservative area, but he threw himself into it and earned his spurs. The next time he tried for a more winnable seat at Netherby. When he came up before the selection committee he was asked how long he had been a member of the Democratic Labour party.

'I joined when I was studying for the Bar. There's a lot of injustice in a courtroom. It moved me to join the party most concerned about social justice. If you will have me, I want to give my all for the people of this constituency. My wife has her own job as a working journalist, but if I am elected to represent the people of Netherby, we will buy a weekend home in Netherby where she would want to join me whenever she could. I want Netherby to be part of a force across the country, for if Demo Labour stands together, we will be in government sooner than some think.'

Luke was selected. When the election came, Blanche played her part in canvassing votes alongside Netherby's Demo Labour workers. But her line was different from theirs when she unlatched the little front gates and rang doorbells. Finding it

slightly demeaning to ask householders to vote for her husband
– it seemed to her obvious why they should vote for Luke – she
said: 'It's your business who you vote for. But I hope you'll get
to the polls and vote for somebody.'

History does not record what effect, other than surprise, this
had on the citizens of Netherby. In any case, Luke won the seat.
But across the country, Democratic Labour was once again
defeated by the Conservatives.

Soon afterwards, Blanche took the train to Netherby to fulfil
Luke's promise to the selection committee. The agent had
placed an ad in the local paper, and there were four possible
houses for her to inspect. The first ones were too big. All she
wanted was a pied à terre – three rooms plus a kitchen and a
room suitable as an office. Luke had specified: 'We do *not* want
a house big enough for entertaining. If we got into that, any
constituent who came to supper would make other constituents
resentful.' The last house on her list fitted the bill. She had taken
ages to find their house in London, but Netherby had a good
deal less variety to choose from.

A town with a population of some 100,000, Netherby was
near the North Sea. Its fleet of trawlers spawned not only the
trade which accompanied each landing on the fish docks, but a
fishmeal factory whose smell overhung the town when the wind
blew that way. Quite a few railwaymen lived in Netherby. Apart
from late Victorian houses of prosperous trawler owners and
Conservative businessmen, the town consisted largely of
indistinguishable terraces built early in the twentieth century. It
was in one of these that Blanche chose a corner house.

Expected to take on a share of constituency responsibilities,
she tried to spend every other weekend there. Once she and the
people of Netherby got used to each other, she liked being part
of the team, however tired she might sometimes be after her
own week's work.

The first time she balked was when she had got back to
Lamont Road on a Friday, yearning to have a quiet weekend at
home to catch up on things. Luke would already be on his way
to Netherby. Instead she found him huddled in his study chair
with a scarf around his throat. He was an 'armchair man' –
preferring to work in the Eames chair, his papers spread out on
its leather ottoman or on the floor around him. One glance told
her that he was feeling sorry for himself.

'Is your throat worse?' she asked, tossing her handbag and
coat on a spare chair.

He croaked his assent, adding in the frog's voice: 'I meant to
catch the late afternoon train. I've rung Harry Camden and told
him I'll have to shorten my weekend at Netherby.' Harry
Camden was the local agent. 'I think I may be running a
temperature. Do you know how to read a thermometer?'

It was lying on the table beside him. She shook it with
ferocious flicks of the wrist – the way her mother had taught her
– cursing the mercury for refusing to fall until the eleventh time
she shook it. 'You have to break your goddam wrist,' she
explained to the invalid.

Sure enough, his temperature was up a couple of degrees.

'Well, you certainly can't go to Netherby tomorrow.'

Luke pressed his lips.

'Do you want me to ring Harry and tell him?'

'Just let me think for a moment,' he croaked.

She sat down in her chair, facing his across the fireplace.

'He'll have to cancel the surgery,' he said gloomily. 'And I'll
never be forgiven if I'm not there to give away the prizes at
Medway School.'

They both sat silent, thinking about all those disappointed
girls and boys.

'Would you go in my place?' asked Luke.

She gave a deep sigh. 'Will it really make that much

difference?' she asked. 'As I walked in the house tonight I thought how wonderful it was to be home for the weekend.'

Luke said: 'Have you no sense of duty?'

Blanche had never been able to stand the word 'duty'. Responsibility, yes. Obligation, yes. But duty sent her up the wall.

'No,' she said sharply. 'Why should I? You're the one elected as MP, not me. Anyhow I hate the word duty. If you'd asked me to go to Netherby out of love for you, I would have done so readily. But I've not the faintest intention of going anywhere when you say it's my duty.'

She got up, snatched her bag and coat from the chair and left the room. Their bedroom was beside the study, and when she entered it she banged the door behind her. Not long afterwards, however, he heard the door open and footsteps padding down the stairs to the kitchen.

Some minutes after that, he appeared at the kitchen door, wearing a conciliatory sheepish smile. Blanche was cooking.

'Will you go to Netherby tomorrow out of love for me?'

Late one afternoon in the office, Blanche was writing up the interview she had done earlier in the day. Since morning she'd had recurrent stabbing pains in her stomach. As they got worse, she left her desk long enough to beg some more Alka Seltzer from the theatre critic.

'You're awfully pale,' he said. 'You ought to go home.'

'I've got to finish this goddam piece. I promised the editor he'd have it for tomorrow's paper.'

Setting her jaw, Blanche finally reached the end and printed it out to take to him. The editor liked to get his first impression from hard copy. By now she was in such pain that she had to concentrate on putting one foot before the other. She handed her copy to the editor's secretary.

'Tell him I'm unwell and am going straight to my GP before her surgery closes.'

'You look awful. Don't you want someone to come down to the street with you and get a taxi?'

'I'll be okay when I get some fresh air,' said Blanche.

Hailing a taxi, she gave the surgery address to the driver before the pain grew so excruciating that she squatted on the taxi floor in an effort to relieve it.

'We're here.' His voice seemed far away.

'I can't walk,' she said. 'Will you get the doctor to come out here?'

The GP appeared, took one look and asked the driver and a passing male pedestrian to help get Blanche into the surgery. By now she was inside the pain and oblivious to all else.

'You have acute appendicitis,' she heard the GP's distant voice say. 'I think it has already burst. We've called for an ambulance. Do you want me to give you morphine?'

'Yes.'

Within moments of the needle entering, the agony began to recede. Blanche would have no recollection of the ambulance or the hospital except when a nurse firmly forced her to swallow a tube.

At some point Luke's face appeared. She wondered why he looked so odd.

The appendix had indeed burst, and she had septicaemia. She was too ill to be told how ill she was. Except for Luke, she could have no visitors. He read her a letter from her editor: 'Your piece was hilarious. We gave it front-page billing. You must have been in terrible pain when you wrote it. Don't dream of coming back to work until you are fully recovered.'

When she could go home, the au pair was looking after things there. Various friends stopped by. Julie Oakes came in regularly. She and Robert were the Daltons' favourite couple. Until

Blanche's illness, the four dined together every few weeks, usually at home, exchanging political gossip – who was in, who was on the way out.

'Wouldn't it be nice,' Blanche said to Julie one day at Lamont Road, 'if our husbands proved that longtime friendship needn't be damaged by inevitable rivalries?'

At this time, Robert Oakes was Opposition spokesman for the Treasury. Luke waited impatiently for the moment he also would be in the shadow cabinet, as Opposition front bench spokesmen were called. Each autumn Demo Labour's members held a kind of beauty contest in which the top twelve chosen by ballot were guaranteed a place on the shadow cabinet. Luke was an effective debater who did not hesitate to speak out on controversial subjects. He was popular amongst his colleagues, most of whom were not turned off him when, after a particularly forceful speech against the Conservative government, the press talked of him as 'a future prime minister'.

'It's a footling remark,' he told Blanche. 'There must be thirty people labelled for each one who actually makes it.'

Nonetheless, he was vastly pleased when MPs and the press spoke of him as one of three Demo Labour MPs who were going far.

The third, Stanley Fox, was already Opposition spokesman for Foreign Affairs. Fox was a loner, widely admired for his acumen but trusted by few.

'All MPs are potential rivals,' Julie said to Blanche. They were having a glass of wine in the Daltons' bedroom. 'It complicates things personally only when they are close friends. I couldn't care less what job goes to that creep Stanley Fox.' She began to laugh. 'He's never forgiven *Robert*, if you please, for a BBC programme I helped produce, which Fox found insufficiently respectful of his great brain. I daresay Robert would feel sick if Fox eventually succeeded Simon as leader.'

Simon Steadfast was the leader of Democratic Labour. Fourteen years older than Robert Oakes, he looked on the younger man as his successor some day in the unknown future. Robert, rightly, had a high opinion of his own intelligence and leadership qualities and thought of himself as a prime minister-in-waiting. This added to the personal hostility between him and Stanley Fox, who had an even higher opinion of himself. Luke believed that Robert would one day be at Number Ten, which made it a good bet that he himself would be made Foreign Secretary, the job he most wanted until – who knows? He might succeed Robert as PM one day. As a famous politician put it fifteen years earlier, any MP who says he doesn't dream of becoming prime minister is lying.

Julie Oakes had cut back on her job with the BBC, working there only part-time so she could be at home when the Oakes's two young sons returned from school. Neither parent believed in sending children away to boarding school. Despite Robert's driving ambition, they were an unusually close family.

Two months after Blanche had staggered from the *Evening Mail* building, she was well and back at work. Her first social engagement was a restaurant dinner with Julie and Robert *à quatre*. The top twelve MPs elected by the party had been announced at its annual conference a few weeks earlier. The leader, Simon Steadfast, had made his appointments.

Robert lifted his glass to both Daltons.

'Here's to Blanche. Long may she thrive. And here's to the new Opposition spokesman for Defence. Long may his ascent continue – so long as he doesn't cast his eye on my job,' Robert added with a chuckle.

Chapter Six

As Opposition spokesman for Defence, Luke made Max Murphy MP his parliamentary private secretary, otherwise known as bag-carrier. Jaspar Byatt was the head of public relations for Democratic Labour, and he and Max trusted each other. As Demo Labour's chief spin-doctor, Jaspar was a magnet for Westminster gossip.

The two men now became good friends of both Daltons. Blanche liked it when Luke would ring her at the paper to say: 'We can escape from the House this evening. Any chance you could produce something from the freezer when you get home from work? I know it's trouble for you, but it'd be so much more agreeable than going out to a restaurant.'

The Daltons had a big Victorian dining table in their kitchen. Luke liked to be in the same room as Blanche when she was at the pots and pans. When they had guests he preferred general conversation to pairing off, and they stayed at table to go on talking over coffee.

That was the stage they had reached this evening when Jaspar said to Blanche: 'Have you and Luke discussed when you should switch to another newspaper?'

She and Luke met one another's eyes and each gave a small smile. 'I'm enjoying writing for the *Evening Mail*.'

Jaspar drank some brandy before he said: 'The time is going to come when it will be an embarrassment for Luke's wife to be writing for a Conservative paper.'

'But I *like* writing across the grain of a newspaper,' Blanche replied. 'My editor has never tried to pressurise me into toeing the editorial line. Anyhow, I write under my own name.'

Jaspar put his elbows on the table, his chin in his hands, looking thoughtful. He had no intention of dropping the matter. 'You've made too big a name for yourself in journalism for most people not to know you're married to an MP, even if they don't know he's a shadow minister. If Luke's career goes as fast as I personally believe it will, and Demo Labour is on the verge of a breakthrough to power, you'll have to reconsider your position, Blanche.'

She turned to Luke. 'Do you feel like that?'

'I take Jaspar's point,' he replied. 'It's all right while I'm an Opposition spokesman. But we'd be asking for trouble if I was in the Cabinet and my wife was writing for the enemy. However, I don't intend thinking about it until the situation actually arises.' He pushed back his chair. 'We've all got a busy day tomorrow.'

The two guests departed and Blanche followed Luke up to his study and sat down in her chair.

'It gives me an odd feeling,' she said, 'to have my job discussed as if I was merely your appendage and my work should automatically depend on what's convenient to Democratic Labour. It's not as if I were a politician.'

'I meant what I said downstairs, Blanche. I'm not going to think about any conflict of interest until I have to.'

'That sounds ominous,' she said aggressively.

'And I'm certainly not going to discuss something that means so much to you,' he said equably, 'when it's late and we've had a fair bit to drink. Let's go to bed.

*

Thaddeus Spearman QC lived in a flat high up in a prestigious block overlooking the Thames, the lift opening directly into his entrance hall. The Daltons were met by an exceptionally pretty young woman who told them Mr Spearman was on the phone. Dressed in black stockings and high heels and a short black dress – not quite a mini-skirt, but nearly – she wore a becoming white ruffled cap and maid's frilly apron. Blanche caught Luke's eye. Everyone knew that Thaddeus fancied the ladies. But this was the first time she'd seen one of them in this guise.

In his drawing room Thaddeus flapped his hand from where he lounged in a swivel leather armchair, revolving it from side to side while he held the phone to an ear. The vision took their order for drinks, but before she could leave the room Thaddeus called out to Blanche: 'Get Bella to make you a martini cocktail. She's the only person in Britain who doesn't shake it and bruise the gin.'

'In that case, let's have two,' said Luke, laughing. He joined Blanche at the wall of glass looking across the water to the Houses of Parliament.

Finishing his call, Thaddeus joined them, putting an arm around Blanche's shoulders as he kissed her on the mouth.

'You were not created to receive kisses on the cheek,' he told her fondly. To Luke he said: 'Well, well, young Dalton. I can't go to my club without someone telling me you are the coming man. Ah.'

Bella had appeared with two gin martini cocktails straight up with a twist of lemon. Thaddeus retrieved his whisky, and the three of them settled in comfortable chairs around a low table by the vast window. Luke had to leave in an hour and a half to be interviewed on BBC2 about the Conservatives' defence policy.

'Let's not hurry,' he said. 'If I skip the pud, I'll be in good time. Blanche can stay and finish her dinner and I'll pick her up after the programme.'

'You'll be surprised to discover that Bella is also an excellent cook,' said Thaddeus.

'Does she live in?' asked Luke, looking innocent.

'Only sometimes,' Thaddeus replied and changed the subject to Blanche's job just as a faint ringing came from Luke's jacket pocket.

'Yes?' he said curtly into his mobile.

'Sorry to bother you,' said Max. 'The presenter wants to change the order of transmission, and it suits our purpose if you come on at the start. Can you reach the studio half an hour earlier?'

'You get the car here and I'll get in it,' said Luke and put away the phone. 'Forgive me, Thaddeus, if I leave a bit before I expected.'

At once Thaddeus went on to Blanche: 'You must have already considered that as Luke becomes better known there will be difficulties entailed in his wife writing for a rabidly Conservative newspaper.'

'Groan,' she replied.

'It isn't as if it were the only paper in London. You are lucky to live in a land where more people read the press than in any other western country. You'll have no trouble getting a job with a centre-left or centre-right position. Either would be acceptable. I'm sure Luke agrees.'

'When Jasper Byatt raised it before,' Luke answered, 'I said I wasn't going to think about it until the situation actually arose.'

'And?' said Blanche a little sullenly.

'And it hasn't.'

Ostentatiously she said nothing.

The car arrived part way through the main course. She and Thaddeus continued with their dinner. The vision tripped round the table, pouring out more claret.

'You've been in London now for twelve years, Blanche. Are

you glad or sorry that you came?'

'Most of the time I'm glad. "On balance . . ." as my mother puts it.'

'The secret to contentment is in those two words,' Thaddeus replied. He sipped his wine thoughtfully before saying: 'You don't seem very pleased at the prospect of changing jobs.'

'It's being told that I'll *have* to change jobs which bugs me.'

'Do you see the reason why it is likely to arise?'

A grudging 'Yes.'

'One other thing on this disagreeable matter. Instead of getting a staff job, you should negotiate a contract as a freelance. It will allow you much more freedom of movement, freedom to accept an assignment or turn it down.'

'That part isn't disagreeable,' she answered. 'Some of the pleasure of going to an office was the sense of comradeship, despite jealous rivalries. That no longer means so much to me; with my growing involvement in politics, I have that comradeship with Luke's supporters.'

'That's settled then.'

Neither spoke further until Thaddeus asked: 'Do you spend many evenings alone?'

'I suppose so,' Blanche replied. 'Actually, I like some solitude.'

'Solitude is one thing. Feeling isolated is another. Have you thought about having children?'

'A lot. It just hasn't happened.'

Thaddeus lifted his brows enquiringly.

After a few moments Blanche said: 'Remember when I was very ill – when my appendix burst and I got acute blood poisoning? No one told me that a side effect of peritonitis is that my ovaries are now blocked. Eventually I went to a well-known gynaecologist in Harley Street who put me in the picture.'

'Can't modern science unblock them?' asked Thaddeus.

Blanche looked away, then said; 'I'm having a go at that. With this same gynaecologist. Good thing I have confidence in her. It's pretty painful.'

'Why can't it be done under anaesthetic?'

'Beats me.'

'I have a view that gynaecologists – female or male – possess a considerable streak of sadism.'

Blanche thought about this but didn't wish to pursue it.

Without transition Thaddeus asked: 'Do you like opera? One reason I was never attracted to going into the House of Commons was those balls-aching hours. If I'd got to opera once a fortnight I'd have been lucky. *Don Carlos* will be at the English National Opera all next week. On Friday Luke will get the whip for next week's business. On whatever night there is a three-line whip, you and I should go to *Don Carlos*. Will you ring me as soon as you know which evening your husband will be incarcerated with those drone MPs?'

Tuesday night had three black lines drawn beneath it, denoting that all MPs must be present to vote without fail. Blanche went to the opera house straight from work. Thaddeus was waiting in the lobby.

'Just time for a glass of wine at the bar,' he said, tucking her arm through his. 'They have a bottle of Cloudy Bay waiting on ice for us.'

He nodded genially to half a dozen other opera-goers, introducing Blanche to the director of the National Theatre: 'Have you met the distinguished profile-writer, Blanche Winslow?' He made no mention of her employer. 'She's also the wife of an MP who's going far – Luke Dalton. Isn't she lovely?'

Blanche felt proud of Luke, and proud of being with Thaddeus this evening. He made everything fun. When they took their seats in a box near the stage, she saw several people in the stalls turn to look at them and then say something to each other.

As the lights dimmed and the curtain rose, she experienced the same tingling sensation as when she and Mavis had gone with their father to the Metropolitan Opera House to see *Tristan und Isolde*. Their mother didn't accompany them on that trip to New York, saying: 'You two girls see so little of your father that I think it would be nice if it were just the three of you.'

When they left the opera house, Blanche was still keyed up by the stimulation of all her senses. Sitting beside Thaddeus in the back seat of his car, she was very aware of his physical nearness, and sensed his awareness of hers. What added a further frisson was the fact she saw him as a father figure. Halfway home he rested his hand on her knee. This is what her father often did when she was sitting beside him consulting him about something. But with her father she was comfortable. With Thaddeus she felt self-conscious and vaguely uneasy. Yet if she moved his hand off her knee, it would be giving the gesture a significance she felt it didn't really warrant. He kept it resting there until the driver pulled up to her front door.

'Don't nag her,' Luke said to Jaspar. 'You've made the point. So has Thaddeus. She won't have forgotten any of it. Wait and see.'

Jaspar was an impatient man. He had wanted Blanche to look for a different newspaper employer at once. Out of the blue assistance now came from another quarter. The editor of the *Nation* rang Blanche to ask her out to lunch with him. She knew him only slightly. They met at L'Escargot and he quickly came to the point. He liked her work and would pay her more than she was getting at the *Evening Mail*. He didn't need to tell her that the *Nation* was centre-right. 'Practically left-wing compared with the *Evening Mail*,' she thought to herself.

On returning to her office she steeled herself to tell her editor.

'I don't know what it says about my character,' she told him, 'but after a while I want to move on to pastures new.'

'I'll tell you the real reason,' he replied, grinning maliciously. 'Luke Dalton doesn't want his wife writing for a right-wing paper.'

'I suppose he might prefer it,' she replied, blushing, 'if I wrote for a more centre paper. But *I'm* the one who decides about my career.'

'Someone mentioned you were lunching at L'Escargot earlier this week with the editor of the *Nation*.'

God, how she hated blushing. 'I'm thinking of giving it a try,' she said.

'You'll regret it.'

Chapter Seven

*I*T was the third fine summer in a row, balmy at seven in the evening. Max Murphy and Jaspar Byatt were having a drink on the House of Commons terrace with the Washington journalist Abe Dixon.

'He's the coming man,' Jaspar said to Abe, his eyes on the Daltons standing farther along at the terrace edge, watching a tug assist a barge downstream.

'How long has he been in the House?' Abe asked Jaspar.

'Seven years. Americans have never heard of any British politician except Margaret Thatcher – and the lamented Princess Diana, whom I include as an honorary politician. But I predict that before this decade is out, the name of Luke Dalton will be instantly recognisable, even on your side of the Atlantic.'

'How's he going to get the leadership?' asked Abe, who had become head of the *Washington Tribune*'s London Bureau a few months earlier. 'Since I've been here, the Opposition spokesman who's had the most serious coverage is Robert Oakes. And Stanley Fox is the best performer in the Commons.'

'We're talking off the record, aren't we?' Max interrupted, taking no chances. 'Fox's reputation for slipperiness will tell against him. And Robert Oakes gives hostages to fortune. He spells out specific policies he will introduce when Democratic

Labour gets into government.'

'If,' said Abe cheerfully.

'Should something happen to our leader, God forbid,' Jasper said in his supercilious voice, 'and Oakes succeeds him, you're right about "if" he could win an election. Except for the liberal chattering classes, most British voters are bored stiff by politics. Luke Dalton doesn't burden himself with off-putting policy detail. He stands for decency, for hard work being rewarded, for a helping hand to those who cannot help themselves – but not too much of a helping hand. Oakes with all his greater-equality policies would scare the shit out of half middle Britain.'

As Robert Oakes and Luke had been friends from university days, Jaspar badmouthed Robert when Luke was not around. He broke off as the Daltons turned and spotted him and Max with Abe Dixon. Luke gave a big smile as he came towards their table.

'We're meeting for lunch next week,' he said as if it might have slipped Abe's mind. The self-confident can afford to be diffident. 'Blanche says you and she haven't met.' Blanche shook hands with Abe and gave a comradely grin to Jaspar and Max.

The fine summer continued, and several weeks later a not dissimilar conversation could have been overheard in the Members' Bar had the speakers not kept their voices low. They were sitting in the alcove overlooking the Thames, and so far no one else had moved in to join them on the window seat. The subject was the leader of the Democratic Labour party, Simon Steadfast.

'He'll be a negative factor in the next election,' Max Murphy said to the *Times* political editor. 'Homespun wisdom and the common man's friend are out of date. No doubt Simon stands for all that's worthy, but when he appears on television, viewers switch to another channel.' Max lifted his brows in despair. 'The public today want a leader who has dash and total confidence and drive – and glamour. Simon Steadfast's wife, whom personally I adore, could be his mother. She may make a great summer pudding, but charisma she has not.'

At that moment Luke and Blanche came in the bar. She was a good advertisement for Luke the husband. She was very American – open and friendly – which put her outside narrow class judgments. They spotted Max in the alcove. 'The bloke with him is political editor of the *Times*. Max says he's never met you,' Luke told her.

They went over to the alcove and Max put that right, adding: 'Can you join us?'

'For fifteen minutes,' said Luke. He turned to *The Times* chap. 'The Commons' hours are not designed for two people who actually enjoy one another's company. I told Blanche nothing except the division bell would interrupt a quiet dinner in the Members' Dining Room.'

Like all skilful politicians, he – and Blanche – sat down and ordered a drink and then focused on the *Times* man. At the end of fifteen minutes, Luke glanced at his watch, got to his feet and said to his wife in a mock authoritarian voice: 'Come on.'

Later that evening at the BBC's Westminster studio, Luke was interviewed about Defence expenditure. As Opposition Defence secretary, he had perfected the 15-second soundbite: 'In our new Britain, previous Defence costs will be slimmed down by cutting away dead wood. I shall focus on qualities central to the needs of our country: Vigilance. Valour. Might.'

In autumn the rain began. Umbrellas dripping on the floor became a regular feature of London life. On one such forbidding evening, Daltons and Oakeses were to meet at the House of Commons for dinner. MPs were on a three-line whip, which meant that when a vote was called and the division bell began its insistent clamour, they had to be in the division lobby in ten minutes flat. MPs who lived within ten minutes of Parliament could go home for dinner, but the Dalton and Oakes households were outside that radius. Both men liked their wives to come to the House for a little time together between votes.

Blanche made her way through labyrinthine corridors and up twisting stone staircases to the Opposition spokesmen's rooms. Unlike the grand suites of high-ranking Cabinet ministers, the shadows' rooms were mere cubicles. When Blanche entered the Opposition Defence spokesman's domain, where Luke was working at his desk, the room became crowded. The walls were so thin that it was impossible not to hear Stanley Fox in his neighbouring Foreign Affairs spokesman's cupboard making his private arrangements for later that evening when the final vote had been held.

Luke glanced at his watch. 'We'd better go. It's already eight.'

They walked to the Members' Dining Room where Julie and Robert were already at the table. Robert looked dreadful.

'Is everything all right?' asked Blanche as she sat down.

'Everything's all wrong,' Robert replied shortly.

'Let's order dinner,' said Julie. 'And plenty of wine. Then we can talk.'

She was the one who told the Daltons.

'I had some tests a few days ago. The doctor told me today: I've got leukaemia. Apparently there's more than one type of leukaemia. I have the incurable one. There's nothing you can say. At least it won't be painful physically.'

Little conversation followed. Robert remained silent, and after a few mouthfuls he pushed his plate away. Blanche put a hand on his arm for a moment. All four steadily sipped their wine.

The division bell clanged raucously and the two men went off to vote. While they were gone, Julie said: 'Unless Robert marries again, Charlie and Nat will have to go to boarding school.'

Blanche started to say 'Don't talk like that,' but didn't.

'Will you and Luke keep your eye on him? He's going to be lonely.'

'Of course,' Blanche replied to both sentences. She reached across and drew her index finger up and down the back of Julie's hand which rested on the table. 'Have you been given any kind of timetable?'

'Maybe six months. Maybe a year.'

Chapter Eight

WHEN the exceptionally cold long winter at last reached its end, Julie Oakes was confined to her bedroom. Often she talked with Blanche about death.

'Losing my strength produces opposite feelings. When I am totally exhausted, I rather welcome death. I think of it as falling asleep and having no more decisions to make, no more effort. Other times when I wake feeling stronger, I look at the treetops moving in a breeze outside my window, and I think how beautiful the world is. That's when I mind dying.'

'Thank God you and Robert have always been aware that you are lucky having each other. Can you imagine if you had never realised that until now?'

'I like to rest in good thoughts about our life together.'

Occasionally Julie's stoicism broke down, although Blanche never saw her cry. Her overriding fear was how Robert and the boys would manage without her.

'Some years ago,' she told Blanche, 'a girlfriend of mine was dying young. Near the end, she said to me: "If anything ever happens to Robert, I wish you would marry Teddy. Then he could stop being sad." Teddy was her husband.'

Blanche sat silent, her hand resting on Julie's thigh. Under the sheet it felt so thin.

'When a man is widowed,' Julie went on, 'people are often bitchy if he remarries before hundreds of years have passed. I've never gone along with that. I think men who remarry soon are the ones who enjoyed marriage. I think the people who can't understand it are the ones who hate their own marriages.' Her voice trailed off. She closed her eyes.

Blanche went on sitting there, deeply sad.

After a while she quietly withdrew her hand and got up to go. Julie opened her eyes.

'Just when we have a chance of winning the next election,' she said, 'I prepare to depart the scene. What a drag.'

'I'm telling you that sooner than we think, Simon Steadfast will have to go. I have a nose for these things,' Jaspar said to Max over drinks one evening. 'Too many of the party believe we can never win an election under his grey leadership. And Robert Oakes is no longer the likely successor. His clarity of purpose – stating that he intends using taxation to narrow the gap between rich and poor – will scare off the Tories whom we've got to seduce if we're to win the election. Now his wife is terminally ill. A grieving widower would make as grey a leader as Simon Steadfast. We can't let that happen.'

'Step from the wings, Luke Dalton,' said Max.

'Stanley Fox is bound to throw his hat in the ring. It will be Oakes, Fox and Dalton plus the statutory woman who hasn't a chance. Demo Labour doesn't have a Margaret Thatcher. Luke carries with him none of the political baggage that his rivals do. He's unspoilt. Naive perhaps. Doesn't belong to a group. It's a man of destiny approach.'

As the weekend neared, Luke decided not to go to his constituency until Saturday morning. He and Blanche needed to have a relaxed Friday evening together at home. He was about to join her in bed when the bedside phone rang. She answered it.

'Blanche. It's just happened.' Robert's voice was strangely soft. 'She looks so beautiful. I can't believe I'll never hear her voice again. All those plans. All that fun.'

'I can be there in half an hour if you'd like me with you.'

'Please come.'

When she reached the Oakes's house, Charlie answered the door. Just turned twelve, he was the older son.

'Daddy's with Mummy,' he said.

They went upstairs together. Nat, now ten, was sitting on the top step with his chin in his hands.

'Shall I stay out here with you?' Blanche asked them.

'We can all go in any time we like,' said Charlie. 'Nat and me have gone in and out of the bedroom all afternoon. Daddy doesn't mind.'

He was lying on the bed beside Julie, his hands folded behind his head, gazing at the ceiling. When he saw Blanche he got up, and they stood with their arms around one another. After a time she said: 'If you'll give me the name of the undertaker, I'll deal with that. Have you and Julie made any plans about how you want things handled?' She didn't notice that she spoke in the present tense.

'She did all that,' Robert replied and lay down beside her again.

'Have you and your father had anything to eat?' Blanche asked the boys.

They shook their heads.

'Let's go downstairs. I'll make a couple of telephone calls from Mummy's desk and then we'll cook some eggs.'

She made the calls with the boys sitting in the room with her. Then the three of them went to the kitchen. She poured a large Scotch and served up some of the scrambled eggs on a plate.

'Here. You two carry these to your father. I'm not sure about the eggs, but the whisky will certainly do him good. I'll keep our supper warm till you come back.'

She had both boys in bed before the undertaker arrived. When things were finally quiet, she said to Robert: 'I'll be sleeping in the spare room. Call me if you need me.'

The funeral was held in Edinburgh where Julie grew up. Late that evening the Daltons took the sleeper back to London. Once again Luke decided not to go to Netherby on Friday.

'I'll get there on Saturday in time for lunch with Harry.'

He had just turned out the bedroom light when the phone rang. 'Oh *no!*' groaned Blanche before answering it.

'Blanche, it's Jaspar. Is Luke there? I know it's late but I need to talk to him.'

Luke, naked, came to the phone: 'Jaspar. Are you having trouble getting to sleep?'

'Luke, we need to meet. Soon. Tonight if possible.'

'What about coming here at nine-thirty tomorrow morning before I go to Netherby?'

'I'll have Max with me. Something has come up.'

Blanche let them in. 'You know your way.'

Watching the two pairs of shoes mount the stairs, she pulled a face. Yet she did not feel real resentment. For she knew that Jaspar and Max believed in Luke's future. Since she did too, it made for a sense of comradeship. Once again she was conscious of her pleasure in having someone in the vacuum formerly filled by family.

Half an hour later, Luke called down over the banister: 'Blanche, can you come upstairs? You'll be interested in what we're talking about.'

When she walked in the study he said: 'Simon Steadfast may have to give up the leadership this weekend.'

'*What?*'

'The *Sunday News* is running a story about him and a prostitute,' said Jaspar.

'I don't believe it.'

'Well, we all know that Simon has this Gladstonian belief that prostitutes can be saved from their profession,' said Max.

'Unfortunately for him,' Jaspar went on, 'a photographer managed to take some pictures in a brothel, which look incriminating even though they are almost certainly innocent.'

'Even if he *wanted* to get up to whatever he is meant to have done,' said Blanche, 'he would never have risked his reputation and the damage to Democratic Labour. Why doesn't he tell the *Sunday News* to go and stuff themselves?'

'You'll know why when you see how the other papers run the story,' Max told her. 'For years Demo Labour has denounced the Conservative government for its moral sleaze. How many times have we complained bitterly that no one ever resigns from the government, no matter how unappetising the latest scandal? Now the shoe is on the other foot. Personally I think Simon Steadfast is guilty of nothing worse than bad judgment. Even so, I don't think he can hang on. Were he more popular, it might be possible. But as things stand, I warrant that on Monday even the broadsheets will be calling for his resignation. By then we'll have nudged the story along until its implications will damage the party further unless we have a leadership election. I reckon there will be a minimum of four candidates. This very moment Robert Oakes and Stanley Fox will be talking to their supporters about tactics.'

'Robert has just buried his wife, for God's sake,' said Blanche angrily.

'All the same,' said Max, 'it is vital that Luke lace up his running shoes today.'

'But he's catching a train to Netherby in an hour,' she answered.

'The best place for Luke to be when the story breaks is in his constituency,' Jaspar replied urbanely. 'We don't want it to look as if he's making an unseemly scramble to replace Simon before

Simon has thought out his position. When Luke is phoned at home by journalists, Blanche, you're to say he's in Netherby but that the callers could try his PPS. Max will stay at home to field calls and keep in touch with Luke in Netherby.'

Driving Luke to the railway station, Blanche asked: 'What did Max mean when he said we'll nudge the story along until it will further damage the party unless we have a leadership election?'

'He meant he and Jaspar will drop broad hints to the media even before the story breaks in tomorrow's *Sunday News*. One of them should manage to get on a Sunday breakfast programme, which by then will want to talk about nothing else. Look out!'

Blanche had taken her eyes off the road to glance at him. She'd nearly run into a car that braked suddenly in front of them.

'Pull over to the side and let me drive.'

He hopped out and ran round to the driver's door.

'And concentrate on the bloody road when you drive home from the station. You can think about the new situation once you're through our front door.'

'I wish you could get back from Netherby soon. Until I have a chance to talk with you about it, I'm going to have some very confused thoughts about the ease with which you've agreed to let Jaspar and Max "nudge" and "manage" the media on your behalf.'

'There's a long history of spin-doctoring in politics,' Luke said shortly.

They drove the rest of the way to the station in silence.

Several hours later the Netherby agent, Harry Camden, and Luke were finishing their pub lunch when the political reporter of the *Netherby Press*, Bud Foster, and the news photographer walked in and made straight for them.

After amiable salutations all round, Bud said: 'It's just come over the wire that the *Sunday News* will be carrying a story about a prostitute, with photographs which will compromise Simon Steadfast and could force him to resign.'

Harry looked at Luke with astonishment and a slightly hurt expression since Luke hadn't told him that a scandal was about to break.

'I got wind of the tabloid piece just before I caught my train,' Luke replied. 'Until it's proved otherwise, I shall believe that Simon Steadfast is totally innocent of any misdoing.'

Bud scribbled for a moment before asking: 'We'd like to take a picture.'

'So long as you're quick about it,' Luke replied. He looked at his watch and said to his agent: 'Let's get our bill. We're due at surgery in ten minutes.'

Inside Democratic Labour's local office, he paused to give a friendly nod to the constituents already seated in the waiting room. He had barely gone into his own room and sat down at the desk when the phone rang.

'You take it, Harry. I don't want to hold up surgery. Tell whoever it is that I'm doing surgery and they should phone back in a few hours.'

'It was the *Times*,' said Harry when he'd ended the call. 'They want to talk to you about the rumour that Simon Steadfast is resigning as leader before the weekend is over.'

Luke pressed his lips together. As the first constituent came in, the phone rang again.

'Let it ring, Harry, while you go into your office. To any press query, say no more nor less than what I said to the *Netherby Press*. I'm switching off the ringer here,' Luke added. He turned to his constituent with a concerned smile. 'How are things going in the hospital, Mrs Deakins?' he asked.

Chapter Nine

*T*HE early edition of the *Sunday News* came off the presses soon after nine on Saturday evening. Half an hour later it was with London's newsagents. The top half of the tabloid's front page bore the huge headline:

SIMON STEADFAST CAUGHT OUT IN BROTHEL

Below that was the second heading:

CAN DEMO LEADER SURVIVE SCANDAL? NO WAY

The rest of the page was filled with a photograph of Simon Steadfast leaving Madame LaFollette's Massage Parlour.

The printing presses for every other Fleet Street Sunday paper were rolling soon afterwards. Each plastered its own front page with its version of the *Sunday News* exposé. Later editions carried comments from members of the Conservative government, Opposition front bench spokesmen, the Archbishops of Canterbury and York. Unnumbered columnists delivered their opinions, the more agile of them managing to produce eight hundred words of moral outrage in thirty minutes flat.

As Opposition spokesman for Defence, Luke's statement

about believing Simon Steadfast was totally innocent appeared in most newspapers. To the inevitable follow-up query – 'If there is a leadership contest, will you run?' – he replied: 'I have no intention of applying myself to a hypothetical question. Simon Steadfast is leader of the Opposition and so far as I am aware shall remain so.'

Sunday breakfast television revealed how fast the story was growing. Luke in the Netherby men's club and Blanche at home in London were both listening to Jaspar Byatt being interviewed:

'I have no doubt that Simon Steadfast is innocent of the spin that the *Sunday News* has put on the story. Yes, he was in that brothel, just as he has visited unsavoury places before in his attempt to redeem some of those who have lost their way. You must remember that he is a practising Christian who believes that we can all be saved. The most anyone can say about the incident is that it shows a lack of judgment: it opens him up to charges that have wrongly been placed against him.'

The next question put to Jaspar was one that he himself had suggested to the presenter just before the interview.

'Mr Byatt, do you think that lack of judgment could be fatal were Simon Steadfast still the leader when and if Democratic Labour is again in government?'

'I have heard,' replied Jaspar, 'that some Democratic Labour MPs are saying that this lack of judgment disqualifies Simon Steadfast from continuing as leader. I myself do not share that view on any evidence we have to date.'

In London, Blanche screamed. It was not a loud scream but a scream nonetheless. 'He plants the thought and then says he does not himself believe it,' she shouted to the empty room. 'It's disgusting.'

Luke caught an earlier train than he had planned and was home by two. 'God it's nice to be here, even though it will be a disturbed afternoon,' he said to Blanche. 'Let's have one teeny drink in the study while we both unwind.'

She sat down in her chair across from his, watching him while he poured them each a small whisky with a lot of soda. When he was settled in the Eames chair, both took a swallow of their drink. She spoke first.

'Did you see Jaspar on that breakfast show?'

'Yes,' he replied without expression.

'Did you find it as disgusting as I did?'

'I found it disagreeable.'

The phone rang. Luke picked it up. 'We were just talking about you,' he said and winked at Blanche. 'Make it three-thirty.' He put down the phone. 'Jaspar and Max are coming round here for a conference.'

'I have a feeling I wasn't cut out for politics,' said Blanche.

'Do you want coffee?' she asked as they traipsed upstairs.

'Love it,' said Max.

When she carried a tray into the study, Luke said: 'Why don't you get yourself a cup and join us? You might be interested in the moral lecture that Jaspar has just delivered.'

'I'll skip the coffee,' said Blanche, sitting down in the unoccupied chair.

'Luke tells me that you and he are not happy about my interview this morning,' said Jaspar in his half-insolent manner.

'It was the part where you planted the thought about Simon's lack of judgment damaging the party and then went on to say you didn't go along with that opinion "on present evidence". It was so sly. You know I share your view that Luke could one day in the future make a good leader. But I find this scheming to hurry things along unattractive – not to say dishonourable.'

'To take up a moral stance that achieves nothing is hypocrisy,' Jaspar told her. 'Since we lost the last election, we've all known that Simon Steadfast, decent man that he is, lacks the force and style to lead us into the next election. Then fate steps in and this fortuitous scandal occurs. If we take advantage of it, Luke may find himself leader long before any of us had imagined. Do you want us to say: "We are too high-minded, too honourable to play politics in order to reach our goal?" What do you suppose the other probable candidates are doing this very minute? If you believe, as I do, that Luke has a vision for this country that will inspire and benefit his countrymen, then it is feeble if not immoral to step aside when the kitchen gets hot.'

'Blanche,' Max put in, 'my ancient mother used to say: "Grasp opportunity by the forelock for he is bald behind."'

This at least made her smile.

Just before Monday's one o'clock news, Simon Steadfast issued a statement saying that in today's intrusive journalism, it had been unwise of him to hold a conversation, however well intended, in the front room of a brothel, and rather than have the demeaning charges dragged out, he was resigning the leadership that day.

On the six o'clock news three further statements were read out – from Robert Oakes, Stanley Fox and Luke Dalton. All three would stand in the leadership contest. A further candidate was expected to throw her hat in the ring. Max Murphy was then interviewed about his man's chances.

'We're going all out to win,' he replied. 'MPs who have already pledged themselves to us are convinced that Luke Dalton – and only Luke Dalton – has the vision for a stronger Britain where enterprise and hard work will be rewarded, and at the same time the disadvantaged will be found work that can free them from dependence on the state. He has the outlook and drive to unite the segments of our country into a national force which will defeat the worn-out Conservative government and begin a new Britain.'

Luke's personal manifesto was not based on ideology. It was based on what he described as his vision of how men and women could live together in greater harmony with satisfaction obtainable by all. He offered something to everyone. His supporters pitched the line that this broad approach gave Democratic Labour a real chance to appeal across the class divide.

Behind the scenes, Jaspar worked tirelessly with a spin-doctor's cunning. 'Robert Oakes's wife has just died. He was enormously dependent on her. It would be a mistake for him to take on the leadership at this time, and so close to an election it would be disastrous for the party,' he said to every media person he spoke to. Max organised committed MPs to rally the support of the uncommitted. The Dalton camp's hopes rose.

Robert Oakes came top of the first ballot with Luke coming second just ahead of Stanley Fox; the sole woman, coming last, was knocked off. On the second ballot, Oakes remained top and Fox came last. That's when the pressure was put on Robert to stand down in favour of the friend he had encouraged as his junior, Luke Dalton. Because of longtime hostility between Oakes and Stanley Fox, most of Fox's supporters would go to Dalton on the third vote. Thus, it was argued, Oakes could not win, and in the interest of comradeship at the top, instead of fighting it out with Luke, he should hand over his support to Luke. If he did, Luke told him, and Democratic Labour won the approaching election, Robert could choose his job – Chancellor of the Exchequer, for which he was superbly trained, or Foreign Secretary, the two highest posts other than the premiership.

'If Demo Labour should win a second election,' Luke went on to Robert in their long and fraught conversation, 'I would consider stepping down halfway through that term of office so that you could have a turn at the premiership.'

With less than happy grace, Robert gave way. By his default his close friend Luke became leader.

Later that night Blanche phoned Robert. 'The trouble with contests,' she said, 'is that only one person can win. Will you have supper with us tomorrow night?'

Chapter Ten

*F*ROM the outset as Opposition leader, Luke used a technique not unlike that of a TV evangelist: he welcomed everyone into the fold. If you were rich, you would take comfort from his assurance that the top rate of tax would not be punishing so long as you provided employment for workers. If you were too poor to buy a superior education for your children, you could rest easy that Demo Labour would reform the worst state schools into proper places of learning. If you were among the shrinking minority who remained left-wing, you were invited to join the Daltonites in the interest of getting into power and then sorting out your differences. Without power, he kept reminding them, your principles were useless.

He responded to the need to change gear at a moment's notice. When he first became leader, one disgruntled left-winger in the party said to another: 'If he thinks he can stand up at the Dispatch Box and talk about sweetness and light, he'll last a fortnight. The House of Commons is love and Christianity once a year. Most of the time it's a bloody zoo.'

Within days Luke changed his style. 'Next thing he's into bashing the Conservatives,' said the same left-winger to his friend. 'He's more competent than I thought. I may not agree with him, but I can do business with him. You can challenge him and he doesn't throw a fit. He holds his own and more.'

On a Sunday evening when Blanche was having a pre-dinner drink with Thaddeus, waiting for Luke to meet her there when he got back late from Netherby, Thaddeus asked: 'Do you find Luke changing in tandem with the ascent of his career?'

'If you mean does he have outbursts of pomposity, the answer is no, thank God. But yes, there are changes as his responsibility increases. Notably, less time for private life. I think I may mind this more than he does. His job keeps his adrenaline charging around. My own job switches on the adrenaline, too, but it's not the continuous souped-up engine that goes with being leader.'

Minutes later Luke arrived from the railway station, and almost at once the talk changed to his recent appointments to the shadow cabinet.

'Nicely considered, young Dalton. Plenty of creative tension there,' said Thaddeus. 'You have followed the cardinal precept of leadership: think of every appointment in pairs. Put two people already wildly jealous of one another in competing jobs. You'll always be able to play them off against each other. I have often wondered if Jesus applied that principle in choosing His apostles.'

From time to time on a Sunday evening, Luke and Blanche had a drink with Robert at one or the other of their houses. Other times she went alone to the Oakes house and saw the two boys as well as their father. Charlie seemed to be doing better than Nat, who was often withdrawn. In the autumn they would start as weekly boarders at a London school. On this particular evening, all four had a takeaway Indian supper in the kitchen. Then Robert said to his sons: 'I'm taking Blanche upstairs to my study. We need to talk politics. Say goodnight down here.'

Glancing at Julie's chair across the study fireplace from his, Blanche sat down in another one. He poured them each a whisky. She noted that his expression was shy. As he walked up and down the room, she waited. When he finally settled in his chair, he took a large swallow of his drink and began to talk in jerky sentences without his usual clarity, sometimes meeting her gaze, other times looking off at nothing in particular.

'I have no one to talk to about my baser thoughts. Except you. When there were things I wasn't proud of, I could tell Julie. Now they just fester. Others might think I am entirely preoccupied by a widower's bereavement. That bastard Fox said to me yesterday à propos of nothing: "Of course it's much better, old man, that you threw your lot in with Dalton. With Julie's death you have enough to cope with."'

He took another large swallow.

'No one seems to imagine that had I become leader as I expected, the demands might have alleviated the emptiness. Not filled the emptiness. But alleviated it. I could have directed all my energy into leading. As it is...'

He threw back the rest of his drink and got up to pour another. Then he continued.

'It's a disgusting thing to say, but as it is, it's like a double bereavement. Of course they are not equally painful, but the political loss compounds the loss of Julie. She would have been so proud if I'd become leader. It was part of the dream we shared. I don't know where she is. Is there truly an afterlife? I wake up in the middle of the night and ask her if she's there. I shout at her: Why won't you appear? Show yourself so I can see you. If she was here, I wouldn't have let Luke persuade me to give him a clear run in the final ballot. He said, Jaspar Byatt said, others who wish me ill said, that all of the votes that had gone to Fox would go to Dalton on the final ballot. It's true that Fox asked his supporters to vote for Luke. If he couldn't be leader, he sure as fuck didn't want me to win. He thought he'd get a better job if Dalton was leader. Anyone but me. A number of his supporters have told me since that they had always intended to vote for me once Fox was knocked off the ballot. If I was leader, my whole style would be different from Luke's. I'd *lead* instead of letting all those bloody focus groups tell me what to do.'

He stopped speaking as suddenly as he had begun. Blanche got up and refilled both their glasses. Handing Robert his, she sat down on the floor beside his chair and silently sipped her whisky.

It was true: Luke constantly used non-politicians to show him which way the wind was blowing at any given minute. Demo Labour regularly polled these focus groups, made up largely of the middle classes, and as soon as a focus group identified a grievance, Luke produced a reassuring answer for the public.

'It's not sleight of hand,' Jaspar assured a sceptical MP. 'The man is sincere. He truly believes he knows the way forward. In some intuitive way, he does.'

Max arranged for twenty Demo Labour MPs at a time to come to the leader's capacious room at the Commons. These sessions acted as safety valves. Luke listened to each MP, did not commit himself, then summed up well. The sessions ended with a brilliant statement about what he wanted from a Demo Labour government. This had nothing to do with anything that had been brought up, but it lifted the whole mood.

Coming back to earth in the Tea Room afterwards, one MP said: 'All policy now comes down from the top. If Dalton doesn't know what he's doing, God help us. I don't know if he knows. I don't know what makes him tick. Is there a machine in there?'

To which his companion replied: 'I'm confident that with him we can win. But we don't know where the shit we'll be when we get there. He's beamed in from outer space.'

Increasingly Luke's ability to get his way commanded respect, however grudging: 'I don't believe in half of what he says,' said one cynic, 'but I respect his ability.'

When the election was finally called, the whole of Demo Labour was fired with wild excitement: they were on the threshold of power at last. Or were they? Could something still go wrong?

'Thank God you have a freelance contract with the *Nation*,' Luke said to Blanche. 'I'm going to need you with me.'

'I can write an article on canvassing in Netherby,' she replied.

Luke called a final meeting of MPs before they went off for the three-week struggle on the hustings to win back their seats. What he told them was recorded on a tape for each Demo Labour candidate trying to overturn a Conservative and enter the House for the first time.

Returning from the Law Courts with his clerk, Thaddeus heard Luke's rallying call on a BBC news report.

The clerk nodded when Thaddeus said: 'Young Dalton didn't put a foot wrong.'

After a few minutes' brooding, he added: 'Too bad he and Blanche haven't children. He can't play the family-is-the-root-of-society card.

Chapter Eleven

*L*UKE didn't need the family card. When the first results came in on polling day, key Conservative seats had gone over to Democratic Labour. As more Conservative seats fell, the realisation grew that Luke's focus groups had done a good job. Each time they had pinpointed a lurking fear that Demo Labour would turn out to be more left-wing than it seemed, Luke had reassured them that their suspicion was without foundation. He made Conservative voters feel that the radical drive he promised for a New Britain was based on conservative values, but more fresh and able and bold than the patently worn-out Conservative leadership.

At Netherby Town Hall, the count was still going on. It was a privilege to be allowed into the count, as the contents of the ballot boxes were separated and deposited in clumps in wooden troughs stretching down tables lined end to end. Even while wads of votes piled up in Luke's trough and his opponent's lagged far behind, he never displayed triumphalist emotions as he and Blanche strolled amongst their party supporters. While they all saw on the television screen what was happening across the country, they were too dazed to be ecstatic. Blanche kept smiling, despite a growing headache which she knew was caused by tension.

'As soon as the count is announced,' she said to Luke, 'can we telephone my father and mother?'

Bleeping his agent, who at once materialised out of the crowd, Luke said: 'Harry, when we get to the Labour Club and I've thanked our supporters, we want to phone the good news to Blanche's parents in Virginia. Make sure a photographer gets a clean shot of Blanche on the phone.'

When the Town Clerk walked on the platform, followed by the Daltons and the Conservative and his wife, a hush fell on the crowd. Blanche knew from the clumps of ballot papers that Netherby had returned Luke as its MP, yet she remained strung tight like a piano wire, and the pain in her head had become like a nail piercing it.

'Luke James Dalton, the Democratic Labour Party candidate: 31,859 votes. Andrew Laurence Symonds Thorne, the Conservative Party candidate: 18,236 votes.'

Following initial shouts of victory, Demo Labour supporters trooped off to the Labour Club. After thanking them, Luke said to Blanche: 'Come on, let's make that phone call to your parents.'

In a side room a photographer was already present. 'Good thing there's a five-hour time difference in Richmond,' Blanche said to no one in particular as she dialled the number. Almost at once her mother's voice answered.

'Mama, Luke has just won back his seat in Netherby,' Blanche said joyously, despite the nail still boring into her head. 'We're waiting for the result across the country.'

'I felt he was almost certain to win back his seat,' said Kitty. 'But it's still a relief to know for sure.'

'I want to tell Daddy myself.'

'He's driving back from Washington. In fact I expected him by now. Where can he phone you?'

'I don't know. We're driving back to Demo Labour

headquarters in London to hear the rest of the results come in. I'll phone again.'

The photographer had taken his picture at the moment that Blanche, laughing, told her mother the news. A smiling Luke stood beside her, gazing down at her fondly. It was this picture that was run on several front pages the following morning.

On the leader's specially converted 'battle bus' was a narrow bed behind a curtain where Blanche lay down on the trip to London. She should have been deliriously happy at Luke achieving his ambition while not yet forty. Instead she struggled with a sense of foreboding. She drowsed fitfully while Luke, at a table with two aides, talked on his direct line to Jaspar. Jaspar was at headquarters.

'Your victory speech in the Town Hall is shown on the news every half hour,' he said. 'You'll make just one more speech tonight when you get here. I've drafted it a couple of times, and the top draft will come over to you in a few minutes.'

Luke was studying the draft when a further call came from Jaspar. 'Blanche's sister Mavis is on the line from Richmond. She needs to speak to you or Blanche. Shall I put her through?'

'Give me two minutes to wake Blanche. She wants to tell her father herself.' He roused Blanche from her uneasy slumber, saying, 'Mavis is on the line.'

At once she shoved the curtain aside and made for the table where, wild-eyed, she snatched up the phone. As soon as she heard her sister's voice she babbled: 'Has something happened? Has something happened?'

'Take it easy, Blanche,' Mavis said. 'Take it easy. I've got bad news. It's Daddy.'

'What's happened? What's happened?' Blanche shouted, bursting into sobs.

Luke took the phone from her. 'Hello, Mavis, it's Luke. What's the matter?'

'Daddy was driving back from Washington. A freight van crashed through the central barrier and hit his car head-on. He's dead.'

After a stunned silence, Luke said: 'Where are you now?'

'I'm with Mama.'

'How is she?'

'Well, you know...'

Her voice trailed off.

'Give us fifteen or twenty minutes. One of us will ring you back.' He put down the phone.

'He's dead, isn't he?' Blanche said in a toneless voice.

'Come on,' said Luke, leading her back to the curtained bed. She was docile, like someone hit on the head. To an aide Luke said: 'Bring us a brandy. Neat.'

He got her to the bed and sat beside her, his arms around her. He repeated Mavis's words. Someone held out a brandy through the curtains, and he took it and put it to Blanche's lips.

Time passed and then in a small voice she asked: 'Did she say if he died instantly?'

'That's what I understood. We'll find out more when we ring back.'

'Where is he now?'

'We'll find out more when we ring back.'

After a time she asked: 'Is Mama with him?'

'She's at home in Richmond. Mavis is with her.'

'I want to go home as soon as possible.'

Both knew which home she meant.

'Drink some more of that brandy,' Luke said. Had she looked into his face, she would have seen his intense concentration. He glanced at his watch as if doing so helped him focus. Finally he said: 'We'll go straight to party headquarters and thank them. I'll make a short speech for the media. You needn't say a word. Just stay beside me. Then we'll walk up Whitehall and Downing

Street where there will be more suppporters. The night air will
do us both good. Then we'll go home – to Lamont Road.' He
paused. 'Can you do that? Out of love for me?'

'I'll try.'

'I'll need you here tomorrow. We'll have to explain to Mavis
that this is a momentous time. But you could catch tomorrow
night's plane to Dulles. You'll reach Richmond on Saturday
morning.'

Luke had just placed the call to Mavis when an aide told him
that Jaspar was anxious to speak to him. Blanche took over the
phone and talked quietly with her sister.

'I can't get there tomorrow. It looks like it will be Luke's first
day as Prime Minister. Or else it will be a crushing disappointment. Either way, he needs me here. But I can fly out
tomorrow night and reach home on Saturday.'

Mavis said nothing at first. Then in a slightly chilly voice she
said: 'Let me tell Mama. She's just in the next room. I'll tell her
you can't make it home until the day after tomorrow.'

Blanche bit her lip.

Her mother was on the line. 'Come as soon as you can, dear,'
she said. 'I need you.'

There was something the matter with her voice. It sounded
hoarse.

Mavis was back on the line.

'I'll see what I can do,' Blanche said. 'I'll phone you again
shortly.'

She put down the phone and waited for Luke to be free.

'Out of love for you' – she smiled wanly – 'I'd like to stay with
you until tomorrow night. But I can't. My mother spoke to me.
She needs me. Now. I'll have to fly out on the first plane we can
book.'

When he was angry, Luke's light eyes looked paler, almost like
ice. How could his wife be so impossible at a moment like this?

What was the matter with her family not to realise that things must be different now?

She saw his eyes and she said: 'I feel I'm being torn in two by wild horses.'

He checked his anger and called an aide. 'Find out what planes go to Dulles or Baltimore tomorrow morning. We need to know as soon as possible.'

Blanche turned her face away from him, resting a cheek wearily against the headrest.

At three in the morning, the Conservative Prime Minister conceded defeat. It was not a natural smile on Blanche's face as she moved through the rest of the night's schedule of events, but everyone put it down to exhaustion. What a strange way to be entering Downing Street, she thought, dazed.

When they finally fell into bed at Lamont Road, they were asleep at once. She was woken by Luke with a cup of coffee. 'I'm going with you to Heathrow,' he said.

The two cars set off, the Cabinet Secretary and a bodyguard with the Daltons, Jaspar and more bodyguards following. Blanche held silently to Luke's hand. The Cabinet Secretary's presence made her even less inclined to talk. Nonetheless, the near future had to be discussed.

'I'll probably be there for a week. Then come back to London and help with the move to Downing Street. When that's under control, I'll go back to Richmond for a little while with my mother.'

'I shall miss you,' he said, lifting her hand to press it against his cheek. 'I'll tell the diary secretary that any plans made for you must be provisional until I say otherwise.'

As they all walked into the airport, two cameramen stepped forward. Luke had made Jaspar swear to alert no more than two, one for TV, one for the press.

Blanche's plane was scarcely airborne when Jaspar issued a statement: 'Mrs Blanche Dalton's father, Nathan Winslow, the Pulitzer-Prize-winning foreign correspondent of the *Richmond Herald* in Virginia, died in a car crash yesterday. Mrs Dalton has flown back to Virginia to be with her mother. The Queen has conveyed her deepest sympathy to Mrs Dalton.'

In the back seat of his car, finishing off a letter with his clerk, Thaddeus heard the announcement that came over the radio.

'Young Dalton got to play the family card after all,' he said without expression.

Chapter Twelve

BLANCHE sat on the arm of the wing chair in Nathan's study, stroking her mother's hair. Perhaps because the chairback was so tall, Kitty appeared to have shrunk. She sat passively, face crumpled like that of an exhausted child.

'Most people never know a love like yours and Daddy's. They've never experienced that connection. You and he had it for thirty-eight years. Can that be of some comfort to you?'

'It doesn't help, dear.'

The Presbyterian Church in Richmond was packed. Blanche hadn't been there since her father gave her away in marriage. This time Kitty was flanked by her daughters. Nathan had greatly liked 'The Battle Hymn of the Republic', but both girls knew their mother would find that unacceptable, as indeed would the rest of the Southern congregation. Instead they settled for 'My Country 'tis of Thee'. The organist pulled out all the stops, and towards the end of the third stanza, Kitty began to tremble convulsively from the effort of not breaking down. Blanche took one of her hands and held it to her in the knowledge that Mavis would take the other.

Two days afterwards, Nathan's ashes were to be buried in his family's graveyard in Vermont. Three planes of diminishing size were needed to get from Richmond to Vermont, and there would be a long drive after that.

'Mama won't be able to bear up,' said Mavis. 'We'll have to break the journey and stay the night en route.'

'That will mean more complications. I'm going to call the *Richmond Herald* proprietor and ask him for help.'

'But you and I hardly know him.'

'Our father was his star writer. Daddy told me once: "In their pride, Southerners are always saying they mustn't impose on others. But they mistake imposing on people with accepting their help. When you're in trouble, let them help you. It gives them pleasure," he said.'

The proprietor's six-seater executive Cessna made the trip in under three hours. The co-pilot, doubling as a steward, produced a box lunch of Chesapeake Bay crabcakes and a bottle of Sancerre. The plane landed on a local airstrip not far from the Winslow cemetary, and Nathan's two brothers met them and took over. Kitty held the small mahogany box of ashes tight against her breasts.

When they reached the peaceful little graveyard bounded by black wrought-iron railings, marble headstones rising against gloomy fir trees, they found that two cousins had dug the grave. Bunches of gladioli and asters were arranged comfortably. A dozen more of Nathan's family stood back until the short service was over and the earth was packed down level with the ground. Only when Kitty and her daughters had stepped out through the wrought-iron gate did the New England aunts and uncles and cousins come forward to embrace them.

They all went back, subdued, for tea and food at an uncle's house. He poured out bourbon as soon as Kitty was seated. Blanche felt as if she were operating on auto-pilot, something in her head buzzing silently. At the end of the afternoon when the three women were back on the executive plane, she found herself suddenly exhausted. Part way through the flight, as the dark closed in, she left her seat to rummage in her carrier bag from which she produced a half bottle of bourbon and three glasses. They sat behind one another in window seats, sipping their whisky, gazing into the black.

A week later Blanche was on a trans-Atlantic plane with her forehead pressed to the window. A full moon rode above dense low cloud.

'Where has all that extraordinary energy gone?' she whispered to the moon. 'Father, where are you now?'

Disembarking at Heathrow airport, she found Luke's private secretary, Andrew Marston, waiting at the bottom of the steps. Beside him was the airport manager. It was a Thursday morning.

'The Prime Minister is in Cabinet,' Andrew said. 'He asked that I bring you straight to Downing Street and he'll come up to the flat for lunch. We've arranged for someone to produce the food.'

The airport manager said he'd send on the luggage when it came on to the carousel. He asked for Blanche's passport so he could go ahead through Passport Control. Andrew skirted the queues and took the Prime Minister's wife through a side door. Even in her robot-like state Blanche noted all this.

Americans who have visited the White House are initially astonished when they see London's unpretentious little street with its 18th-century terraced houses. Downing Street was one of the places Blanche visited when she first came to London, guidebook in hand. Today when the car turned off Whitehall and the barrier was raised, the Prime Minister's house had taken on a dimension which she hadn't seen before. Perhaps it was the policeman saying 'Welcome, Ma'am.' Or the big door swinging open at once. Or the Special Branch officers, lounging in a corner of the entrance hall, suddenly standing erect. Or was it simply that Number Ten was now home?

'Do you want to walk through the State reception rooms on

the first floor?' asked Andrew. 'Or shall we go straight up to the flat?'

'The flat, please.'

They took the lift.

'The Prime Minister said to warn you it doesn't look like home. He said you'll put that right as soon as you have caught your breath and can go back to Lamont Road to decide what objects you want to bring here. Clothes, for instance,' Andrew added cheerily. 'You'll have help with the packing up and moving things to the flat. Here we are.'

Unlocking the front door, he led her in. She found herself in a five-star hotel suite with comfortable armchairs and sofas, some fine furniture, period mirrors and original paintings. She made for one of the dormer windows and looked down on a large garden.

'That's your garden. It's where the IRA mortar bombs landed. The Cabinet was very lucky. If we open a window so you can lean out, you can look down on the Cabinet Room. That's where the mortar bombs were aimed.'

'Is everything that's here permanent?'

'You can make some changes if you wish. Other prime ministers and their wives have often chosen different pictures from the Government Stores. One prime minister's wife brought three flying ducks with her to decorate the drawing room wall.'

'It's slightly spooky. Little sign that anyone has been here. Luke must have eaten with friends.'

'Not to mention official dinners. A number of engagements made for the previous prime minister are now in your husband's diary. And yours.'

'Where's the kitchen?'

She opened cupboard doors until she found where the glasses were kept. Taking one to the sink, she ran cold water and drank glass after glass.

'Who's been keeping house? Everything's spotless.'

'We've had a housekeeper coming in daily. You may want to keep her on or not. You don't have to decide that at once. The bedrooms are through that door.'

Tactfully he didn't accompany her lest the main bedroom display too intimately the Prime Minister's personal habits. When she saw his hairbrushes on the chest of drawers and a small framed photograph taken on their honeymoon, her heart turned over. Hearing a bleeper in the other room, she rejoined Andrew.

'Here comes your lunch,' he said, whereupon the doorbell rang.

'Hello,' said Blanche. 'Just leave it in the kitchen, thank you.'

Andrew's bleeper went again.

'Your luggage from Heathrow is on its way up.'

'Hello,' said Blanche. 'Will you leave them in the main bedroom?' She followed the porter. 'On second thought, put them in the other bedroom. I shan't be unpacking straight away.'

As she returned to the drawing room, she heard the bleeper again.

'Cabinet is finished. The Prime Minister will be joining you in a few minutes. I hope you'll be very happy here, Mrs Dalton. I've put your card with next week's appointments on the coffee table,' Andrew said, and let himself out.

Keys turned and Luke was there. Closing the door, he stood looking at her, smiling, and tossed his jacket on to a chair.

'Hello, Prime Minister.'

She ran to him and put her face in the tender bit where his jawbone met his neck. Soundless tears coursed on to his collar. 'I hope I won't always have such a melancholy effect on you,' he said, drawing her away from him enough to kiss her.

Still crying, she began to laugh as well. 'What are we doing here?' she asked.

'I've counted the days until you got here. Shall I make us a tiny drink and you can tell me about Richmond?'

There was an armchair either side of the fireplace. Guessing which one he had already bagged, she took the opposite one. They lifted their glasses to each other.

'To Nathan,' he said, 'whose influence on you and untold others will last for ever.'

He lifted his glass a second time. 'To our new life together.'

As soon as they had eaten, Luke looked at his watch. 'Robert is coming to see me downstairs in a quarter of an hour.' Blanche already knew that of the two jobs Luke had said were on offer, Robert Oakes had chosen to be Chancellor of the Exchequer. 'There won't be time to take our clothes off, but let's lie down for a few minutes as we are.'

They lay atop the bedspread, speechless in each other's arms. Ten minutes later he untangled them. 'Why don't you stay where you are and catch up on a little sleep?'

She got up with him. 'I'm too excited to sleep. I want to take a look at the rest of this amazing house.'

He went downstairs to the Prime Minister's official study, and not long afterwards Blanche was wandering through the State reception rooms, marvelling at their beauty and grandeur. When Luke returned to the flat for a drink and dinner, she was in a state of exhilaration, describing some of what she'd seen, bombarding him with questions about what went on at Number Ten.

As he left the flat to go downstairs the following morning, Luke said: 'I told Michael to ring you soon after nine.' Michael was the Prime Minister's diary secretary. He had more engagements to check with Blanche.

For the rest of that day she moved about in a trance. On the day after that, she fell into depression. She went to see her GP and burst into tears. 'I keep waking up at four in the morning and I can't get back to sleep.'

'My dear girl, what you need is something to make you go back to sleep at four o'clock.' She wrote out a prescription.

Blanche got some sleep.

Several evenings later, in a long beaded silk sheath, she stood in the White drawing room between Luke and the guest of honour, the Italian Prime Minister, who was in London for an official visit without his wife. They greeted some forty guests who went through to the Blue drawing room (Blanche's favourite) and on to the Pillared drawing room. Among the guests was the celebrated barrister Thaddeus Spearman, who winked at Blanche and kissed her warmly on the mouth as he went through the reception line. Luke beetled his brows but almost immediately had to turn his attention to the next guest.

When at last the welcoming trio could move on to mingle with the party, waiters passing silver trays with champagne, Blanche was expected to fend for herself with the aid of the head of the Civil Service. Jaspar Byatt, now the Prime Minister's official spokesman, came up to make further introductions. She was not raised in the South for nothing: she was at ease with anyone, even though she rarely caught their names.

When dinner was announced, Luke turned up beside her with the guest of honour. Some gliding, others shuffling, everyone went into the State dining room. Blanche was put between the Italian Prime Minister and the Chancellor of the Exchequer, Robert Oakes.

'Oh, Robert,' she exclaimed. She hadn't seen him since he had moved into Number Eleven. It had a connecting passage with Number Ten, largely used by the Chancellor on his way to Cabinet or by government officials of the two great departments. 'I haven't rung you since the election, because my family have had a tragedy and I had to go home for a while.'

'I know,' said Robert and briefly laid a hand on hers. 'I heard you were back.'

Blanche changed the subject. 'What's the domestic side of life like in Number Eleven?' she asked. For some reason unknown to her, the Chancellor's flat was much larger than the Prime Minister's.

'The place is bigger than I need,' Robert answered, 'but it suits me: I've always wanted to have work and home under the same roof. I just use the rooms I need and leave the others with their doors shut.'

'Do you ever think about marrying again?'

'Not really – though I often think how different Number Eleven would be if Julie were alive to share it with me. Mind you,' he added, switching to a jocular tone, 'I'm told that all Chancellors' wives have moaned about no help being provided. What they mind most, apparently, is providing and installing lavatory paper for three bathrooms and the lavatory just inside the flat's front door, which is used by all the plainclothesmen.'

'May I come and see you soon at Number Eleven?' Blanche asked.

'Will you ring my private office tomorrow and fix a time with them? I can't even blow my nose without informing the diary secretary first.'

Reluctantly she turned to talk to the Italian Prime Minister. Throughout the evening, except when she was gossiping with Robert, Blanche had the now familiar sense of being on auto-pilot. Perhaps after a few more nights of taking the GP's pill, she'd wake feeling more tuned in.

'I was very proud of you tonight,' Luke said when they were finally inside their own flat. 'There's just one thing: you mustn't encourage Thaddeus to kiss you so familiarly on public occasions. "Caesar's wife must be above suspicion."' He used the quote only half-mockingly.

This was the first time Blanche had known him to be pompous.

'I didn't encourage him,' she replied tartly. 'If now that you're Prime Minister you don't like the way your old friend greets your wife, *you* tell him how you want him to behave.'

Chapter Thirteen

'L UKE, what are we going to do about that bastard Oakes?' Jaspar Byatt demanded angrily. They were in the Prime Minister's study. 'When you made me your official spokesman, one of my first directives was that all ministers must obtain advance clearing from me for any interview they proposed to give to the press. Oakes gives a major interview without clearance whenever it takes his fancy. His press secretary spurts far more leaks than I do.'

'Robert came to see me when you first issued that instruction and told me candidly that he doesn't expect as Chancellor to be told what to do by you.' Luke gave a wintry smile at the thought of his old friend Robert's outrage. 'However desirable it is to keep ministers on message, Robert and the Deputy Prime Minister are outside your domain.'

'They're not outside your domain. You should have a talk with each of them.'

'You seem to forget that you and Max and I have agreed that I be kept clear of these little squabbles. That's what you're in business to handle. I want to talk about something else. Namely Blanche. As you know, since before the election she has been pestered by journalists and TV editors wanting her to grant them an interview. Her secretary handles the correspondence, but Blanche has to take the decisions. The requests she finds particularly embarrassing to turn down are from journalists she already knows. Make an appointment with her when I'll be able to attend. We need to work out a long-term strategy for her.'

The three of them met in the same room. 'It's not wholly chance,' Blanche said, 'that I chose a career in which I would be writing about other people. Having someone interviewing me is the opposite of that. It's like having my nature turned inside out. I dread it. And I know all the journalistic tricks of getting someone off her guard and then leading her to say something that will include a single sentence which, printed in isolation, makes a jackass of her – or, worse, makes a jackass of her husband.'

Jaspar drummed his fingers on the arm of his chair thoughtfully. 'Jackie Kennedy made a virtue of remaining a woman of mystery,' he said. 'Except when she gave the press a tour of the White House after she had it redecorated, she never opened her mouth to a journalist. None of them ever had the chance to discover that her first priority was always money. Nor were they allowed the opportunity to observe that apart from her ability to attract rich men, she wasn't all that bright.'

'If I needed a higher profile,' Luke said, 'like the Opposition's weird leader, there'd be some point in exploiting Blanche, encouraging her to give press interviews however much of a strain she'd find it. As she *is* bright, I would take the risk of her possibly stubbing her toe.'

'But it's not a question of stubbing my toe,' Blanche said. 'It's a question of putting myself in the power of a journalist that I've usually never clapped eyes on. If he or she decides to insert the old stiletto, I'm helpless.'

'Let me finish,' said Luke. 'I don't need to exploit my wife. I've already reached the top. If she does the official entertaining and makes official visits in style and attends a certain amount of school events or hospital wing openings or art exhibitions, she has absolutely nothing to gain by giving an interview. If she feels strongly about a subject and wants to express her view, she has a column in the *Nation* to do just that. If she wrote something highly controversial, no doubt other papers would pick it up, but it would be *her* words.'

'All approaches to Blanche,' said Jaspar, 'will henceforth be re-directed to me. I'll reply on her behalf.'

He scribbled on a piece of paper and handed it to Luke, who read out the scrawled draft to Blanche: 'Blanche Dalton is not at present – or ever – going to give an interview to the media.'

Blanche's contract for the *Nation* was for thirty-eight columns a year. As she was freelance, she could work from the study in the Downing Street flat, fitting in interviews and her writing with the demands of her official diary. Using the same technique she had always employed – self-mockery – she found she could write about all manner of things, from abortion to lunch at Buckingham Palace. In the latter instance, the trick was not to quote anyone directly, above all not to quote the Queen.

'Eleanor Roosevelt had a daily column called *My Day* while her husband was President,' she wrote to her mother, 'and I'm experimenting with a less frequent version of that. Mind you, the Roosevelts' enemies ridiculed her, so I'll have to expect some of that. At least I undertake it as a professional journalist.'

M. le President de France had graciously condescended to visit Britain, even to put up for a few nights at Buckingham Palace. On day one, the British Prime Minister and Mrs Dalton gave a splendid lunch for twenty in the State dining room in Number Ten. The two heads of government sat side by side in the middle of the long table, facing a magnificent portrait of the Duke of Wellington.

At Buckingham Palace that night, the Queen gave a State banquet for the French. M. le President sat on the Queen's right, the Prime Minister's wife on his other side. Blanche hugely enjoyed the fanfare and glitter; as a child, *Alice in Wonderland* had been one of her favourite books. She was surprised and entertained by her turns at conversation with M. le President. In his careful faultless English, he complained that he had been grievously offended by the earlier lunch in Number Ten, as he had been forced to look at the painting of an arch-enemy of France.

'How do the English imagine the French President can enjoy his food in such an insulting position?' he asked.

'What do you do with your portraits of French heroes who would hardly be the favourite of a visiting English statesman?' Blanche enquired, genuinely curious. 'Like Napoleon.'

'We cover them with a curtain, of course,' M. le President replied, astounded that such fundamental courtesies need be explained two centuries after Waterloo.

The following morning at Downing Street was occupied by top-level policy meetings with the French. Lunch in the State dining room found the previous day's seating arrangement inverted: Prime Minister and President now sat with their backs to the Duke of Wellington.

When it was M. le President's turn to talk to the Prime Minister's wife, he had a fresh list of complaints.

'Buckingham Palace provided grossly inadequate security for the French entourage,' he declared. 'Not only that, I am very angry that my foreign minister was asked to give two of France's highest orders of merit to the Lord Chamberlain and the Mistress of the Robes to the Queen.'

Blanche confined her comment to a rueful, 'Oh dear.' She hadn't the faintest idea which of the various royal functionaries would be appropriate recipients of France's high orders.

When she and Luke returned to the flat that evening, there was a message for her to ring Mavis in Richmond. It began with the words: 'Don't panic. Nothing has happened. I've got to make some plans with you.' Mavis went on, 'Mama is adamant that she wants to move out of the house and into an apartment. We need your help.'

'Of course I want to come,' Blanche replied. 'How long do you think we should allow?'

'Certainly two weeks. At least.'

'I need to phone you back tomorrow, Mavis. There are bound to be official engagements.'

'Well, do your best. It's already enough of a strain for Mama without our now changing dates around.'

'I've got to tell Luke, for heaven's sake, that I intend being away for a couple of weeks.'

A silence.

'I'll phone you tomorrow, Mavis. Goodnight.'

'What was that about?' asked Luke.

Blanche told him.

'She can't expect you to take off for at least a fortnight just like that,' he said sharply. 'She's got to be made to understand that your life has changed. You have obligations to carry out here.'

Blanche looked utterly wretched.

'How can I possibly refuse her? Most of the time it's Mavis who has the full responsibility for Mama's care.'

'Tomorrow is another day. We both need some sleep. Are you coming? You have obligations for the rest of the French visit. Some of them far from disagreeable,' he added, to remind her of the privileges and pleasures she enjoyed as his wife.

Normally it delighted him that she shared excitements neither had known before. 'What are we doing here?' she had once again teased them both, the first time they stayed at the Prime Minister's country house, Chequers. Yet at this moment he thought her ungrateful and unappreciative. They fell asleep not touching each other.

Between his preliminary morning meeting with the Chancellor, Robert Oakes, and the arrival of the French President and his entourage for economic talks, Luke hurried upstairs to catch his wife before she set off to escort the President's wife to Tate Modern.

'Blanche?' he called from inside the front door.

'I'm in the bedroom. I just laddered my tights.'

He stood watching her strip them off.

'And the car's coming in five minutes,' she muttered.

'When we've quarrelled and not made up, a black cloud hangs over my whole day,' he said. 'I've just come up to tell you that I was an insensitive lout last night. Will you forgive me?'

With one leg encased in the new tights, she hopped off the bed to press her face against his neck. Drawing away, she saw the red streak on his collar.

'Oh God. I've put lipstick on your shirt. What will M. le President say?' Holding the loose leg of her tights she ran to a mirror. 'And I've got to re-do my mouth. Otherwise *la femme formidable* will raise those arched brows at me.'

Her brother-in-law, Bolling, met Blanche's plane at Baltimore airport. From there the interstate highway to Richmond was directly south. As they drove up to the house that she had lived in all her life, Blanche felt an ache, almost like a blow, in the centre of her diaphragm. Queenie opened the door and Blanche flung her arms around her. 'How's Mama?'

'Miz Winslow she doin' pretty good. I jes take her a cup of coffee. She like to sit in that tall chair in yo father's study.'

Blanche ran upstairs.

'Why, dear, how lovely to see you,' Kitty said, as if her daughter had just called in from a few streets away in Richmond.

Mavis came up from the cellar with lists in her hand. After dinner, Bolling returned home to fend for himself and their two children.

Each evening over cocktails, sooner or later Kitty said: 'I think of family furniture and pictures as symbols of continuity. It makes me happy to know which things you girls would like.'

In her bedroom, Blanche wrote to Luke, giving him a lighthearted account of what was happening in Richmond, no matter that much of it was heartrending.

When he telephoned her, he too recounted his news as if the whole thing was a comic charade. Most nights when she fell into bed exhausted, she thought of him and Nathan, and again in the morning when she took her coffee out on the side veranda. But mostly she stayed focused on her mother and the dismantling of their home.

Near the end of the second week, Blanche was working in a top floor room known as the sewing room when Mavis appeared in the doorway.

'I think Mama has gone crazy,' she said. 'Come and look at the books.'

Nathan's notable collection of American history and biographies had been removed from their shelves. In the sitting room, directed by their mother, Queenie was piling up those that Kitty wanted to take to her apartment – prized volumes on Robert E. Lee, Stonewall Jackson, Jeb Stuart, Jefferson Davis, and so on.

Stacked on the dining room floor were books that Kitty wanted given to the Good Will Charity. Among them were the six volumes of Sandburg's *Abraham Lincoln*, collectors' items about Sherman and Ulysses S. Grant, and any other book about Northern heroes, even Benét's epic poem *John Brown's Body*.

'Well, then, let's divide them up and take them ourselves,' said Blanche, slightly dazed by the pocket of Southern bitterness unexpectedly revealed in her sweet-natured mother. But before they could do so, they had errands to run for her and were absent for a couple of hours. When they got back, every book stacked on the dining room floor was gone.

'Mama?' Blanche shouted.

'I'm in my bedroom,' her mother called down.

Blanche ran upstairs two at a time.

'What's happened to Daddy's books that were in the dining room?'

'Oh, the Good Will truck came while you were gone,' her mother replied.

'But Mavis and I wanted them,' Blanche said.

'Why, dear, I'm so sorry. I had no idea you children were interested in those old books. The Good Will truck left here only twenty minutes ago. What a shame.'

On the morning of the final move, Queenie gave the sisters a note from their mother.

'I don't want anything said about it,' they read.

When the moving van finally pulled away from the house, Kitty was on the front step, watching it go, watching until it was out of sight. Watching her, Blanche needed all her will power to keep from breaking down.

Chapter Fourteen

'No one doubts the Prime Minister's sincerity,' the Opposition leader declared in the House of Commons, 'least of all himself.' Conservative MPs' braying laughter in the background. 'He believes he was sent amongst us to bring joy and prosperity to all. Alas, he has not the foggiest idea how he will bring this about. He is against schools which fail to educate children. He is against long waiting lists for overcrowded hospitals. He is against poverty.' Long pause. 'Who isn't?' More brays. 'Instead of leading us into the brave new tomorrow he promised, he has proved to be a kiddies' conjurer. Ministers appointed by the Right Honourable Gentleman are as toothless as their master.'

Blanche's face burned. She had asked the driver to turn on the six o'clock news as he drove her to the Middle Temple. 'It makes more sense if the car collects you from Downing Street and then comes for me,' Thaddeus had said. 'My chambers are only a few minutes away from the opera house.'

When he climbed in the back seat beside her, he leant to kiss her mouth and felt her stiffen and draw away.

'Has the Prime Minister given you a lecture about Caesar's wife's public demeanour?' he asked caustically.

'Do I warrant a lecture?'

'Not to my knowledge. But that's irrelevant. I've known Luke a long time, my dear girl. The trouble with these idealists is their belief in perfection. And they decide what is perfect. It's often said that worse than marriage to a sadist is marriage to an idealist. Ah. We're here.'

Mounting the stairs to the Crush Bar, Blanche said little as Thaddeus greeted every fifth person. When called upon to acknowledge an introduction, she gave a quick bright smile, reminding herself of Luke's quick bright smiles when his mind was elsewhere. Thaddeus tucked her hand through his arm and pushed his way to the bar. Without asking her what she'd like, he ordered two gin-and-French. 'Best drink for heightening emotions.'

The first bell began to ring. 'Plenty of time. Finish your drink. No point in coming to *Don Carlos* unless you're in a mood to agonise over every betrayal and torment.'

The final bell was clanging when they made their way to the box. As before, Blanche saw people in the stalls look up at them and comment to each other. She had an overwhelming desire to lean towards Thaddeus as if they shared a secret. It was to spite Luke and his concern about Caesar's wife.

Not until they were in the car on their way home did she speak of how dismayed she was by the adverse press that Luke had been receiving lately. 'After months of his seeming invincible, everybody is saying Luke's a fraud. I hate it.'

'Few of them really think he is a fraud. But they resent Jasper Byatt's endless spin-doctoring when Luke hasn't put muscle behind his rhetoric.'

Blanche bit her lip.

Thaddeus continued. 'His appeal to the public is an emotional appeal – he's going to do something for each and every one of them. But he has an intellectual void when it comes to planning how he's going to do it. Other than Robert Oakes, the whole

Cabinet expresses good intentions without a proper analysis of how to achieve them.'

Blanche looked unseeing out of the window.

He patted her knee. 'You mustn't worry that beautiful little head of yours. There is nothing wrong with Luke's brain power. It's just that he applies it to presentation. Once he and Jaspar realise that presentation is not enough, I'm confident he will get down to some real thought and action.'

Blanche pushed his hand off her knee.

'Any more words of reassurance?' she asked sarcastically, continuing to gaze out of her window until the car turned into Downing Street.

The seesaw bore her up again. They were in a specially converted VC-10, their own inner sanctum behind the cockpit, the Prime Minister's aides and bodyguards sitting in the body of the plane along with platoons of media. The inner sanctum contained a sofa, table for four, two berths behind a curtain. At present the table was occupied by Luke and Blanche and Jaspar Byatt. The two men were discussing how to maximise Luke's publicity during this three-day visit to Washington.

'We're playing to two audiences,' Jaspar said. 'British voters. Americans who matter. In both cases Blanche as the American wife should be exploited.'

'Any time, Jaspar,' she said drily.

They landed at Andrews Air Force base where the Vice-President and his wife waited, she half hidden behind the enormous bunch of flowers she carried to present to Blanche. The four of them climbed into a giant helicopter which disgorged them alongside the Washington Monument. A limousine took them the short run to the White House, where the front was permanently protected by discreet blocks of concrete positioned to make it impossible for a terrorist's four-wheeled motor vehicle to approach with a bomb. The Daltons were taken in by the east side entrance and escorted to the Rose Garden at the precise moment that President Richard Monroe Masters and his wife Meredith came down the outside stairs from the Oval Office to welcome them.

After their initial formal greeting, President Masters set the tone by calling the British Prime Minister and his wife by their first names. The two couples went into the President's Oval Office, where Blanche's eyes fixed at once on the big desk beneath which a ladyfriend of the President used to gratify him while he conducted statesmanlike telephone calls above her head.

The First Lady showed Blanche to the Daltons' bedroom.

'I know if I were you I'd want to rest before dinner,' Meredith said. 'You can phone the housekeeper for tea or coffee or whatever you want. Here we are.'

She pushed open a door into a room dominated by an enormous bed with a dark, ornately carved rosewood headboard rising half as tall again as the one used by Blanche's grandmother.

The First Lady chuckled. 'I took a chance in putting a Virginian in the Lincoln Bedroom. Mrs Lincoln is believed to have bought the bed shortly after the Civil War began.'

'Good thing my father was a New Englander,' Blanche replied, laughing.

When she was alone, she lay atop the bed, her eyes moving around the room at the dark-stained American Victorian furniture. Throughout her Richmond upbringing she had seen similar furniture. 'But not this grand,' she said to herself. It would be something to tell her mother tomorrow, when Blanche was to be excused from the official schedule so she could visit Kitty in Richmond.

Pre-dinner drinks that evening were in the Rose Garden

before some sixty guests moved into the State dining room. Glittering tables laid with the Reagan red-bordered china service awaited them. Above the mantelpiece hung a contemplative portrait of President Lincoln, painted posthumously, not long after his assassination. President Masters made a pretty speech without notes, making much of the British Prime Minister's American wife.

Afterwards they all trooped into the White House movie theatre where a celebrated Hollywood comedian stepped out on the stage to entertain them. Luke found it a bit corny, but it provided an opportunity to be silent after the hours of concentrated talking with American industrialists, Supreme Court judges, leading politicians, media proprietors *et al.* When the lights lowered, they were shown excerpts from Charlie Chaplin's silent movie *Modern Days*, and Rita Hayworth in *Gilda*, pumping her hips in the most erotic dance ever filmed, and the latest *Star Wars* sequel. It was during Gilda's dance, which inevitably unsettled everyone in the audience, that Blanche became aware that the President, in the seat on one side of her, had moved his hand on to her thigh. After a minute or two of uncertainty, she leant towards him in the dark, clucked her tongue in lighthearted parody, and moved his hand to rest on his own thigh. He turned to meet her eye and gave an amused smile which might almost have been collusive.

In their formidable bed that night, Luke drew Blanche to him. 'Do you suppose Abe Lincoln and his wife got up to the same things we do?'

Kitty was sitting in the wing chair from Nathan's study, very much the Southern lady. Her chestnut hair, now streaked with grey, curled prettily and her smile gave the heart-shaped face a radiance.

'Why, dear,' she said to Blanche who at once perched on the

arm of her mother's chair, 'where have you two girls been?'

'I live only a few streets away,' Mavis answered. 'I came to see you yesterday, Mama. Blanche lives in London. Her husband is the British Prime Minister.'

'Why, of course I know that,' said Kitty. 'How silly of me to forget.'

Blanche stroked her cheek.

'Luke and I have flown to Washington to stay for three days with President Masters and the First Lady. Wouldn't Daddy have been interested? You'll never guess what bedroom we've been put in. Lincoln's.'

Kitty's eyes went vacant.

'Do you remember how Grandma used to say that Lincoln was the Devil?' said Blanche.

Her mother's eyes focused again. 'Your grandmother shouldn't have told you children that,' she said benignly.

The telephone rang and Mavis answered it. She frowned. 'It's a reporter from the *Richmond Herald*,' she told Blanche. 'She's at the front desk. A Mr Jaspar Byatt told them that you were visiting our mother today. There's also an AP photographer who'd like to take a picture of the three of us together.'

Blanche gave an almost imperceptible nod.

'Do you remember, Mama, all those years that Daddy worked for the *Richmond Herald*?' she said. 'That's where he met you when you were a reporter. When Mavis and I were growing up, he used to go away on foreign assignments for the *Herald*, and we always had a big celebration when he came home.'

The doorbell rang. A pleasant young woman reporter and a male photographer came in. When introductions were being made, Kitty gave the newcomers her lovely smile.

'We don't have long with our mother,' said Blanche, 'before I have to be back at the White House to change for our return dinner for the President. It's being given at the British Embassy.'

She knew that the quickest way to get rid of a reporter was to give her a quote, however mundane.

The photographer asked Mavis to lean over the back of her mother's chair. Scribbling on a notepad, the reporter went on asking Blanche questions. Then they were satisfied and said goodbye to Kitty, and Mavis took them to the door, after which she made some tea. As Blanche kissed her mother goodbye, she said: 'I'll be back soon, Mama.'

'That would be delightful, dear.'

Before her return journey alone to Washington, the sisters found a bench on the front veranda of the apartment house.

'Obviously I'll have to discuss it with Luke. But I'd like to stay over for two extra nights and have some time with Mama. I could sleep in the second bedroom.'

Blanche barely had time to dress for Luke's return dinner for the President. A small cavalcade of limousines and outriders left the White House and made for that sweep of Massachusetts Avenue known as Embassy Row. Of all the national showcases lining each side, the most impressive was the British Embassy, its red brick walls and white columns rising dramatically below Sir Edwin Lutyens' great pediment.

On their way into dinner, the Ambassador showed Blanche the spot on the marble floor where the wife of an earlier British Foreign Secretary had fainted on a State occasion and broken her jaw, ending up in the President's suite at Bethesda Hospital. Blanche muttered to President Masters: 'It's only my adrenaline that has kept me from doing the same thing on this marathon.'

'I'd be only too happy,' replied the President, squeezing her hand, 'for you to have the suite that's kept reserved for me at Bethesda. So far, thank God, I've had no use for it.'

As soon as they were back at the White House, the Daltons

bid their hosts goodnight and went up to the Lincoln Bedroom, where Blanche told Luke about the visit to her mother.

'She's going farther and farther away so fast that I want to have a little more time with her while connection between us is still possible.'

Exhilarated by the evening's success, Luke immediately phoned his private secretary who was staying at a grand mansion called Blair House, another home-away-from-home for foreign dignitaries on official visits to the United States.

'Andrew, my wife wants to stay over for a couple of nights with her frail mother. Can you see any reason why this shouldn't be possible?... I'm sure you can fix that.' He put down the phone and said good-temperedly to Blanche: 'Of course you can stay over with your mother. You have nothing in London that can't be postponed. Tomorrow, get my staff to arrange your air ticket.'

From the hallway between their bedrooms, Blanche liked to watch Kitty, dressed in a silk kimono, sitting at her dressing table, brushing her hair upside down. She would then give it a shake and move around her bedroom with her hair standing on end 'until it has lifted by the roots, dear'.

On the third day, Blanche phoned her mother's housekeeper to confirm that she was returning to London that afternoon. When Kitty went to her bedroom to rest, Blanche leant over the pillow to kiss her goodbye.

'I'll be back before very long,' she said, and Kitty looked into her daughter's face and gave her beautiful smile.

Chapter Fifteen

O<small>N</small> the morning that Luke and Jaspar returned from America, the *Times* gave prominence to a long letter signed by ten left-wingers in the party. It began by calling for much more money for the National Health Service. Halfway through, it changed tack, criticising the Prime Minister for 'his love affair with the American President and for his overt imitation of the presidential system of government. The Prime Minister cannot be allowed quietly to curtail our long history of parliamentary democracy. The letter ended with the words: 'We have reason to believe that we have the private support of the Secretary for Health.'

Within hours the Health Secretary put out a statement claiming that though he was aware of the letter, he had not read it.

'Sack him today so he'll have time to take reading lessons,' said Max Murphy, who was with Luke and Jaspar in the Prime Minister's study.

'Let him gnaw his nails for a few weeks. I'll get rid of him in next month's re-shuffle,' Luke answered calmly, cold-eyed. 'I only put him in Cabinet to demonstrate how I've so enfeebled the left that I can afford to give one of them a job – providing he sticks to the project. *My* project.'

'You turn your back for a minute and the bastard bites the hand that feeds him,' said Jaspar. 'I say sack him today.'

'Then the media will claim yet again that I'm an over-sensitive control freak. There are other ways to torment him before the re-shuffle.'

'Leave it to me,' said Jaspar.

Late that night, alone in the flat, Luke lay back in the Eames chair, gazing at the ceiling, a glass of wine beside him. He was reflecting on his feelings about President Richard Masters.

Luke was still new enough to office to be dazzled by proximity with the most powerful leader in the world. He was charmed by Masters' manly charisma and personal boldness. Those three days in the White House had made Luke feel they could be partners on the international scene when an appropriate opportunity presented itself.

He was able to set aside his contempt for Masters' compulsive sexual promiscuity and lies. All leaders had to lie at some time. Any boundary between spin-doctoring and lies was not easily discernible. Masters, however, got caught out in his lies. Yet when the President was dangerously threatened by personal scandal, with careful words Luke gave him support: 'He has lifted the American economy to its highest level of prosperity in the last twenty-five years. On the international scene his presence has guaranteed peace throughout most of the western world.'

Thoughtfully he sipped his wine. If only something could arise in the world which would require international action. America would, of course, be senior partner in any such operation. But Luke would voice a warrior's leadership – and moral leadership. Margaret Thatcher had led Britain into the Falklands War and won it. On the strength of that, she had gone on to achieve moral leadership. What destroyed her in the end was her own hubris. Luke would match her achievements, excel them even, without succumbing to that hubris which throughout history has brought down seemingly invulnerable leaders.

Relaxed in his chair, his feet propped on the ottoman, he tried to visualise an international crisis that he alone had the force of character to resolve. He spoke aloud a few ringing phrases, improved them, spoke again. There were some dreams of glory that a leader would not whisper even to his wife. Tonight a new thought surfaced: before his first term in office was out, he must win the Nobel Peace Prize. Who could question his authority then? He would be bound to go on and win the next election. Even the one after that. His dream for a more just Britain, where men and women might fulfil their potential, and useful enterprise would reap reward, would come to pass. Unconsciously he adopted the evangelical's vernacular.

Blanche arrived back in Downing Street at the weekend. Luke was in his constituency. She wandered through each room of the Downing Street flat, not yet feeling jetlag, tingling. After a time she went down to the State reception rooms, suddenly running upstairs again. She examined her Netherby train timetable. She knew Luke would be watching the home team play Laresby. She got through to the agent.

'Harry, it's Blanche. I'm back. I'm catching the next train to Netherby. Make sure Luke stops by our house after the football match.'

Two hours later she was upstairs in the cosy terrace house when she heard its front door slam and Luke's voice shouting: 'Blanche?'

She flew down the stairs.

'It seems as if I stayed behind much longer than three days,' she said into his neck. 'Maybe it was because the days before that were so surreal I might as well have been on a different planet. I'm so glad to see you.'

She drew back from him to check he looked the same.

'God, I'd like to spend the rest of the afternoon here.' He looked at his watch. 'I'm to see the Town Clerk at five to discuss the new development. Come too. What made you decide to join me here?'

'I couldn't wait until tomorrow.'

It was eleven o'clock when the last of Saturday's constituency commitments was behind them, and Blanche was surreptitiously yawning.

'Goodnight all,' Luke said to the others. 'I have a jetlagged wife.'

Lying side by side in bed, he told her about the end of the White House visit which she had missed, and she told him about Richmond. Laughing she added drowsily: 'Remember that movie in the White House? Remind me to tell you tomorrow about your hero playing footsie.' Resting her head in the crook of his arm, she reached out a hand to his body. In the next instant she was asleep.

Over breakfast the next day he asked her about the 'footsie' episode with the President. When she told him, she made it sound ridiculous – as indeed it was. She was interested to note that Luke was wholly amused, without a flicker of resentment. He was possessive of her, she knew, yet he had no difficulty in accepting the President's overture as comic. None of the Caesar's wife business. She realised he had double standards when the man was President of the United States.

Constituents had often asked her: 'What's it like to be the Prime Minister's wife?' This time they wanted to know: 'What's it like to stay in the White House?'

Frequently she used her newspaper columns to answer their questions – up to a point. She was a natural essayist, and the columns were informative and entertaining. She was not a fool:

she had no problem in separating confidential conversations from material for her writing.

Normally the column came out each week. But as most of her life had little pattern, she might produce nothing for a week or so and then bunch several columns together – as she did when writing about the visit to Washington. She used her experiences to illustrate fundamental differences between Americans and Brits.

If she had not quite finished her writing, she grumbled when she had to break off to host a lunch for the German Chancellor's wife. But by the time she got back to the Downing Street flat, she had already thought out a way to use the lunch as a springboard for describing distinctive German characteristics.

'That's too close to the bone,' Jaspar said to Luke when he first saw the columns in print.

'Take it up with Blanche, not me,' Luke replied.

That was easier said than done, Jaspar knew. Blanche was prickly about him interfering in her work. She finally agreed what she called a compromise with him. At the same time as sending her copy to her editor, she sent a duplicate to Jaspar. Should Jaspar object to something, very occasionally she altered the offending sentence if the piece lost nothing by doing so. More often she told him: 'I thought about the way you suggested I change it. I like my way better.'

She seldom protested when Downing Street's official social demands conflicted with interviews which her own work required. For she knew that if she complained, she could jeopardise keeping her job. Having a job of her own not only gave her satisfaction. Without it, she might become like those spouses who resented their appendage position, however privileged it might be.

'I'll tell you what Luke and Robert Oakes are like,' she said to Thaddeus. He was at the Downing Street flat for dinner.

'They're like that two-headed Indian creature with bodies joined together. They live here cheek by jowl. When they want to argue out some economic point, Robert comes through the connecting passage into the PM's part of the body. Afterwards, he goes back through the passage and their two heads function independently again.'

At that moment, Robert was with Luke downstairs in the Prime Minister's study. When their talk ended, each would return to his private flat, Luke to the top floor of Number Ten, Robert to Number Eleven. Meantime Thaddeus was having a drink with Blanche.

'It's a system that works very well,' he said. 'The Prime Minister has to support the Chancellor in Cabinet. But then if fiscal policy comes unstuck, the Chancellor alone bears the responsibility. Bye, bye, Chancellor.'

'When does the Prime Minister take the rap for something going wrong?'

'If Jaspar Byatt does his stuff, never,' Thaddeus replied drily, 'though if Democratic Labour should ever split over major policy the way the Conservatives did, not even Jaspar could conceal that. Luke could then be in deep trouble at the next election. But that's unlikely to happen when you have a Prime Minister as authoritarian as this one.'

The key turned in the front door lock.

'Ah, this must be young Dalton now. Your wife has just compared you and the Chancellor to a two-headed monster.'

Luke gave his big white smile. He was always glad to see Thaddeus.

The public was generally bored stiff by the minutiae of politics – often by the entire subject – but the inhabitants of Westminster and their hangers-on never tired of their game of snakes and ladders. This time their gossip concerned the approaching Cabinet re-shuffle.

'I still haven't finalised it in my mind,' said Luke, 'so most of them are entitled to feel on tenterhooks. Not more than three or four are safe, with the Chancellor the safest of all. Robert has masterminded an economic situation that would have been the envy of any other Labour government. He is virtually unsackable.'

'Does it ever give you an odd feeling to know your next door neighbour would love to see you stub your toe so badly that a leadership election would be called?' asked Thaddeus.

Luke shrugged.

'No one should ever forget that it happened to Mrs Thatcher when she thought she was invincible,' Thaddeus reminded him.

Blanche strolled to the kitchen to get supper on the table. She had peppers baking in the oven and water boiling in a big pan in readiness for pasta, and suddenly the room felt intolerably hot. She was trying to open the window – she'd have to get someone to loosen it tomorrow – when Luke and Thaddeus heard a crash. On reaching the kitchen, they found her crumpled on the floor.

'Get the fucking window open,' Luke said, crouching beside her to lift her into a sitting position against his knee. Thaddeus demonstrated an unexpected domestic side by turning off the boiling water before helping Luke carry her to the drawing room. At the very moment they laid her on the sofa, she came around. 'Try her with a little brandy,' said Thaddeus. Luke brought a glass of brandy and a tumbler of water. She sipped both.

'I don't know what happened.'

'You've been under a lot of stress,' Luke answered. 'Everyone says that politicians' spouses feel the strain more than the politicians. Take another swallow.' He pushed back the wet strands of hair that clung to her damp face.

'I'm all right now,' she said, trying to sit up. Luke put a cushion against the sofa arm so she could gradually get upright.

'Could someone turn off the water that was boiling on the cooker? And turn the oven down?'

'That's my new role,' said Thaddeus. 'You never guessed I was a master chef, did you?'

He was soon back.

'There are enough baked peppers in the oven for a meal in themselves, and they smell delicious. I've taken them out and put the garlic bread in their place. Presto. The perfect supper.'

Blanche smiled wanly.

'We'll eat it in here,' said Luke.

Thaddeus left soon afterwards.

'I'm going to have an early night with Blanchie,' Luke told her. When he switched off the bedside lights and took her in his arms, he said: 'I'd be much obliged if you didn't scare me like that again. You must ring the GP first thing tomorrow.'

Next day Blanche went to the surgery. After taking blood samples, the GP asked: 'When did you last go to the fertility clinic?'

The following morning Blanche was in Harley Street. When the gynaecologist had completed her tests she gave a wintry smile of satisfaction: 'You're pregnant,' she said.

Blanche burst into tears of relief and joy.

Luke had never fully shared her desire for a child. 'If you want it so much, then I hope that doctor can get your ovaries open,' he had said more than once, 'but if she fails, it will be on your account that I'll be disappointed, not mine.'

He couldn't explain his lack of enthusiasm.

'I wonder if other men care less than their wives about having offspring,' he suggested, 'but don't say so.'

'Quite a few women don't want children,' Blanche replied. 'I see nothing terrible in taking that decision. It's just that I *do* want your child.'

'Perhaps I'm less keen because we have such a close marriage. Inevitably a child will make a big change in that.'

'Would you prefer to put all your energy into your career and me?'

'Possibly.'

She hadn't talked to him much about her visits to Harley Street. When he'd made his own visit to have his sperm stored, he described the scene to her in a self-mocking way.

'Do you think your lack of enthusiasm has something to do with my being unable to be impregnated directly?' she asked.

'Don't know.'

'It's not as if you were impotent.'

What she believed would happen – *if* she could be successfully impregnated – was that once he saw her pregnant he would be greatly moved.

On her way home from Harley Street, she longed to tell him her news, certain it would deepen still further his love for her. He had flown to Cologne for the G8 Summit meetings with President Masters and six European heads of government, but he would get back to Downing Street late that night. She visualised his hand laid tenderly on her belly.

She was propped against the bed pillows reading, waiting to hear the front door lock turn. He came straight to the bedroom to greet her, still carrying his overnight bag and Prime Minister's box.

'I have something to tell you,' she said softly.

'Come into the next room and I'll pour us each a tiny drink.'

In her bare feet she padded into the drawing room and took her chair, expectant and proud.

'I can tell from your face that it's good news,' he replied with a smile.

'I'm pregnant.'

In the silence that followed, he pursed his lips and a deep scowl drew his brows together.

'We'll talk about it tomorrow. I still have work to do,' he said.

Chapter Sixteen

*T*HE next day found Blanche subdued and depressed. She sat down to write a column, staring at her computer, willing herself to think of a subject, only to have her concentration crack as her hurt broke in again.

She didn't see Luke until seven, when he came up before going on to a working dinner with the Lord Chancellor about the still unfinished reform of the House of Lords. 'I need to speak to you before I leave,' he told her. 'Can you come in the bedroom while I change my shirt?'

She sat on the side of the bed and watched him. His eyes met hers in the mirror over the mantelpiece. He looked away, frowning slightly as he appeared to concentrate on his tie.

'Each time I think of last night,' he said, 'I wince. I keep seeing you waiting up for me, waiting to tell me your news.' He gave his head a quick shake of disgust and turned to meet her eyes directly. 'My reaction was boorish, revolting, in every way horrible. What wouldn't I give to be able to replay that scene? I must have known at the time that I was hurting you. Why should I have wanted to do that? Can you ever forgive me?'

Looking down at her hands, she turned them palms up and studied them, as if they held the secret of the universe. When she raised her eyes she said: 'What's there to forgive? You can't help it that you don't share my feelings about a baby.'

'They're not the same as yours, but neither are they as different as my behaviour suggested. If you will give me a little time, I'll show you.'

She got off the bed and stood silently in front of him, barely against him, raising her face to rub her cheek against his.

'Like a pony,' he said.

After some moments, she moved back. 'When you return from the Lord Chancellor, let's start all over again.'

He pressed his hand against her cheek, rested his mouth on hers and left.

On his return, she was sitting up in bed reading. She closed the book. 'I have something to tell you,' she said, the corners of her mouth turned up at their collusion in play-acting.

'I know from your face that it's good news.'

'I'm pregnant.'

He crossed the room to sit on the bed beside her. He put out his hand and gently laid it on her belly. They remained like that for some minutes until at last she lifted his hand and held its palm against her mouth.

The following evening they were dressing for a dinner they were hosting for the President of the European Union when the private telephone rang. Luke took it.

'It's Mavis, Luke. I'm glad I could reach you. Mama isn't very well.'

'Blanche is right here if you want to speak with her.'

'Probably better if I tell you first. When her housekeeper arrived two days ago, she found Mama lying on the floor in the sitting room. In her nightdress, so heaven knows how long she'd been there. She didn't know how she got there. Her hip was broken. She's in hospital and has been safely operated on.'

Mavis paused. Luke waited. Blanche crossed the room and

stood beside him. 'What's happened? What's happened?'

'Your mother has broken her hip. She's been operated on successfully. Let me finish talking with Mavis and then I'll hand the phone to you. She was in the middle of telling me something. Mavis. Go on.'

'The doctor says we must face the fact that our mother will never be the same again. She'll be able to walk, but the shock has taken a dire toll on her mind. When she leaves hospital, she will need round-the-clock nursing care. Indefinitely.'

'I see.'

'Shall I speak to Blanche now?'

'She's next to me.'

He handed over the phone. 'Tell me from the beginning.'

When Mavis had finished, Blanche asked: 'Shall I come now?'

'There's no point yet. She's really out of it.'

'How?'

'Each time somebody enters her room she asks when Daddy's coming home. She asks if anyone has told him she has hurt herself. When she's able to walk on one of those frames, she'll go back to the apartment and I'll arrange for nurses. It may prove a short-lived phase. I'll start looking into the question of nursing homes.'

When Blanche put down the phone, Luke said: 'Perhaps it's a good thing you have to be hostess tonight. It may take your mind off your mother.'

'It's Mavis who has to do all the managing because I'm here.'

After some weeks and numerous telephone calls between the sisters, Mavis rang to say that it was not working out at the apartment.

Blanche felt the tension known to everyone who's in the middle, but she controlled it and waited for a good moment to tell Luke she had to leave again. This time he didn't complain.

Once back in Richmond she slept in her mother's apartment

in one of the twin beds in what was now the night nurse's bedroom. Her mother knew her and seemed glad to see her. Each time that Blanche left the room for a few minutes, when she returned Kitty said: 'Why, dear, how lovely to see you. Where have you come from?'

All the while conscious of her sister's full-time responsibility, Blanche went to inspect the spacious nursing home which Mavis had chosen. Once a convent, it stood among rolling green hills outside Richmond.

When the morning for the move came round, Blanche woke sweating with nausea. Crouched in the bathroom, she saw she wasn't bringing up food. When the retching stopped, she still felt so sick she had to lie down again. Kitty's nurse brought her a dry biscuit. Not long afterwards, Blanche felt strong enough to get up and face what lay ahead.

She told her mother of the move ahead to the nursing home: 'You'll feel safer there.'

'That's not necesssary, dear. I like it here.'

While the nurse took Kitty for a walk on the frame to the old-fashioned drugstore where they had an early lunch, the moving van came for her bed and other pieces of furniture and rugs and sentimental objects. Returning with the nurse, Kitty noticed the Victorian wing chair was gone. Blanche told her it was being taken to her new home. Mavis drove them there.

Kitty's room looked cosy with the familiar furniture. While she sipped tea, her daughters rearranged the furniture and knick-knacks, hung the pictures, set up the family photographs.

Kitty declined to have another cup of tea, saying: 'This has been very nice, children, but I think we should be getting home now.'

After an excruciating silence, Mavis said: 'This is to be your home now, Mama.'

'It has been very nice, but I think we should be getting

home,' her mother said firmly. The next time she repeated it, a note of panic was in her soft Virginia voice.

Two days later, Blanche took the evening flight from Baltimore airport to Heathrow. Halfway across the Atlantic, she woke aware of strange sensations in her belly. She made her way through the dimmed lights to a lavatory, reaching it just when sharp, hard contractions began. With gasping groans of horror, she miscarried into the lavatory bowl.

Chapter Seventeen

LUKE'S dream of a humanitarian colossus bestriding the world stage seemed to be moving towards reality through Jaspar's calculation. British television news had latched on to the savage cruelty of 'ethnic cleansing' in the Balkans. For as long as anyone could remember, Muslim Albanians and Orthodox Christian Serbs had lived in a sporadic truce in Slavonia. Now President Vronovik, the Serb dictator of Slavonia, was 'cleansing' the province of Begova of its Albanian population, ie, massacring them or driving them out of their homeland. Mutilated bodies, children with stumps for arms, refugees with their pathetic belongings on their backs were nightly fare on British television.

'It has everything,' Jaspar told Luke.

The Prime Minister seized the opportunity with both hands, bombarding the American President, whose active cooperation was essential, with urgent telephone calls.

'Dick,' Luke said yet again to the President, 'I've been brooding about our conversation yesterday.' They were speaking on the scrambler between Number Ten and the Oval Office. 'How much longer can you and I do nothing to force NATO's hand? All right, it is internationally illegal to interfere in a sovereign state. Yet every night the British and American public see mass murder in Begova, unspeakable atrocities,

Albanian villages in ruins. We have got to intervene on humanitarian grounds.'

'Eighty per cent of any NATO military intervention would have to be undertaken by American planes. And the last thing the American people want is to be dragged into a new Vietnam,' President Masters replied, not for the first time. '"What's it got to do with us?" is their attitude. The United States is a helluva long way from southeastern Europe.'

'Those nations that have the power have the responsibility to do what needs to be done.'

'Look, Luke, we are talking about a religious conflict within a sovereign state. They've been murdering each other for centuries. If it were a once and for all operation, it would be easier to persuade Americans to take an interest. But even supposing this mayhem could be ended by our bombing the shit out of the heart of Slavonia, we'll destroy as many Albanian villages and refugees as President Vronovik's troops are doing now. Possibly more. If we are not to lose bombers, they must stay too high to pinpoint targets accurately.'

'We cannot call ourselves humanitarians and stand by doing nothing,' Luke repeated doggedly. 'We have to show barbarians that there is a new internationalism that will not tolerate these atrocities.'

'We'll speak tomorrow,' said Masters.

Conventional bombing alone could not win such a war. Nor could a war on the ground be won; it would oblige NATO troops to remain in a devastated Begova indefinitely. Nonetheless, most Britons watching their television screens said: 'Something must be done.'

This decent emotional response was shared by Luke, and quickly he picked up the banner and placed himself at the forefront. Military critics could carp all they liked about this 'witless war' that he was promoting. Polls showed that Dalton's popularity remained strong.

'He's like a *Boy's Own* hero,' Max Murphy said to Jaspar. 'The public still have idealistic feelings buried beneath their cynicism. Human beings need to believe in somebody or something. Luke is tapping into that need.'

'I wonder if he has thought the thing through,' Jaspar answered in a detached voice, producing a quill pick to clean his teeth while he reflected.

'Probably not,' Max replied. 'Never forget that after the age of four he saw his parents once a year, and they died when he was nine. He must have lived in his imagination more than most boys. The commonest fantasy is being a leader and saving the world. Luke still gets carried away by the dream. He wants to turn fantasy into reality.'

Jaspar examined his toothpick before returning it to his pocket. 'Does that lessen your opinion of him?'

'On the contrary. It's his boyish vulnerability that makes him lovable. You feel he needs you. If along with his high ideals he appeared to be an unblemished man, he wouldn't command the same loyalty. An unflawed leader makes his men feel superfluous.'

'No fear of that with President Masters' men,' Jaspar commented drily. After a silence he went on: 'When Masters was most endangered by sexual scandal, I believe Luke was entirely sincere in giving the President his public support. He doesn't expect the same standards of others that he has set for himself.'

'Except in his wife.'

Now another sex scandal erupted in the White House, President Masters desperately sought to distract public attention from it by launching a small war. He put a call through on the scrambler to the British Prime Minister.

'You'll be pleased,' he said to Luke. 'Forty-eight hours from now, our bombers go in. My private guess is that they'll bring President Vronovik to his knees before three weeks are out.'

Luke's announcement to the House of Commons that day was highly emotional. 'Age-old international law is being challenged. We are saying to a sovereign state: "You can no longer brutalise a large section of your own people. We will stop you." We pray that the cost to our gallant troops will be minimal. They know that we undertake this war with right on our side.'

Two months after this exultant proclamation – long past the three weeks duration that President Masters had so optimistically predicted – NATO's largely American air power further accelerated its bombing of Slavonia. Regrettably, countless bombs fell on the Albanian hordes fleeing Begova, the very people whom NATO was trying to help.

Since the disaster during her flight back to London, Blanche had been uncharacteristically irritable. Long into the conflict in Begova, she said to Luke: 'Occasionally I get the feeling that you don't see me as a real person, that you see me as your ideal of a politician's wife.'

It was a Sunday evening, and to unwind he had chosen to stroll the short distance from Downing Street to Thaddeus's flat. The tradition in Britain is not to have excessive security. Instead, two bodyguards walked far enough behind to allow the Prime Minister and his wife to have a private conversation, and more bodyguards were in a car that followed at a walking pace.

'I hope you don't mean what you say,' he replied.

She didn't answer. When they reached the centre of Westminster Bridge, they stopped and leant on the railings, looking down at a tug leading a barge beneath the bridge, Big Ben and the Houses of Parliament just beyond.

In a less than amiable voice she said: 'Funny to think how much water has flowed under this bridge since we first looked down together at the Thames.'

Ignoring her tetchy tone, Luke said: 'This evening is a little demonstration to ourselves and our watchdogs that we don't always have to be ushered swiftly from the car into a building. If anyone wants to pop me off, it can be done in the seconds it takes to cross the pavement, as too many American politicians have discovered.'

She made no comment.

He glanced sideways at her. 'Are you getting your period?'

'I wish you wouldn't ask that every time I fail to please you,' Blanche replied sharply. What made it doubly irritating was that in fact she *was* getting her period.

They crossed the rest of the bridge in silence, indifferent to any cars slowing down while their occupants took a second look.

Approaching the handsome tower block where Thaddeus lived, Luke said: 'We haven't that much opportunity for a normal social life. Let's decide now to enjoy our evening with Thaddeus.'

'Okay,' she replied in a conciliatory tone.

Stepping from the lift directly into the entrance hall, they were met by Bella's successor, she too dressed in singularly fetching maid's attire. Luke remarked to the two bodyguards who remained in the lift: 'You can see I'm in safe hands now.'

The current vision showed the Daltons into the drawing room as if they'd never been there before. As usual, Thaddeus was on the telephone, swinging his swivel armchair from side to side as he completed his conversation.

He jumped to his feet to embrace Blanche, only then addressing the Prime Minister. 'Dear boy. How very agreeable to see you without Jaspar hovering. You've met Marcia. Marcia, would you kindly mix up three gin martinis in the way we discussed yesterday evening? Above all, remember not to put them in a cocktail shaker and bruise the gin.'

Crossing to the big window and looking out, Blanche found any residue of her grumpiness vanishing. This flat had a glamour all of its own; the view over the river was quite spectacular. She suddenly felt as though she were on holiday from the Houses of Parliament opposite and the constrictions of governing that she associated with them.

Settled with their drinks, they turned at once to NATO's continuing bombing of Slavonia, which was answered daily by President Vronovik stepping up the slaughter of those Albanians who chanced remaining in their homes in Begova. Undeterred, Luke had just given yet another gung-ho interview, this one to the *New York Times* around the theme: 'Dictators can no longer with impunity persecute their own people to stay in power.'

'Where do you stand, Blanche, on the great divide? Do you see young Dalton as the fearless warrior who believes every tyrant can be flushed out and run to ground? Or is he a naive do-gooder whose interference is causing greater havoc to the very people he is trying to help?'

Blanche looked uneasily at Luke. 'I admire Luke's championing of those who are being abused.' She paused. 'But as it has led to many more abuses, I'm not sure what the point is.'

Luke bristled. 'One would think you were being paid to act as Vronovik's propagandist.'

Blanche flushed.

'Well, what is your answer to the fact that President Masters has promised his voters that American ground forces will never be used in Slavonia?' asked Thaddeus. 'NATO's bombing has not brought Vronovik to his knees. All it has achieved is increased slaughter of the people you meant to help. Where do you go from here?'

Luke's expression darkened. 'You would have preferred me to see no evil, hear no evil,' he replied sulkily.

'I would have preferred you to discipline your desire to rush into the affairs of other countries. You have gone for the melodramatic action which achieves nothing.'

'Between you and Blanche,' said Luke petulantly, 'any hope of a few hours' respite from international problems has been wiped out.'

Rising from his chair, he suddenly looked exhausted.

'Come on, Blanche. I've got plenty to do at Number Ten. Let's go.'

Blanche stood up and said to Thaddeus: 'Please apologise to Marcia. Even if we stayed for dinner, it'd only be a strain for all of us now. What on earth would we talk about?'

She lifted her face to kiss him. At that moment, she admired him more than she admired Luke.

There was no interest on either side in a romantic walk back across the bridge. They had barely got in the car when Luke bleeped Jaspar at his home.

'Sorry to disturb your evening, but I need you at Downing Street. I'll be downstairs in the study.'

At his press briefing the next morning, the Prime Minister's official spokesman let it be known that Britain would be sending combat troops and tanks to Begova against Vronovik's thugs, who continued to rape and kill and burn.

'It has become evident that bombing alone will not drive Vronovik's Serbs out of the province. The Prime Minister will not stand by while the barbarities continue. On humanitarian grounds, he plans to send in fifty thousand British soldiers to restore peace and civilisation to Begova.'

As the representative of a distinguished British newspaper, Mark Fleetwood attended these daily press briefings, but Jaspar refused to accept any questions from him. Mark had stopped trying 'to catch the official spokesman's eye' except to amuse himself and his fellow journalists by the futility of his efforts. His revenge was his column the following day:

'By flying at the safe height of 15,000 feet, NATO's bombers managed to kill five times as many innocent civilians as did Vronovik's military forces. Now Crusader Dalton yearns to have a go on the ground. Even his silver tongue has failed to persuade any of Britain's NATO partners to send combat troops into the province. Never mind. In his over-excitement, the Crusader now plans to send 50,000 of our own soldiers – ie, the entire British Army – to invade the province and drive out Vronovik's marauders. When the inevitable cycle moves on and surviving Albanians wreak a savage vengeance on any Serb they can lay their hands on, what will the Crusader think up then?'

Chapter Eighteen

ROBERT Oakes bided his time. Five years had passed since he had been prevailed upon to withdraw from Democratic Labour's leadership contest. Perhaps because his wife had died only days before, he had let himself be persuaded that Luke's extrovert charm and skill at courting the media were more likely to win over the Conservative middle-class vote in the general election. Robert's own serious setting forth of principles, it had been said against him, might well have made them wary. His heart remained bitter. From the moment he became Chancellor, he made himself a powerful, invaluable and potentially dangerous Number Two.

Luke talked emotionally about the radical changes his Government was making in education, health, social services, the environment, the police. But he restrained the ministers of those same departments from taking the radical long-term decisions which in the short term might be unpopular.

His style of political management was in fact conservative: he believed in waiting as long as possible to see if circumstances would improve. After two years in Government, the radical reforms that Democratic Labour had promised were still a mirage. While Jaspar continued to exercise his hypnotic powers over the media, and polls showed Luke's personal popularity remained high, the public itself could not but notice that schools, hospitals, social services etc remained as lamentable as before.

The Chancellor's approach to Government was the reverse of the Prime Minister's. Robert took crucial decisions as soon as possible, while the new administration was still enjoying its honeymoon phase, before things had a chance to go wrong. In the first year, he made radical changes in economic policy and taxation. Were there a way for him to grasp the premiership, he knew he would make the better statesman. But how to get there?

'Dalton may stub his toe sooner than we thought possible,' said Roly Barksure, Robert's media manager. They were alone in the Chancellor's study at Number Eleven. Roly would have liked to have been the Chancellor's Jaspar Byatt, 'official spokesman' for his master, but Robert said waspishly that he preferred to be his own spokesman. Roly had to content himself with running around pointing out to the media how exhausted the PM looked these days, how he had aged ten years in two, how unnamed MPs were asking whether he had the staying power necessary. None of the derogatory asides he fed the media were to be attributed, of course.

'Paradoxically,' said Robert, 'while Luke drags his feet over vital domestic decisions, he rushes into international affairs as if he were in a race for the Nobel Prize. Convinced that he can put the world to rights, he imagines that intervening in Begova is as simple as playing toy soldiers. Unfortunately he has persuaded NATO HQ to listen to him.'

All but two of the Cabinet bowed to Luke's eagerness to crusade against the dictator Vronovik. Robert kept his silence. Did he perhaps hope that Luke's great new adventure would fail? Stanley Fox, the Foreign Secretary, was equivocal, playing it both ways.

He too had not given up his ambition for the premiership. If Luke failed in Begova, Fox would let the media know that he had feared this all along. Even though the Defence Secretary, who dealt directly with NATO, would probably have to carry the can, Luke's lustre might be irredeemably tarnished. On the other hand, if Luke emerged the hero of Begova, he might well punish Robert Oakes for his lack of support, and make Fox his Chancellor and heir apparent. So far the dictator showed not the slightest sign of collapsing beneath NATO's rain of bombs.

At the weekly meetings of the Cabinet, other ministers were intimidated by the power Luke had gathered at Number Ten. With Jaspar Byatt sitting in at Cabinet, taking notes throughout, ministers rarely spoke except to voice agreement with the Prime Minister. Luke's contempt for the House of Commons, which he attended as little as possible, deprived ministers of a Commons base to bolster their confidence. All these factors reduced boldness in mastering their departments with sufficient skill to carry out the promises made before the election. Only the Treasury was run with clear direction and panache. Should the electorate turn against the Prime Minister, the one member of the Cabinet who could challenge him was the Chancellor, despite the Foreign Secretary's dreams.

State reception rooms at Number Eleven were few compared with Number Ten, though the Chancellor's private flat was much larger than the Prime Minister's. Had it come to Robert sooner in his life, there would have been four people occupying it. But with Julie dead and his sons away at school as weekly boarders, most of the time he lived in a home which was far too big for him. He went on working at his boxes while he was there and welcomed the undisturbed quiet.

Yet he was not a recluse. He enjoyed feminine company. He wished he could take a woman friend to the opera without reading about it the next day in the gossip columns, for the publicity encouraged speculation that the widower might soon marry again. At present that was not Robert's intention.

Rebecca Knight, a solicitor, had enjoyed a year of being his sometime companion. Attractive and unmarried, she was often asked to Dorneywood, which at that time was the Chancellor's country residence. A Queen Anne mansion in Buckinghamshire, Dorneywood was one of the most desired perks of high office. It was where Robert's young sons joined him on those weekends that he was able to get away from London. Rebecca took the responsibility for planning menus in advance with the housekeeper. When Robert was working on his ministerial boxes, she and the boys went to the billiard room to play for 5p a point. One way and another, she hoped to make herself indispensable.

The largest State room at Number Eleven was where the Chancellor held his annual drinks party for the media. On this occasion, Rebecca was present as unofficial hostess. Part way through the evening, the Chancellor's next door neighbours called in to join the party for half an hour, accompanied by Jaspar Byatt. As they normally did on social occasions, Luke and Blanche moved off in different directions.

At once, Rebecca came up to Blanche. 'I'm so glad to have a minute with you,' she said. 'I greatly enjoy your column and learn more from it than I do from the stuff written by most of the press that accompanies you and your husband to the places you describe.'

Blanche beamed with pleasure. 'Thanks.'

'I wish it were possible some time,' Rebecca went on, 'for you and me and Robert and your husband to have a meal together some place. I believe you used to do so frequently in Opposition. I know from Robert how much he admires you.'

'He hasn't told me,' said Blanche, laughing, 'but I'm honoured if that should be his opinion.'

A couple of journalists came up to join them. Blanche knew almost as many members of the press as did Luke. She was at ease with all of them. Few gatherings are more bibulous than those for the media. Each time a waiter with a silver tray was within reaching distance, Mark Fleetwood, the most eminent of Luke's few critics in the press, helped himself to another glass of champagne. Making his way to join the little group around Blanche, he presented himself to her. 'As a fellow journalist, I hope I am allowed to talk to you,' he said to her.

She had a sneaking regard for his column, even though his acid witty criticism of Luke was too often near the bone. It was so beautifully written and well argued that she was curious to know him. If his analysis of Luke sometimes got under her skin, out of pride she would not let Mark Fleetwood see it.

'I gather you do not care for my husband,' she said jauntily.

'On the contrary, I cherish him,' replied Mark. 'Without him, my task of entertaining the readers would be far more toilsome. Tell me, how do you manage to write such an informative column without giving away state secrets?'

'I wish you would repeat that to Jaspar Byatt. He sometimes gets a little twitchy.'

'Speak of the devil,' Mark said with a snort of a laugh.

'I've been delegated to take you from these reptiles,' Jaspar said self-importantly. 'You and the Prime Minister are already late for your next appointment.'

Blanche looked at her watch. 'I'll join him in five minutes. I can see where he's standing.'

'It would be better if you came now.'

Out of the corner of her eye she saw Mark Fleetwood raise his brows.

'I'll join him in five minutes,' she repeated, turning back to Mark.

Pursing his lips, Jaspar went away.

'Does he always nanny you like that?'

'He tries to,' she replied, leaving Mark to interpret that as he wished.

When their car pulled out of Downing Street and made for the Mansion House, where the Lord Mayor was giving a banquet for the Prime Minister to address the capital's financiers, Blanche lifted her pocket mirror to look at the bodyguards' car following behind them. As usual Jaspar was with them. She stuck out her tongue at her mirror.

'What's that *à propos* of?' Luke asked.

'Nanny Byatt. Most of the press are frightened he will tear a strip off them, but to me he's like a mother hen. Cluck cluck cluck. Why did he say we were late when we weren't?'

'He thought it unseemly for you to be making yourself so conspicuously charming to Mark Fleetwood. Did you see what he wrote about me this morning?'

'I think it would have been a good deal more unseemly if I'd slapped his face.'

'Other modes of behaviour do exist.'

'Okay. I could have looked at him icily and put my hands behind my back. Or I could have screamed and rushed away. Personally, I think it's more of a putdown if I act as if his column is of no consequence.'

Luke turned away and looked out of his window silently.

On their way home from the dinner, both were more relaxed. Luke had given a first-class speech about the vital role which financiers played in the new Britain. One of them came up to him afterwards and said: 'As a lifelong Conservative, I never thought the day could come when I would want to contribute to the war chest of another party. Your treasurer will be hearing from me.'

Stepping from the car to enter Number Ten, Blanche glanced

at Number Eleven. 'What time did the party end?' she asked the policeman at the door.

'Soon after nine, Ma'm.'

They took the lift to their flat. 'Did you talk with Robert's solicitor girlfriend tonight?' she asked.

'Not much more than hello.'

'She wondered if the four of us might go out to dinner together some time.'

'When Robert and I need to talk about economic policy, we meet in my study. We see each other at Cabinet. That's enough, I should think, for both of us.'

'We used to go out together when Julie was alive.'

'We were in Opposition then. In Government we're not so comfortable with one another. Each of us has deep reservations about the other. I know that Robert hasn't given up his ambition to have my job. He alone amongst Cabinet ministers has remained totally silent about my pushing for NATO to send combat troops into Begova. If we fail to bring down Vronovik, it will damage my international reputation. I think Robert hopes for that, unpatriotic though it may be.'

'What's it to do with patriotism?' asked Blanche. 'Begova has nothing to do with Britain. Or with the United States, which is why your friend President Dick is not going to involve his country in a war on the ground. Do all the Cabinet except Robert acclaim what you're doing in Begova?'

'Certainly – though Fox, as usual, equivocates.' He looked at her sharply. 'You surely can't think I have made a mistake, can you?'

After a long hesitation, without looking at him she answered: 'I don't know.'

Chapter Nineteen

A T his media briefing some days later, Jaspar announced that the Prime Minister would be going to Begova at the weekend to see for himself what was happening in that tragic land.

'Would you like to go with me?' Luke asked Blanche when he got back from the House of Commons late that evening.

'Oh yes,' she replied without hesitation, sharing his excitement at the prospect.

That night, however, she lay awake thinking about it. It would make a terrific column, perhaps two. She'd often thought about being a war correspondent. But then the uninvited thought pressed in: she wasn't going to this stricken territory as a *bona fide* war correspondent. She was going as the wife of the man who was leading the international argument for NATO to send in troops on the ground, to join the British soldiers already there.

Her mind moved to Jaspar. Was it his idea? She could see the picture he would set up: herself doing an imitation of the late Princess Diana in her Queen of Hearts mode, sitting on the edge of the debris of a destroyed house, her arm around a child with bandaged stumps for legs. She could see the whole thing.

'It's disgusting,' she said aloud, and Luke shifted in his sleep.

In the morning she told him she'd changed her mind. 'There is one purpose only in my going: for Jaspar to get a picture showing how much I care about those mutilated children. It is arrogant and offensive to imagine my compassion can alleviate their tragedy in any way.'

'What makes you so certain it wouldn't give comfort to them to know we care enough to be there? When Princess Diana went to hospitals to comfort the sick and injured, their families said it made a real difference to them.'

'Maybe. But you know and I know that the main point is to be photographed doing it. I think it's cheap and shoddy to exploit these people's misery to show what a wonderful person I am.'

'Then don't come,' Luke said impatiently, leaving the room without further words to gather up his things and go downstairs for a meeting with the Israeli Prime Minister.

'I'm turning into a harridan,' Blanche said to Thaddeus. She had asked him to come to supper that Sunday. They could watch the news together and see Luke in Begova.

Although she had friends in London, it was not like the United States where there was the family. In Richmond she had Mavis, although loyalty to Luke would prevent her from being totally candid with her sister. Funnily, she could discuss some things more freely with Jakie's father. Among her own father's New England family, she had an aunt to whom she could tell just about anything.

But in London there was only Thaddeus to fill the role. The fact that he thought women existed primarily to be groped did not lessen her regard for his judgment in other matters. She thought that he understood Luke better than anyone did except herself, maybe even better than she did.

'You don't look like a scold,' Thaddeus replied.

'At this rate, I soon will. Perhaps any two people who have been together for fourteen years get to know too much about each other.'

'Only a most exceptional couple can avoid that.'

'But we did avoid it until we moved into Downing Street. Since then, qualities – flaws, if you like – that used to be endearing have sort of ballooned. The more power he has, the more authoritarian he becomes, the more certain that he is invincible. I adored Luke, warts and all. I loved adoring him. I don't want to grow cynical.'

She lapsed into strained silence. Thaddeus held his tongue.

'He truly wants to make the world a better place,' she burst out. 'But it's as if he gets a rush of blood to the head and believes he can put everything to rights just by saying that he's going to do so. He doesn't seem to realise that some sort of intellectual analysis is necessary if he's to judge whether his actions will actually accomplish what he had in mind.'

'Luke is very clever, which is something I first saw when he was in my chambers. However, he has never shown the discipline of analysis that a war leader requires. In many ways he has a deceptive personality.'

'Do you think so? I find him very open, even though I may not like what he is saying.'

'I didn't say he is deceitful. On the contrary, he sincerely means whatever he is saying at the time it comes out of his mouth. I meant that his charm of personality is such that most people exposed to it would never guess how ruthless he is in getting his way.'

She got up to turn on the television. The first news item showed Luke in Begova. He was smiling broadly as he raised his arm triumphantly in an athlete's 'high five' greeting and slapped palms with an Albanian standing before rubble that had been his family's home. The man grinned back, as if his life were not in ruins. In the background children chanted 'Luke, Luke' in the way that one of Jaspar's aides had coached them.

From the corner of his eyes, Thaddeus glanced at Blanche. Her profile was expressionless.

Later in bed, she lay awake, trying to suppress her cynicism of the stunts she'd watched on television. All politicians, she knew, had to go in for play-acting. Almost all: the Chancellor came into her mind. Robert Oakes remained the most commanding figure in the Government apart from the Prime Minister. He refused to go in for stunts. Perhaps it wasn't so necessary to be a showman at the Treasury.

She wished she could see Robert more often, but he was always so busy. The last time she had had a drink with him at Number Eleven, only one bedroom was in use, with Charlie and Nat away at school. Robert, always a workaholic, told her he was thankful his job at the Treasury was all-consuming. 'During those years in Opposition after Julie died, work kept me sane. Most of the time. In Government, work is at an infinitely higher pitch, for which I'm grateful.'

Luke, Blanche tried to convince herself, was not ruthlessly exploiting a war-ravaged people; rather, he was manifesting a boyishness which had for so long appealed to her. She thought again of what she'd said to Thaddeus: 'I don't want to grow cynical.'

She shifted the blame to Jaspar. He was the one with an uncanny ability to persuade the media that black was white and white was black. How then, she said to herself, could anyone wonder that Luke was flattered into believing what he saw on television and read in the press about his negotiating skills and courage, despite each week of the Begova horrors showing that the war he had pressed for was counterproductive? Even someone less convinced of the validity of his own point of view than Luke would be susceptible to the daily spin-doctored version of himself.

Might she also be to blame for her present doubts? She had adored Jakie. She had adored her father. In retrospect she still adored them. She had focused her capacity to love unconditionally on Luke. The difference was that she and Luke had spent fourteen grown-up years together, bound to reveal cracks which youthful adoration had disregarded. He was a human being, for God's sake. In this way Blanche dealt with bouts of disenchantment.

When Luke returned from his short visit to Begova, he was still running on adrenaline, gratified by television clips of his walk-about in a mine-infested land (though that piece of terrain had, of course, been thoroughly searched for any unexploded landmines), proud of his high-five slapping of palms with an Albanian survivor of a NATO bomb, excited by the children chanting 'Luke, Luke'.

Blanche was waiting for him at the Downing Street flat. Within minutes of arriving there, he turned on the answer machines, unfastened her skirt and drew her down with him to the sitting room carpet. Had he not known so well where to touch her, his urgency would have made him come alone.

Not so many days later, Blanche received a letter marked 'Personal' from the editor of Mark Fleetwood's newspaper: 'We are all aware that you do not give interviews. But I would like to invite you to be my guest of honour at an entirely private lunch. Six times a year I give such a lunch in a private room at the Savoy. My last guest was the conductor Sir Simon Rattle. It is an opportunity to exchange your ideas with six members of my staff and myself. If, as I hope, you would find this of interest, perhaps your secretary could ring me to discuss a date convenient to you?'

There was no hard and fast rule about letters marked 'Personal' getting unopened past Blanche's secretary, who in turn might or might not send a copy to Jaspar's office when the writer was a member of the press. Blanche had made it plain at the outset that her secretary's first loyalty was to the Prime Minister's wife, not to the Prime Minister's official spokesman. The secretary, screened by Jaspar when she first was employed, felt she was walking a tightrope.

'I'd like to go,' Blanche said to Luke. 'It's fun being with journalists when they're confined to confidentiality.'

'Find out which of the staff will be there. That bastard Fleetwood has never heard the word "confidentiality".'

'I'll make sure that before the lunch I receive a list of the journalists who'll be present.'

'That's not the same thing. You ought to know before you accept.'

'I think that's undignified and insulting to the editor.'

'Look, Blanche, he will be thrilled to have you accept. You can impose any conditions you like.'

'What you mean is that I should stipulate that his political columnist cannot be present,' she said indignantly. 'I find that demeaning. Of course the editor is not going to invite me to a private lunch and then permit one of his staff to report our conversation.'

'I hope you know what you're doing. When we first met and you took me to that whirlpool, you were courting disaster. Over the years I hoped you had outgrown that urge.'

'This is getting a little melodramatic. You talk as if instead of going to the Savoy for lunch, I was about to fly to Begova to walk among a field of landmines.'

Luke flushed. When he had done his walkabout in Begova, he knew the area had been thoroughly searched for landmines. This was nothing to be ashamed of: to endanger the Prime Minister's life would have been madness. Even so, he felt there might be a sting in his wife's words.

'I must soon go across to the House for Prime Minister's

Questions,' he said testily. At the best of times he resented the centuries-old tradition of being questioned by the House of Commons. In his present mood of personal bellicosity towards Vronovik and irritation with his own wife, his sense of aggrievement was considerable as he left the room.

She chose a date at the first gap in her diary, for summer was approaching. The House of Commons would rise at the end of July for the August holiday. This year Blanche and Luke were taking their holiday separately. He would be looked after in the villa of a hospitable Italian grandee who lived not far from Florence. Luke had a passion for architecture which he enjoyed on his own; his bodyguards would see more than enough cathedrals and castles for the taste of most of them. Meanwhile Blanche could return to Richmond for a couple of weeks and make regular visits to her mother in the nursing home, while Mavis and her family took a break for their own holiday.

When she reached the Savoy Hotel, she found her host waiting for her in the lobby. The rest of the party was already assembled in a private dining room. The editor made the introductions. Mark Fleetwood's leisurely gait in coming forward matched the drawl with which he greeted her. The editor set the tone at the outset, steering the conversation into comparisons between America and Britain. This was right up Blanche's street: American idealism compared with British pragmatism; direct action with caution; the work ethic with mockery of work; boastfulness with sly diffidence.

'According to your distinctions,' Mark said to her, 'your husband might be an American.'

Surprised, Blanche considered this, her face tilted to one side. She gave a broad grin. 'I'd never thought of it before. There's something in what you say. Why should that be?'

'The influence of his American wife?' Mark suggested.

'Except that Blanche isn't boastful,' the editor interposed.

'Nor is Luke in private life,' she replied. 'It's Jaspar's briefings which are boastful, but then that's the point of spin-doctoring.'

In this relaxed manner, she was led to talk more freely about Luke than she had expected, though always remaining within the bounds of loyalty to him.

Afterwards Mark said to the editor: 'It was useful. I learned a couple of things about the PM, and rather more things about his wife.'

In the remaining weeks of July, Blanche saw little of her husband. It was the time of year to jam everything in before MPs rose for their holiday. Luke flew to Presnia for a peace summit on the future of Eastern Europe. He paid a second fleeting visit to Begova to see British troops, meet political leaders and make contact with people in the capital, who cheered him ecstatically.

Blanche studied the newspaper photographs closely. When embracing an Albanian child returned now to a homeland ravaged by Serbs and by misdirected NATO bombs, Luke's expression was almost beatific. In several photos, clearly not staged by Jaspar, where Luke's face was captured when he was away from the adulation, he looked utterly exhausted. It was these latter pictures which brought tears to her eyes.

She remained in London until he set off for his three weeks in the peaceful eighteenth-century Tuscan villa. The following day, she flew to Baltimore airport, and from there took a small plane to Virginia where Mavis met her. As they drove into Richmond and the humid heat pressed down upon them, Blanche looked around her with nostalgia. The plan was that she stay with Mavis for a night or two, and when Mavis left for the cool of the north with her husband and children, Blanche would move in with Jakie's father.

'You'll find Mama much changed,' Mavis said.

In the morning they drove to the nursing home on the green

outskirts of the city. On the way from the lift to their mother's door, Mavis sent Blanche ahead while she had a word with the nurse in charge. In the corridor Blanche passed a number of old ladies sitting in a row of chairs against the wall. From the corner of her eye, she noticed a thin lady who sat very erect, her expression blank, like a statue, and Blanche thought to herself: 'I'm glad Mama doesn't look like that.'

Kitty wasn't in her room. A few minutes later Mavis came in, pushing before her a wheelchair with the erect old lady whom Blanche had walked straight past. Blanche still didn't recognise her mother. It may have been the way a nurse had swept back her hair from her forehead, making the top of her face look much taller than her own heart-shaped one.

For an hour they sat together, and Blanche still didn't recognise Kitty – except her hands. When Blanche touched one of them, her mother drew them back against her.

'They do that,' Mavis said, 'when they don't know who you are.'

At lunch in the dining hall where she let Mavis feed her, perhaps two spoonfuls, Kitty kept staring at Blanche, occasionally nodding thoughtfully. At one point Blanche looked into her mother's eyes and nodded back. But as that nearly made Blanche go to pieces, she didn't try it a second time. By the end of lunch, she could just make out her mother's jawline. Otherwise she didn't recognise her.

When the two sisters left Kitty sitting in the corridor, Mavis said: 'She'll go to sleep now. Do you remember how she could sleep in a car by just closing her eyes, always sitting with her head erect?'

They looked back and Mavis said: 'Oh. Her head has fallen backwards.' She looked like a broken doll.

Chapter Twenty

B LANCHE returned to London a few days before Luke was due back from Italy. She slept a great deal, wrote her column, and went to the National Gallery – where going up the stairs she met Mark Fleetwood coming down.

'What are you doing here?' she asked, making less than a total effort to conceal her delight.

'Pretending to be a tourist,' he answered carelessly.

'That's what I'm doing too.'

'Why not give the National Gallery a miss and join me in a boat ride to the London Dungeon?'

For a moment she thought she would stick to her original intention. Her next thought was what fun it would be to act spontaneously, without reference to any official diary for the day.

'Is that the only place you can think of?' she asked gaily. 'I've never been inside it and feel I haven't missed anything.'

'What about the Black Chamber, then? It houses torture instruments and such. We could take a boat from Charing Cross Pier and decide when we reach Tower Bridge.'

This time she didn't hesitate. 'Okay.'

They strolled along to the pier, running the last fifty yards when they saw the boat preparing to depart.

'I love boat rides,' she said as St Paul's drew closer on their left. Except for outbursts of chatter provoked by something she saw, they talked very little. When Tower Bridge loomed ahead, they disembarked at the pier and set off for the Dungeon. Blanche felt about thirteen years old as they climbed into a long boat with pairs of seats, like one of the rides at Frayling's amusement park in Richmond, and glided along a narrow outlet from the river, deeper and deeper into the black.

Her recent visits to her mother haunted her, but it was not until she was staring into a windowless cell, where a replica of a not-quite dead prisoner lay, that she wondered whether that was what it was like for Kitty in her pre-death limbo. Emerging into daylight, they climbed on to the embankment wall to watch the water traffic pass, and she told Mark of her morbid imaginings.

Presently he replied: 'My father has had a massive stroke. My mother nurses him devotedly rather than devotedly helping him die. He's paralysed and can't speak, but he can hear and his eyes are open. I want to ask him so many questions, but he has no way to communicate back except by a strange strained sound in his throat. Recently I did ask him what he saw. Myself? The window with the sky outside and clouds moving across it? The walls of his room? Something quite different which I couldn't see? The only time he made that sound in his throat was when I said the walls of his room.'

Neither spoke further until Blanche said: 'I had a cousin whom I worshipped. I've just remembered one of my dreams after his death. We lay in closed coffins on the side of a bare hill. Though we were only a foot apart, we could not see one another or communicate. I knew we would be lying in those two boxes for eternity, each of us in absolute isolation – and aware.'

Some minutes passed before Mark said: 'Come on. Let's get the next boat back to Charing Cross pier and take a taxi to the

Ritz. What we both need is a glass of very cold champagne.'

In the end they shared most of a bottle before Blanche got up to leave. Sinking back in her taxi, she felt excited and reckless. Perhaps this was in part a reaction to the deep sadness of Richmond. She didn't know what she thought of Mark Fleetwood. Yet she knew he was going to be a player in her life.

That evening she went to *Tosca* with Thaddeus. She always shivered with horror in the scene where, to force Tosca to submit to him, Scarpia lets her hear her lover's screams from the dungeon where he is being tortured. Tonight she found the scene so disturbing that she closed her eyes to try and banish thoughts produced by the off-stage cries.

On their way back to Downing Street, Thaddeus told the driver to take them to the Ritz instead.

Blanche gave a short laugh. 'I might as well set up a camp bed in the Palm Court.'

They took a table not far from where she'd sat that afternoon.

'What I need is a very cold glass of champagne,' she said in imitation of Mark.

Once he'd ordered, Thaddeus asked: 'You've been here often lately?'

'This afternoon. With a fellow journalist. Mark Fleetwood. Do you know him?'

Thaddeus lifted his brows. 'I hadn't realised you have a taste for Don Juans.'

'I didn't know he was one.'

'His wife gave up and moved to America. The young woman journalist who had been his lover for years finally gave up too and married a less attractive man.'

'Does that make him a Don Juan?'

'Possibly not. It might be more accurate to describe him as bad news.'

She welcomed the champagne set before them.

'Are you interested in him?'

'I never thought I'd hear you sound like my lovely mother.'

Blanche's smile was soft at the recall of Kitty's voice as it used to be.

They sipped their champagne in silence.

'When does Luke get back from Italy?' Thaddeus asked.

'At the end of the week.'

'Does he still believe he has forged the one thing he has desired most since his election: the leadership of Europe?'

'Probably.'

'Certainly he played a major role in making Vronovik's Serbs withdraw from Begova. But no one except Jaspar Byatt would call it an unconditional surrender. It was no more than a ceasefire. And Luke has no coherent plan for the peace. He has simply left the British army bogged down in one of the most hopeless territorial disputes in Europe.'

'Mark Fleetwood wrote the same thing not long ago,' Blanche said drily.

'I never suggested there's anything wrong with Fleetwood's powers of logic.'

'And Luke's?' she asked tetchily.

'You tell me what you think about Luke's present powers of logic.'

'Sometimes I hate you, Thaddeus, for being so reasonable.'

She drank some more champagne, replacing the glass with a whack.

'Why do you say his *present* powers of logic?' she continued.

'Barristers may be immoral, but they normally are logical. I saw Luke's mind work in those years he was in my chambers. It's his present certainty that he alone can save Europe that has eroded his logic.'

Nothing further was said until she remarked: 'I must be going.'

In the car he put his hand on her knee, and the image recurred of her father doing the same thing affectionately when they were having a serious conversation. But Thaddeus was not like her father, she knew.

She had made an appointment with a distinguished psychoanalyst, not to talk about herself, but to get material for a column about males' manifold sexual deviations versus females' two or three. When she got back to Downing Street the policeman on the step told her that the Prime Minister had arrived from Italy half an hour earlier.

Luke was putting his papers in different piles when she reached the flat, and when he came to kiss her, his face was tanned and rested and young. He looked a different person from the exhausted, petulant man she'd seen off three weeks before. Her heart lifted. They would start afresh.

She cooked a simple supper and they exchanged reports of their holidays. He listened closely to her account of Kitty, and she had a stab of shame that in the past months she'd grown sceptical about his Prime Ministerial preoccupations. They went to bed early, happy to be back in each other's arms.

The next day's newspapers carried a front-page picture of Robert Oakes laughing. The first of the Cabinet to make a post-holiday statement, he announced his intention to take another penny off income tax in his autumn Budget. Inflation had been kept low while economic growth rose, thus making it possible for him to hold to his objectives and at the same time reduce the taxpayer's burden. Roly Barksure ran around briefing individual journalists about how only the Chancellor's skill and boldness made this good news possible.

'Too bad Oakes got in first,' Max Murphy grumbled to Jaspar Byatt. Nor were they pleased by Mark Fleetwood's column the following morning:

'The Prime Minister's well-wishers will be happy to know that he has returned from his holiday refreshed and fit. Let us hope that this means he can at last set aside sentimental rhetoric for some hard analysis.

'Thus far the only member of the Cabinet who shows a capacity for systematic thought is Chancellor Robert Oakes. Yesterday he announced the fruits of his summer concentration: another rise in economic growth, another penny off income tax, a steady hand on the tiller as he makes for his objectives.

'After two years of unfulfilled promises from our starry-eyed Prime Minister – education worse, hospital waiting lists longer, crime increasing – how many of the public would again choose a charmboy to run the country? Were a leadership election to be held tomorrow, the less glamorous Oakes would be the front-runner.'

'Prick,' muttered Jaspar, drumming his fingers on his thigh. 'With Begova now at stalemate, the public has forgotten about it. We need another war.'

'Any ideas?' asked Max.

'Get me the *Times Atlas* from the PM's study.'

When the massive book had been laid open on a table, Jaspar turned first to southeastern Europe. No new site immediately presented itself for another bellicose drama. Almost lovingly he ran a finger around Begova.

During the next weeks, Blanche took on everything that the Prime Minister's diary secretary suggested. The more acid Mark Fleetwood's column was about Luke, the harder she tried to be a supportive wife. Yet each time her own column appeared, she imagined Mark Fleetwood reading it. She wanted his good opinion.

One day she received it. She was interviewing the latest climber to reach the top of Everest and come down again. She intended making comparisons between him and ambitious politicians. Having found that all interviewees – bishops or prostitutes – talked more freely when enjoying an expensive lunch, she'd booked a window table in the Savoy restaurant. Her own food was chosen for simplicity of eating, as she continued to scribble on a pad. Suddenly something made her turn and look behind her.

Several tables away, a Conservative politician was lunching with Mark Fleetwood. Unlike Blanche, Mark rarely wrote down more than a few phrases in a small neat notebook he removed from his pocket. As he talked he was looking at her. He gave a supercilious little bow which broke her concentration completely. Blushing, she quickly turned back to the mountaineer.

When she was settling the bill, Mark appeared beside her table. 'I wanted to congratulate you on your last column,' he said. 'And I also hoped you would introduce me to your distinguished guest.'

This time when her face grew hot the cause was pleasure.

The three of them left the dining room together, and when Blanche had said goodbye to the two men, she slipped off to the ladies room. When she came back out, Mark was standing in the lobby waiting for her.

'Do you have to be somewhere else?' he asked. 'Or would you like to go with me to Tate Britain? It's almost the last day of the Blake exhibition.'

She had already seen it, but she was eager to go again. She found William Blake's visions wildly erotic, and she rather fancied having Mark beside her as she stood before the naked succubus crouched over a sleeping woman.

They moved slowly past the paintings, and her excitement grew. She remembered what she had said to Luke on that first day together in New York. Now, after a moment's hesitation, she said much the same to Mark, because it was true, and because she felt like titillating him.

'Do you find that if a painting excites you, you become sexually moved as well? I'm sure it has nothing to do with another person: it's because your senses are all connected.'

'Now that you mention it.'

They continued around the room, sometimes standing a long while before an astoundingly erotic vision of angels, neither of them speaking again.

When they started down the front stairs, Blanche stopped and sat down on a step beside one of the stone lions to look at the Thames flowing by.

'Did I tell you I live just the other side of Whitehall from you?' said Mark. 'It's a big anonymous-looking mazelike place called Whitehall Court. Why not stop in on your way home?'

'Maybe some other time,' said Blanche. 'I want to transcribe my notes before I get ready for a dinner we're giving for the Spanish. If I wait until tomorrow, I won't be able to figure out my scribbles.'

'You industrious Americans,' he remarked languidly.

'I'll drop you off there if you like.'

'I'll walk,' he said. 'I want to call in at the House of Commons on the way.'

'That sounds pretty industrious to me.'

She wanted to look back from her taxi, but thought better of it. Had she done so, she would have seen him sauntering along Millbank, his hands in his pockets, whistling a tune.

Chapter Twenty-one

*T*HE German Chancellor, Herr Schlosser, and his party were met at Northolt airport by the Foreign Secretary, Stanley Fox, and the Defence Secretary. The motor cavalcade set off for Chequers, the Prime Minister's official country retreat in Buckinghamshire.

Built in the sixteenth century, its last family-owner had given it to the nation in 1921. No alterations to the Tudor exterior were permitted, but successive prime ministers had redecorated inside, built an outdoor heated pool, upgraded a tennis court – in short, made it everything an incumbent might desire to ease weary bones at a weekend. But not this weekend. The Germans had arrived for a mini-Summit on the intractable problem of keeping peace in Begova. Each week returning Albanians took their turn at committing barbarities against Serbs, who had always lived in the province too.

Luke and Blanche were standing in the front hall to greet their guests. She did her best to seem welcoming to Stanley Fox, but his sinuous personality slightly repelled her. Even when he had patently made a mistake, he slid away from acknowledging it. While the staff showed the rest of the party to their rooms, Blanche took Chancellor Schlosser to his suite. An unusually large man, he beamed when he saw his bedroom, dominated by a seventeenth-century four-poster with a tapestry canopy. Over the years the sides of the bed had been lengthened to take into account the fact that the human race was steadily growing taller. Herr Schlosser put out one huge paw and patted the bed appreciatively.

'You will imagine, Mrs Dalton, how often when travelling I am faced with a bed where I have to hang my feet over the edge. You Americans handle these things well. Take the White House. My wife and I were put in the Lincoln Bedroom where the bed was so large there was no need for my wife and myself to roll into each other all night.'

'We slept there too,' Blanche replied brightly, not mentioning that she and Luke slept together in the middle of the large expanse. 'When you're ready, come down to the Grand Parlour for drinks.' She started to add a teasing remark about the ostentatious name, but as the guests were German she let things stand.

Joining them for drinks, she found most of the party had got down to business at once. English aides talked with their German opposite numbers. The Foreign Secretary, having engaged the German Chancellor in high politics, beetled his brows ferociously when Herr Schlosser turned away from him to chat further with his hostess about the White House.

'Did you go into the Oval Office?' he asked her.

'Oh yes,' she said, guessing what would come next.

'And you examined the desk under which the lady crouched?'

'I looked at it with interest,' Blanche replied, quite enjoying this German Chancellor. She also felt an unworthy amusement at seeing Stanley Fox's brows still drawn down fiercely as he waited for the Chancellor to turn back to him.

Luke, who had been moving about from group to group, now said goodnight to Blanche and, putting a comradely arm through the Chancellor's, led the men to the dining room where the two leaders would direct general conversation as they all enjoyed their food and wine. When coffee was served at the table without brandy or port, they got down in earnest to the start of two days' work.

Blanche went off to the master bedroom where her dinner was served on a table. She enjoyed not having to make conversation. She turned on the radio for the beginning of *Lohengrin*, which was being broadcast from the Metropolitan Opera House in New York. When the ravishing tones melted into one another as they climbed and fell, her mind wandered back to the last time she had seen Mark Fleetwood.

If they met again, she would take him up on his invitation. There was nothing odd about calling on another journalist at home. Even as she thought it, she knew she was not being wholly honest with herself. Going to his flat was asking for trouble. Yet that fuelled the desire to go. To see what would happen? Her gaze roamed about the room. She loved the huge canopied four-poster. How long had it been here?

Thaddeus had said Mark was bad news. Yet that didn't deter her. Was it because of Luke's almost sanctimonious self-certainty? Or was it because of what he'd called her earlier self-destructiveness? Was self-destructiveness like an infection that could be suppressed but still lie dormant inside you, waiting to drag you down again some day? One of the staff came to clear the table and bring coffee. Blanche got ready for bed, and though it was not late she turned out the lights to lie awake in the dark. Elsewhere in this immense house were the German Chancellor, the British Prime Minister, the Foreign Secretary and Defence Secretary discussing how to get NATO out of the peace-keeping mess that, egged on by the British Prime Minister, they had created in another land. As well as physically separate, she felt emotionally unconnected with these men playing soldiers downstairs, albeit humanitarian soldiers. She had a moment of shame at being so frivolous about politicians whose actions had measureless consequences for good or ill. Then her thoughts returned to Mark Fleetwood.

Not many weeks later, Blanche was crossing the central lobby of the House of Commons to go up to the gallery and hear Luke make a statement on Begova. Given his increasingly presidential style of government, his appearance in the House was a major event. From where she looked down on the chamber, the press gallery behind the Speaker's Chair was within her view. Making his way along its benches was Mark. While waiting for the Prime Minister to begin, she glanced again at the press gallery and found Mark's eyes resting on her. As before, he made a formal little bow. The Prime Minister rose.

'Madam Speaker. I have not weakened in my resolve to keep our troops in Begova until a lasting peace has been achieved. At present the dictator Vronovik awaits the British Army's departure so he can with impunity renew his ethnic cleansing of the province. No decent-thinking man or woman in our country would want us to permit again the abominable abuse of Muslims in that tortured land.'

The Leader of the Opposition caught the Speaker's eye.

'Mr Wellright.'

The Prime Minister sat down as the Conservative leader stood up.

'Madam Speaker. Will the Prime Minister explain how he selects foreign countries to save from themselves? Is it because Sodugur is in Africa that he takes no humanitarian interest in the vile barbarities practised in *its* civil war?'

Wellright sat down and the Prime Minister rose.

'The Right Honourable Gentleman has a way with words. Only he would drag an offensive racist innuendo into a life-and-death subject.'

'Hear, hear,' bayed Democratic Labour's backbenchers. On the front bench, the Chancellor of the Exchequer sat poker-faced. Luke went on with his statement, a rhetorical balancing act between 'human decency, strength of purpose, courage' and 'evil, sadism, brutality'.

As Blanche listened to him, something drew her glance to where Robert Oakes was sitting. He was looking up at her. When their eyes met he gave a crooked smile before turning away to resume his deadpan expression.

'As usual,' Mark Fleetwood's column began the next day, 'the Prime Minister delivered his statement, which told us nothing new, with commanding self-confidence and emotion which may have been deep-felt. Who is to say?

'Curiously, he avoided any mention of the fact that the Albanians returning to the province are now ethnic-cleansing those Serbs who remained because Begova has long been their home too. As most Serbs who are natives of the province have now fled, the Albanian avengers have had to make do with mutilating, drowning and burying alive those too old or too young to escape.

'Anyone less self-righteous than our Prime Minister would be sickened by the evidence that we have replaced one injustice with another, after ourselves helping NATO bombers slaughter thousands of innocent people.'

'Since you lost the baby,' Luke said one night, 'you have never spoken of going back to the fertility clinic.'

Blanche wanted to say that her desire for a child had been knocked out of her, but even as she thought it, she knew it was mean and provoking. 'Thank you for speaking of it,' she replied instead in a low voice.

'I know you sometimes must be restless, despite your job. I'm away or preoccupied so much of the time. If you could become pregnant again, and this time run to term, I think you would be much happier. How do you feel about it?'

'I don't know. I've thought about it sometimes.'

'And when you thought about it, what did you feel?'

'Yearning – to have a baby. At the same time, I felt it would never happen.'

'Why not?'

After a long pause she said: 'Because of being the only one who really wants it.'

'As this time I am asking you to do it, will you think about returning to Harley Street?'

The following day, Blanche was going out the front door of Number Ten when the front door of Number Eleven opened and Robert Oakes stepped out, accompanied by Charlie and Nat. They went over to speak to her.

'They're on their half-term holiday. We're going over to the House so they can have the dubious pleasure of listening to their dad make a statement.'

'I think all three of you are lucky,' Blanche said, and Robert detected a note of wistfulness.

'Why don't you come too?' asked Nat.

Robert and Blanche laughed. Then, to his surprise, she said, 'Okay,' and hopped into the Chancellor's car beside the boys. Except when terrorism was rampant, the Prime Minister's wife only had a government car for herself when she was on government business.

They entered the Commons by Westminster Hall, and Robert stopped by the slab where Charles I had been beheaded. Although they had seen it many times before, both Charlie and Nat looked properly awed.

In the Visitors' Gallery, Blanche sat between the boys. As Robert took his seat on the government front bench, he looked up and grinned. In the Press Gallery Mark Fleetwood watched this little piece of theatre impassively.

Not long after the Chancellor's statement, the trio in the Visitors' Gallery slipped out and made for the stairs. The Chancellor's room in the House was not far from the Prime Minister's. Blanche delivered the boys to the detective sitting in the anteroom outside the Chancellor's door and went on her way. Re-crossing Central Lobby she was not entirely surprised to see Mark Fleetwood standing near the policeman. Smiling, she changed her course and they met halfway.

'I didn't know you were fairy godmother to the Chancellor's sons.'

'I was a close friend of their mother. They're very likeable.'

'And their father?'

'We've been friends for a long time.'

'Even though he's biding his time to replace your husband?'

'Lots of people want to do that,' she answered, wondering if Mark might take that as double-edged.

'For myself,' he said, 'while I've toyed with the thought of supplementing him, I'd never be so arrogant as to suppose I could replace him.'

As they strode away from Central Lobby, she listened to her heels click-clacking on the stone floor. She turned to go down the stairs into Westminster Hall, Mark staying with her. When they came out of the sunless hall into bright sunshine, she said: 'I'll say goodbye here. I'm walking back to Downing Street.'

'I'm walking back to Whitehall Court. The last time I asked you to call in for a cup of tea, you said perhaps some other time. This is some other time.'

She laughed, feeling lightheaded, and said nothing further as they walked past the policemen at the gate of Palace Yard. They started up Whitehall, Downing Street ahead on the left, and at the first little turning right, Mark took her arm and steered her into narrow streets, round the back of Inigo Jones's Banqueting

House and finally into an enclave where an eight-storey exuberant Gothic fantasy rose before them. Built in 1884, its wings appeared to go every which way, each adorned by pyramid roofs, balconies and loggias.

'If you get lost in here, you'll never be seen again,' he said easily.

By the time they reached his door, she felt that every hair on her body stood alert with expectation. Inside, beneath high and ornate ceilings, were rooms furnished comfortably and with the feel of a bachelor's flat. She walked across the drawing room to windows overlooking the Thames. 'Time like an ever-rolling stream bears all its sons away...' she sang in a voice not very different from a hum.

'What can I offer you?' Mark asked.

'Coffee?'

'What about a brandy or a glass of champagne?'

She laughed. 'My head is already doing something very peculiar. I think I'll have coffee.'

'Pity,' he said.

As he ambled from the room she called out: 'May I come see your kitchen?'

'By all means.'

'I like to see how other people live. Especially now when I live in such a peculiar place.'

'Do you want something to eat?'

'Have you such a thing as a cookie? I know you call it a sweet biscuit, but cookie sounds more inviting.'

He opened a packet of shortbread fingers. 'Wrong shape,' he said, 'but they taste like cookies.'

He carried the tray into the drawing room where she started to go to the sofa and then chose an armchair instead.

'You don't mind if I sit on the sofa?' he asked mockingly.

She stuck out the tip of her tongue at him. Noticing a framed picture of a small girl on the table beside her, she picked it up to examine the solemn little face.

'She lives with her mother in Washington,' said Mark.

'Do you get used to her absence?'

'If she died, that would be horrible. But knowing I can go over there several times a year makes the spaces in between all right. Remember, I've been brought up in a country where parents send their children away for most of the year.'

She put the picture back.

'Didn't you want children?' he asked.

'Yes. I do now. But peritonitis from a burst appendix wrecked my ovaries. Everything else functions normally,' she added.

'Does being unable to conceive make you readier to have an affair if you're attracted to a bloke?'

'The thought has arisen too seldom to say. I seem to be monogamous by nature.'

'There was a Scottish psychoanalyst who made his name writing books about the distinction between monogamous and monoerotic – how a person who believed in one marriage could be polyerotic as anything.'

'I understand the distinction, yet in my own marriage I felt I was both monogamous and monoerotic.'

'You use the past tense.'

'Freudian slip?' She stood up. 'On that note I'll take off, Mr Fleetwood. I don't want to mess up my life with Luke.'

'Maybe he'll mess it up one day.'

'Not the way you imply. He believes in marital fidelity, and he tends to practise what he believes in.'

'I wasn't suggesting that he would have a sexual romp with someone else. I had in mind that it must sometimes be off-putting to live with a man who is carried away with saving those parts of the world that he deems deserving.'

'I find most of your columns enjoyable because they're

insightful and funny. But I don't like your putting down Luke to me. Thanks for the cookies.'

With the slightest shrug he got up and walked to the door with her. 'Can you find your way out?'

'If I can't, I'll come back and eat humble pie.'

'Take this,' he said, putting a business card in her hand.

She took it and left him.

The phone was ringing as she unlocked the flat door.

'Blanche, it's Robert. You made such a hit with my sons that they're keen for you to come to Dorneywood some weekend soon. You met Rebecca Knight at a Number Eleven drinks party. She'll be there too. Maybe one or two others. Why not look for a weekend when Luke will be away, as he sees quite enough of me already.'

When she put down the phone, she gaily picked it up again to ring Luke's diary secretary.

'Michael,' she said, 'I'm looking for a weekend when my husband will be away so I can accept an invitation that would bore him.'

'He has a mini-Summit in Paris the weekend after the coming one. The next one he's away is a fortnight after that.'

'Right. I'll try to fix it for one of them.'

She rang back the Chancellor's office.

'He has someone with him, Mrs Dalton, but if it will be a quick call I'm sure we can interrupt him.'

Robert came on the line.

She set out the alternatives.

'Let's go for the earlier one,' he said. 'And bring a swimming costume just in case. The pool is heated.'

Chapter Twenty-two

'A FUNNY thing happened to me today,' Max Murphy told Jaspar Byatt. 'In the tearoom. A Liberal MP came up, grinning, and said: "I didn't expect to see Blanche Dalton keeping company with Mark Fleetwood. The Prime Minister must be a tolerant chap."'

'*What!*'

'"She sees lots of journalists,"' I replied casually, not wanting him to think he was telling me something I didn't know. "Where did you run into them?" I asked.'

'Well?' Jaspar could feel the litle vein in his left temple throbbing.

'He was taking a back way to the National Liberal Club and happened to notice them going into Whitehall Court.'

'Maybe they were going to see someone they both know,' said Jaspar. Even as he said it he was reaching for a bound notebook which held home telephone numbers and addresses of senior journalists. He pushed it across the table to Max. 'Look through this while I return an urgent phone call.'

Uneasily Max turned to the Fs, hoping to get his overriding fear out of the way. Farmer. Fellowes. Fleetwood. He stared, mesmerised, at the address: Whitehall Court.

It was such a convenient address, he told himself, that more than one journalist might live there. Oblivious to Jaspar's voice grating on the phone, Max started at the beginning of the alphabet, running his index finger down each address. He stopped in the Ds, a hope in his heart as he read 'Whitehall Court'. Then he saw it belonged to the *Post*'s American correspondent and was in Washington D.C.

Intently he turned the pages, stopping at Fleetwood along the way, glaring at his address. When he reached the Vs, foreboding deepened. Only a couple of letters to go. Finally Young. He turned back to Fleetwood and pushed the open book across the table. After one glance, Jaspar ended his phone call. Staring at the page, he pressed his lips.

When he looked up at Max he said: 'Let's not panic.'

They sat in silent thought until Max said: 'Journalists aren't like other people. They go where their work or their whim takes them without concern for how it might appear to others. We shouldn't read too much into it.'

'What we cannot do is mention it to Luke. He already has enough fucking problems without having to hear tittle-tattle from some Liberal prick.'

'I say put it in the back of our minds until something further comes to our attention.'

'Do you remember when Robert's girlfriend asked if we four could have dinner one evening?'

'Vaguely,' replied Luke.

'You said you and Robert saw more than enough of each other. Well, he and Rebecca will be at Dorneywood while you're in Paris, and they're having a few people there. Robert asked me, and I said I'd love to come. I intend to drive down on Saturday.'

It was a fine morning as she wound along curving roads through the verdant hills of Buckinghamshire. On either side trees of tender green were stippled by the springtime sun. Occasionally stopping to check the map she had been sent from the Chancellor's office, she felt lighthearted as she resumed her drive. She'd heard that Dorneywood was more domestic in its scale than some of the sought after grace-and-favour houses in the gift of the Prime Minister. Chevening, for instance, the Foreign Secretary's country house, was so big that a guest could easily get lost.

On one side a stone wall had run unbroken for some while; she knew she was nearing her destination. She braked. A horrid security barrier stood impenetrably where wrought iron gates had once offered a friendly view of the Queen Anne manor house beyond. Terrorism had put an end to such civilised English habits.

Noting the security camera out of reach, she hopped out to press a device on the wall and a gate rolled back, humming. When she drove through, hundreds of acres of gardens and woodland spread before her. The stone manor house stood peacefully amidst the green.

A boy came out on to the gravel drive to meet her. She saw it was the ten-year old, Nat.

'I'm acting as doorkeeper,' he said. 'Do you think a doorkeeper should call you "Mrs Dalton"?'

'Only if you feel as doorkeeper you should be called Nathaniel.'

'Just while I'm doorkeeper. Charlie's gone to the greenhouse to choose flowers for tonight's dinner table. I'll take your suitcase . . . Mrs Dalton,' he added with an almost imperceptible smile.

Together they entered an inviting central hall with a honey-coloured glow upon Regency furniture, silk-covered walls and a graceful staircase. There were none of the yawning spaces and chilly furniture which characterise too many official homes. Just inside the front door, Nat stopped to bang his fist on the closed door of a sideroom.

'Come in.'

The boy led the way into what was little more than a walk-in cupboard large enough for an armchair and desk. 'This is Winston,' he said to Blanche. 'He's the one who let you in the front gate.'

Winston looked up from the book he was reading and nodded to Blanche as she eyed a panel of blinking lights and a small screen on which she saw the security gate.

'Have any other guests arrived?' she asked Winston.

'No, Ma'm.'

'I'll take you to your room . . . Mrs Dalton.'

'That would be very nice, Nathaniel.'

As they started up the stairs, another door opened and Robert ambled into the hall.

'Welcome.'

He was dressed in tweed trousers and an open-necked shirt. 'I'm trying to get one box finished before lunch and the grand tour.'

'Nathaniel is giving me an initial tour.'

Robert looked amused. 'We're putting you in the Chinois room because it's the prettiest bedroom in the house,' he said. 'Come down whenever you're ready. Lunch is at one. We might first have an aperitif in my study.'

'We could go for a walk or play billiards,' put in Nat.

The Chinois room was ravishing, with its painted bamboo furniture and windows looking in three directions over the park.

'Daddy would have used this room if the trustees had allowed him to swap these twin beds for a double bed.'

'I thought your father usually got his way,' said Blanche.

'Not when it comes to Dorneywood's trustees. They're stricter than my headmaster. Shall I leave you to unpack?'

'Thank you, Nathaniel.' As she did so, she thought how happy Julie would be that Robert and his sons were so relaxed in one another's company.

Downstairs she found both boys lounging on chairs in the hall. They got to their feet, and she remarked to herself once again that their parents and their boarding school had taught them good manners without squashing them. 'Hullo, Charlie.'

At that moment the study door opened and Robert appeared, grinning. 'Drinks time,' he announced, and as he led her within he said to his sons: 'We'll see you two at lunch.'

All around an armchair the floor was covered with piles of briefs. Two red boxes stood open, a third one shut. Robert nudged it with his foot: 'That one's done.'

She walked to the French windows to look out on the front garden. He took a bottle from a wine cooler on the drinks table.

'Chablis,' he said, handing her a glass.

'Where's Rebecca?'

'She couldn't come.'

Blanche was uncertain whether his normally ruddy complexion deepened.

'And I decided not to invite anyone else. I hope you don't mind. It's rather selfish, but I thought a quiet family weekend would be the nicest of all. I'm treating you as honorary family.'

'Actually, I'd like that too. I don't see much of family life except when I go back to Virginia.'

Despite the size of the dining room, Blanche didn't feel like a pygmy. The table had been reduced so that the four of them seemed cosy as they tucked into roast pork and sweetcorn. She told them how sweetcorn grew so profusely in the United States that it was fed to the animals, making pork, for instance, particularly succulent.

'What else is different?' demanded Charlie.

'Well, electricity is cheap because of all the rivers with their waterfalls generating so much electricity that people can use all they want. And taxes – hem, hem,' she said, looking at Robert, 'are much lower than here.'

Robert at once reminded his sons of the benefits of Britain's welfare state.

A woman servant swooshed in and out through a swinging door, clearing away everything in readiness for the summer pudding.

'We'll have coffee at the table,' Robert told her, 'before we take Mrs Dalton into the gardens.'

'Don't you want to get back to your boxes, Daddy?' said Nat as they left the dining room. 'Me and Charlie can show Blanche around. And after she's had a rest, we're going to play billiards.'

'Thanks for your consideration,' Robert replied, laughing, 'but if you don't mind I'll come too for the first part of the tour.'

When they all returned to the house, Robert peeled off to the study to resume his boxes. Nat called after him: 'Can we show Blanche the brown room?'

At the top of the staircase was a corridor with doors closed in the English manner along each side. The boys began at the end where her own room stood, and opened each door as they moved along, every bedroom having its own personality though all had the grace of the eighteenth century. Near the other end of the corridor, Charlie said, 'Wait for it,' and Nat with a flourish threw open the door to 'the brown room'.

Its presence was overpowering: dark Victorian furniture throughout, heavily carved headboard looming over the outsized bed, tall mahogany-framed mirror on casters, Robert's clothes strewn about. Nat at once pushed the mirror to the bed where, lying down, he propped himself on an elbow and made a face at his own reflection. The Victorians' heightened sense of virtue and vice permeated the room. Round its walls, engraved

Victorian statesmen looked out of their frames observing what went on below them. Directly facing the bed stood Charles James Fox, that fast liver from an earlier era.

Blanche thought of Robert in this room – and Rebecca, too, presumably – with all these statesmen, like voyeurs, gazing at them. It gave her an odd feeling. That's not at all how she had thought of Robert.

As if reading her mind, Charlie said: 'Don't forget that the room was like this before Daddy moved in.'

More than a month had passed when Blanche opened a letter marked Personal and forwarded from her newspaper. It was written on a piece of unheaded paper and signed M. She smiled at his taking no chances if the letter were opened before it reached her.

Dear Blanche – Would you have time for me to pick your brain for a piece I'm writing about the American South? Over lunch, perhaps? Getting through to you is so uncertain that I'd be grateful if you could ring me at the paper or at home. In trepidation lest you slung the card, M.

They met at a small unfashionable restaurant in Soho. If someone recognised her, so what? She couldn't be expected never to meet her friends, even if one of them wrote about her husband with less than respect. Was she meant only to go out with people who were Democratic Labour?

After they'd placed their order, he said: 'Let's do our work first. Otherwise you'll suspect me of getting you here under false pretences.'

Mark really did want to ask questions about the South. He could not have had a better person to give him a rundown on the Southern psyche. With her father's family living in New

England, Blanche could describe fundamental differences in manners and mores and above all the difference in psyche, between a defeated people and those who had never known defeat except far away in Vietnam.

The little tutorial lasted through most of the meal. Mark closed his notebook. 'Let's order a pudding and change gear.'

In fact, they didn't really change gear, for he wanted to know more about her family upbringing – Nathan and Kitty, the extended family in Richmond, the family in the north. She mentioned Jakie but didn't go into what happened.

Mark said nothing about going back to Whitehall Court.

A fortnight later they met again for lunch. This time she told him about Jakie. That was a sign, she realised, that Mark was becoming important in her life: she didn't run around talking to everyone about her dead cousin. When she finished he asked: 'Did it make you self-destructive too?'

'Consciously for quite a time.' Without any gradual transition of mood, she laughed as she told him about her first date with Luke. 'I took him to a whirlpool not far from college. When we climbed over the security barrier, I sat down on the edge with my legs hanging over the water. He sat down too, warily, keeping a big space between us in case "one of us", as he tactfully put it, got the urge to push the other in.'

'Did he even then think he could make the world a better place?'

'He didn't go on about it, but it was there. He was always an idealist. In that boyhood without a family – unless you count two stern aunts – he may have daydreamed even more extravagantly than most of us. When I was about nine, I used to daydream I was a Joan of Arc figure on a white horse. Luke's daydream has never ended, I suspect. It's one of the things I loved about him.'

'You use the past tense.'

She ignored that. 'In some of his dispatches, my father wrote about the damage wreaked by idealists. Only lately has Luke been in a position to put his humanitarian ideals into practice.'

Mark decided it was bad tactics to press into the opening.

It was after her next lunch with him that Luke said one evening: 'I'm told you're being seen around with Mark Fleetwood.'

'Who on earth told you that? I have lunch with him from time to time, but that's hardly what you mean by being seen around. It sounds like a Jaspar turn of phrase.'

'You have a good ear. But he wouldn't have said it if he weren't genuinely concerned.'

'Why don't you tell him to stuff himself? You can't expect me never to have lunch with another journalist.'

'Is there a reason why you've picked a journalist who consistently denigrates me?'

After a long pause she answered: 'I'm not sure. But I *think* it's to show some independence from Downing Street-Fleet Street politics.'

'You already skim close to the line in your column. Do you really think it's a good idea to set tongues wagging by meeting Fleetwood so often?'

In part because of a sense of guilt she lost her temper as she said: 'When I first came to London, the greatest joy was the sense of freedom. I could go where I liked, do what I liked, meet for lunch with anybody I liked without tongues wagging, to use your phrase. In Richmond, if you had lunch alone with a man, tongues wagged all right. Everybody knew everybody. It made me feel confined – though the funny thing is I didn't realise how confined I felt until I came here and nobody knew me. I was anonymous.'

'Now you are not. And much as you may regret it, a responsibility goes with your position.'

'At least you didn't use that loathsome word "duty",' she said sullenly.

'Would it be such a sacrifice to see less of this man?'

'It's the idea that I *have* to which I resent.'

'You didn't object when I first stood for the leadership. You knew then it carried obligations.'

'That's true. I was proud of you. I found it exciting. And it was thrilling when you became Prime Minister. But no one ever really imagines in advance that of course there's a price to pay.'

'It's only in the past months that you have seemed to grudge paying a price,' Luke persisted.

Defiantly she answered: 'Maybe that's because I don't believe in what you're doing now – delivering heroic speeches while you mess about in another country and make things worse for its people.'

'Is that what you and Mr Fleetwood discuss over your lunches?'

She flushed. 'No, it isn't. This conversation doesn't seem to be going anywhere.' She got up. 'Let's get some sleep.'

'I still have work to do.'

'I'll say goodnight then.'

Chapter Twenty-three

*I*T was a tremendous coup to have the Summit held in London. The American President, the German Chancellor and the Russian President would be bringing their wives. Already the Foreign Office was in a stew about the visit of such an unpredictable man as President Milochki.

During the two days that the Summit talks took place, Blanche was to escort the wives to the Victoria and Albert Museum and other prized centres of culture, along with a matinée of *Cats*.

On the first night, the Daltons hosted a dinner at Inigo Jones's Banqueting House. As Blanche stepped through its front door, her mind switched briefly to the afternoon she had skirted the back of the Banqueting House on her way with Mark to Whitehall Court. When she and Luke now greeted the American President and his wife, Dick Masters' eyes met Blanche's with a curiously collusive expression. She wondered whose thigh would be the object of his attentions tonight. Mrs Milochki's? Probably not.

The Russians arrived next, the President wrapping Luke in a bear hug, then lifting Blanche's hand to his lips for a wet kiss. At table she had President Masters on one side, President Milochki on the other, the latter's interpreter seated just behind him. At once Milochki began to talk to her in rapid Russian. 'The President says,' said the interpreter, 'that he gets on better with American women than with English women. You Americans have so much vitality.'

'What about the Queen and Lady Thatcher?' Blanche said, looking into the President's face, which had a merry expression. 'If I tried to keep up with them, I'd stretch out on the floor in a faint. And if you visited Virginia where I was brought up, you'd find the summer heat turns us all into wilted flowers except when we're swimming.'

The interpreter emitted a flow of Russian which led the President to beam. Emptying the glass of white burgundy at his place, he turned back to Blanche and addressed her flirtatiously, pawing the air in alternate strokes of his arms.

'The President says,' said the interpreter, 'that he too likes swimming, and when you and your husband visit Russia, he will take you swimming.'

At this point, thankfully, twenty waiters set plates for the first course before the diners, immediately followed by waiters with platters of poached salmon. Blanche took a large swallow of wine and turned to her other table partner at the same moment that he was turning to her.

'Do you speak English?' she asked.

He replied with a grin and the movement of his leg, so that his foot pressed against hers.

'Does being married to the Prime Minister ever make you want to break loose?' he enquired, his eyes, the corners crinkling with amusement, studying her face as she ate some salmon and considered her next move.

'Is that a personal question or a general one?'

'For me,' he said, 'the general situation of being President increases my desire for free-spirited women.'

'In reaction to restraints imposed by your office? Or out of self-indulgence which your power allows you?'

'Both.'

She moved her foot away from his. He grinned again, unabashed.

A clatter of china rose in unison around the great table as the fishplates were whisked away. One thing was to be said for official banquets: no one was given time to linger over the courses. People had to go to work in the morning. The Russian President's glass was never empty without him wheeling in his chair and beckoning across a wine waiter.

Such was the security that when the evening came to an end, even though the Banqueting House and Downing Street nearly faced each other across Whitehall, the Daltons climbed into the bullet-proof Jaguar to return to Number Ten.

Blanche, still keyed up, broke into chatter. 'I can't vouch for Chancellor Schlosser, but the Russian and American Presidents are definitely sex-mad.'

Halfway through the next afternoon she was escorting the three visiting wives to the Turner rooms at Tate Britain when a security man brought her a message. 'Your sister in Richmond has phoned you. She says it's not urgent, but could you ring her before you begin your evening engagement?'

Some time ago, Blanche knew, her mother had entered a different phase. As soon as she was back in the flat she rang Mavis.

'I don't think she will live a lot longer,' Mavis said.

'Shall I come as soon as I can?' asked Blanche, knowing the answer before asking the question.

Mavis's husband, Bolling, met the plane. Over dinner at the Richmond house, they talked about Luke, Blanche's life in London, Washington and Virginia gossip. When they were going upstairs to bed, Mavis said: 'Sleep as late as you can in the morning. It doesn't really matter when you get to the nursing home. Don't expect her to know you.'

Anxious lest her sister be shattered by the change, Mavis went with her the first time. Their mother lay on her back in a child's cot with the sides up, tiny. The front of her gown had fallen open, and there were only nipples where her warm breasts had been. She made Blanche think of a little monkey.

When Mavis and Blanche were children and their mother took them to the Washington Zoo, she declined to go with them into the monkey house, affronted by 'our so-called cousins making such a spectacle of themselves'. On an earlier visit, she had taken particular offence at a baboon displaying its blue bottom to her. So she sat on a bench outside the monkey house, waiting for her children, her hands in their little white gloves folded in her lap.

She opened her eyes in response to Mavis's voice, and for a moment a ghost of the radiant smile appeared, this time broken by the gaps in her teeth, but even so transforming her face into something recognisable for that fleeting instant.

'I'll come back for you in about an hour,' Mavis said quietly.

When Blanche was alone with her mother, a nurse came with a tray of mashed-up food. Even though Kitty kept her jaws fastened tight, the nurse got the syringe through the gaps in her teeth, and if she didn't swallow she choked. Throughout the feeding she kept her eyes open, fixed on Blanche's face, their expression saying: 'Why are you letting them do this to me?' After it was over, she closed her eyes. She didn't smile again.

The following morning when Blanche returned, she asked the intelligent and sensitive matron, Mrs Spalding, if they could talk privately.

'Why must my mother be forced to swallow all those calories when she doesn't want to?'

Mrs Spalding didn't answer directly. Instead she said: 'We can feed her by spoon. She likes ice cream. She might take a few spoonfuls.'

They discussed the implications of this – that Kitty would then die rapidly.

'Would she be thirsty?'

'We would keep her lips moist.'

Blanche took the decision.

Only then did Mrs Spalding say: 'She doesn't want to eat. If she were my mother, I also would want her to have this choice. It's the only freedom of choice she has left.'

Early that evening, lying on Mavis's big bed, a bourbon on each side table, Blanche nervously told her sister what she had put in motion. For a while Mavis made no response. Then she said: 'I don't know why I didn't think of it, though even if I had thought of it, I couldn't have done it. I'm glad you did. Do you remember what Grandma used to say of a person who'd come for a visit and something momentous became possible as a consequence? "She was sent for a purpose."'

The next day Blanche found her mother didn't look very different, as there was so little of her left anyway. Her eyes remained closed. Blanche tried to spoon-feed her some ice cream, nudging the spoon against her lips, but she wouldn't open them. Mrs Spalding put her hands on Kitty's chin and jaw and tried to open her mouth. Her jaw stayed clamped. 'She knows we're here. She doesn't want to eat. She's not going to eat if she has her way.'

Before dawn the following morning, it was over.

Four days later, Blanche and Mavis and her family took the ashes north. A Winslow cousin had already dug the hole in the same grave as Nathan. Afterwards the cousin said to Blanche: 'I'd expected to come back and settle your mother's box in its permanent position, but it never moved as we filled in the hole. It stayed in the place where I first put it. Right up against your father's box. It was as if it were held by a magnet.'

Blanche's plane came into Heathrow on a Saturday. A car met her and drove her to Chequers, where Luke was staying for two days. 'The flat seemed so empty without you,' he told her.

He spent most of the afternoon working in the library where two red boxes stood open, files fanned around his armchair, two more boxes waiting their turn. An hour before dinner he moved into the small sitting room and poured out two whisky and sodas. Blanche was sitting in the armchair across the fireplace from his. 'Welcome home,' he said affectionately, pressing a hand against her cheek.

They always exchanged news when one of them had been away. This evening they started with Blanche's account of Richmond. She managed not to break down as she told him about Kitty's final days. She longed to be reassured by him – for him to tell her she had made the only decision that a daughter who loved her mother could make. As she described her conversation with Mrs Spalding, Luke's eyes were fixed on her intently, then with distaste.

He jumped to his feet and paced the floor. Stopping before her, he looked down on her and said: 'You have acted as if you are God. That's what your cousin Jakie did. Now you have done the same, each of you ordering death as you see fit. I find that arrogant and presumptuous.'

Had he struck her across the face with the flat of his hand, she could not have been more stunned. She burst into wrenching sobs.

'Well, what's done is done,' he said, returning to his chair. 'We'll say no more about it. I think the best thing now is for me to work until we have dinner.'

'I don't want any dinner,' cried Blanche between her sobs, and fled upstairs to the bedroom.

Half an hour later, there was a knock on the door. A servant brought in a tray with soup and a light supper and a small carafe of wine. 'The Prime Minister asked me to bring this to you, Ma'm. I'm sorry you are worn out from your journey.'

In the morning, they returned to Downing Street together, each speaking little, Luke reading the newspapers, Blanche gazing out at Buckinghamshire's lush green. She thought of Dorneywood, but that relaxed family weekend seemed too long ago to dwell on. As they neared the outskirts of London, she picked up one of the newspapers, but after staring unreading at the print, she went back to looking out of the window.

Later that day, alone in the flat, she dialled Mark Fleetwood's office. He wasn't there, but the newsdesk said he was in London. She didn't give her name. Trying him at home, she got the answer machine. How many weeks had passed since she had heard his voice? Six? Eight? Longer? She left an impersonal message which wouldn't put the wind up his daily, suggesting that they meet at Charing Cross Pier two days later at one o'clock.

They arrived almost simultaneously. 'Which way do you fancy?' he asked.

'Upstream? We could go to Kew Gardens.'

They bought sandwiches and settled on the upper deck where the breeze lifted their hair and the sun felt good on their arms.

'I've seen pictures of you once or twice. What have you been doing lately?' asked Mark.

'After the last Summit, I went back to Richmond. My mother was dying. I helped her on her way. Luke disapproves. He says I was playing God – like my cousin.'

Mark glanced at her. She appeared focused on unwrapping her sandwich. After eating some of it, she asked: 'What have you been doing?'

'Nothing out of the ordinary. Deploring President Masters. Badgering your husband. That sort of thing.'

They went on with their lunch.

'I want to run away,' she said simply.

'Literally or metaphorically?'

'Certainly the second. But at this moment the first as well.'

'If you ran away to Whitehall Court, you could disappear into that maze. Then if you changed your mind, you could get back to Downing Street in ten minutes flat.'

She gave a quick small smile. Immediately she had an image of Kitty's brief broken-toothed smile near the end. She shuddered.

'Kew's rather a long way. Shall we get off at Putney and head back?' asked Mark.

'I suddenly feel done in. You decide.' Before he could speak, she added fiercely: 'That's a copout. I'll decide. Let's get off at Putney.'

They took the open upper deck again for the trip downstream. Conversation was almost non-existent, though when the sun set fire to St Paul's dome up ahead, she spoke of it. This trip seemed much faster to her than the first one. They got off at Charing Cross pier and he led them through a back footway into Whitehall Court.

Closing the door of his flat behind them, he said: 'Make yourself comfortable. I must ring the paper and tell them I'll be filing late.'

When he returned to the drawing room, he was carrying two glasses of chilled white wine. 'Come into the bedroom, Blanche, said the spider to the fly.'

She gave a wild laugh and followed him. Any sense of weariness vanished. She was crazily exhilarated, crazily released as the barricade she had put around herself fell apart and she stepped through.

Taking his time, he undressed her. When she was naked he said: 'When you first met me, did you guess what a patient man I am?'

He pulled off his trousers and, turning her back, she rubbed herself against him. She turned again and began undoing his shirt. 'I like unfastening buttons.'

He threw the bedcover off. 'Lie that way,' he directed.

'It's the first time I've been naked on a bed with a man without his ever having kissed me.'

'We'd better do something about that.'

Later, lying in one another's arms, they kissed each other's mouths for the first time.

'I've never been interested in one-night stands,' she said huskily. 'Is it customary not to kiss the mouth until the end?'

'Can't remember. Though it's fair to say that I hadn't considered this as a one-night stand, and none of the ways we have proceeded is customary for me.'

Chapter Twenty-four

*I*T was dark when she left Whitehall Court and made her way back to Downing Street, where the policemen at the barrier saluted. Unhurriedly she strolled up the little street, pretending to herself that she was an American tourist seeing it for the first time.

She had just said 'Good evening' to the policeman outside Number Ten when the door opened and Jaspar Byatt hurried out. 'Good evening,' she said to Jaspar, stepping past him into the entrance hall.

He turned and followed her.

'We were getting worried,' he said in a voice that trembled with anger.

'Why was that?' answered Blanche, not breaking her stride. 'I knew that Luke was tied up this evening.'

'It would have been helpful if you had told someone when you'd be back. The Prime Minister's wife cannot simply roam around London as if she were a tourist.'

Blanche burst into slightly mad laughter. 'You must be a mind-reader, Jaspar. That's exactly what I was pretending. I went to Kew Gardens.'

'Why didn't you take your mobile? That's what mobiles are for.'

'That's why I didn't take it. As I already knew the Prime Minister's schedule – ' with a magician's flourish she plucked the printed list from her handbag ' – the only calls I would be likely to receive would be about some footling detail that could happily wait until tomorrow. Where's Luke now?'

'I just left him in his study. I'll say goodnight.' The back of his neck rigid, he stalked to the front door and out.

Blanche climbed the stairs to the first floor and tapped on the study door. 'Yes?' came an impatient voice.

'It's me,' she said, opening the door. 'I just bumped into Jaspar, who told me you were in here.'

Luke remained at his desk, signing the last of a pile of letters before wheeling in his chair to look at her closely. 'Where have you been?'

'I had no official engagements so I took a boat to Kew Gardens.' Not a total lie, it was nonetheless sufficient to compel her to add details in a nervous attempt to make it more believable, as she used to do when as a teenager she lied to her mother. 'I thought I could turn it into an item for my column.'

'My office was trying to reach you to tell you that my evening engagement with those industry leaders has been cancelled. The host's wife committed suicide this morning,' he added drily. 'It seemed a shame to miss the opportunity for us to have sups *à deux*.'

Blanche flushed. 'Well, here I am. I'll go up to the flat and get something out of the freezer. Will you be up for a drink before long?'

Both were determined to keep acrimony out of their evening. His dissatisfaction with her attitude was kept under wraps. She in turn, partly from guilt, felt much warmer towards him than she had for some time. The excitement of her hours with Mark and the relief of giving in to her desires made her more inclined, not less, to reassure Luke. They might have gone over his cold-hearted response to her account of helping her mother die, yet Luke didn't want to expend energy on a moral debate with his wife, and Blanche thought the subject best avoided since she had used it as a catalyst for infidelity.

In the morning he said: 'I forgot to tell you, Thaddeus says he thinks it's time you and he went to the opera again. You'll see from next week's diary that I'm in Germany for a couple of nights.'

She took the underground to Kew for a stroll in the serene gardens, stepping into the glassed Palm House to converse with a gardener, stopping for lunch in a cafeteria where she could overhear conversations which might be useful. Belatedly she was getting her material for the column she had mentioned to Luke. Even if he didn't notice it, that bloody Jaspar would.

'I chose to take your column this morning as a personal message,' Mark said when he phoned. 'If you made up those conversations at Kew, you should be a novelist. They sounded absolutely authentic.'

She laughed with delight. 'They were. I took the underground there the next day to put down some footprints.'

'You'd make a good criminal.'

'So would you. I know why you risked phoning this morning. Thursday is Cabinet morning.'

'As criminals, we'd make a good team.'

'Luke will be in Germany next week. I could be free either Tuesday or Wednesday evening. But you have to choose now. One of those evenings I'd better go to the opera with Thaddeus Spearman.'

'I've missed you,' said Thaddeus on Tuesday evening, patting her knee as his car made its way to Covent Garden.

'Did I ever tell you,' said Blanche gaily, 'that President

Masters is a great thigh-patter?'

'You surprise me that he should confine his self-indulgence to anything so prim. What did Luke say about it?'

'As I recall, he laughed. He makes moral distinctions between the American President and an English barrister, however celebrated.'

The performance of *La Traviata* was electric. When Violetta made her heartbreaking promise to Alfredo's father to give up his son who adored her, tears came down Blanche's cheeks. Since the afternoon at Whitehall Court, she had been in a state of heightened emotion. The beauty of the voices and the sacrifice that Alfredo's father required moved her deeply. She felt sexually moved too. This link between her senses led to images of Mark as the sublime notes soared and fell. She basked in the knowledge that she would be with him in Luke's absence the following evening.

'You look radiant,' said Thaddeus in the interval. 'Anyone would think you were in love.'

'Violetta always makes me feel like that,' Blanche replied.

Sipping wine in the Crush Bar, Thaddeus was like a magnet for his friends and acquaintances, who always liked seeing him and wanted to meet Blanche. Not until they were in his car did they have any sustained conversation.

'If you had known Luke was going to be Prime Minister, would you have married him?' asked Thaddeus.

'Oh yes. I was in love with him. It was not until he entered the House of Commons that I realised he might be Prime Minister one day. Neither of us imagined it would happen when we were so young.'

'Do you get restless having him so preoccupied and away so much?'

There was something about the barrister's unemotional interrogations that made them inoffensive to Blanche. They didn't come over as intrusive because they didn't seem personal. In addition, they gave her a chance to clear her mind.

'Rarely. I've been proud to be his wife.' Thaddeus noticed the tense. 'And don't forget how many excitements for me come with his job. Places I would never have seen otherwise. People I would never have met. Peculiar as it is to live in Downing Street and Chequers, I still get a buzz when I walk through their front doors.' She paused. He waited.

'What has cast a shadow,' she went on, 'is the effect of power. People say power corrupts. What I see is its effect on one's sense of self. Since Begova, Luke has seen himself as destined to bring peace and prosperity to all. His blinkers keep him from seeing that his mania for armed interference led to more deaths and destruction in Begova than if he and NATO had minded their own business.'

Thaddeus leant forward to tell the driver to go around Parliament Square and along the Embankment while he and Blanche finished their conversation.

'If people will insist on marrying for love,' he said, 'they are bound to experience disillusion. Ask my former wife. But you'd be wrong to let a little disillusion – ie, reality – blind you to what a remarkable man Luke is. No one else in Democratic Labour could have won the last election with that thumping great majority which enables him to behave like a president.'

'Apart from the half-witted war in Begova, what has he actually done in office? What has he changed for the better in Britain? His evangelist rhetoric makes his achievements sound so splendid, but when you examine them, nothing has really happened. He and Jaspar Byatt have reduced British politics to the level of a McDonald's advertising campaign. The only person who has achieved anything to boast about is the Chancellor of the Exchequer with his hard, gritty intelligence.'

Thaddeus turned to examine her profile. 'You wouldn't be

developing a soft spot for Robert Oakes, would you?' he commented.

'I've always liked him a lot – and I respect him,' she answered. 'I'd better get home. Before I go to sleep, I want some time on my pillow to brood about Alfredo's honcho father using emotional blackmail to bully Violetta into wrecking her life.'

Thaddeus directed his driver to turn back.

The phone was ringing when she walked in the flat. 'The Prime Minister is calling to speak to Mrs Dalton.'

She frowned with unease. Normally Luke didn't phone when he was away for only a few nights.

His voice came on the line.

'Has something happened?' she asked.

He laughed. 'I've had such a successful meeting with the Germans that I wanted to speak to my wife and tell her so.'

She found herself very touched and wondered if she had been too critical of him. 'Remember the best scenes to tell me when you get home,' she said affectionately.

'Have you and Thaddeus been to the opera yet?'

'I just got in from *La Traviata*.'

'Good, because I find I can get back tomorrow evening.'

Her heart sank. 'I thought you were coming back a day later.'

'I was, but tonight advanced things so far that I can cut tomorrow evening's meeting. I ought to be home by nine.'

When she put down the phone, she bit her lip with chagrin. She rang Mark, finding him at his office.

'Luke's coming back early,' she said gloomily. 'I have to be here tomorrow evening.'

'And I can't rearrange my work schedule to bring our date forward to the afternoon. *Tant pis.*'

In bed a little later, she reconstructed their conversation, examining each inflection to discern whether his disappointment was as great as hers. Then she recalled the pleasure in Luke's voice when he told her he'd be home soon, and she felt a stab of shame.

It was her third afternoon visit to Whitehall Court since her return from Richmond. She had just swung her legs over the side of the bed to start dressing when Mark said: 'Deep down, do you want to be found out by the Downing Street mafia?'

She dropped back alongside him as he lay contemplating the ceiling. After a silence while she gazed at the elaborate cornice, she said reflectively: 'I *think* the answer is no.'

'But if we *were* found out, what then?'

'I don't think about that.'

'Normally,' said Mark, 'I avoid too much introspection. But then normally one isn't making love to a prime minister's wife.'

He reached for a cigarette and lay back with an ashtray on his chest.

'What I like about our situation,' said Blanche quietly, 'is that it's not going anywhere. We enjoy it for itself – which heightens it.'

He pulled a wry face. 'That makes a change. Any other woman I've known is obsessed with commitment. "This is not going anywhere,"' he mimicked.

'If you demanded commitment of me, I'd be off,' she said. 'I'm a happily married woman. Remember?'

He put out his cigarette, removed the ashtray and turned to kiss her. After a few moments she drew away.

'The odd thing,' she said, 'is that the more I see you, the better wife I am to Luke. I keep my views about Begova to myself. Quite often I take the initiative in bed. At official dos, I'm the perfect consort. Actually, I always was pretty good on those occasions: I didn't want to let Luke down. Yet I'm evidently quite prepared to be unfaithful to him.'

'He wouldn't be the only prime minister to have his wife cuckold him.'

'I hate that word. Do you have to put it like that?'

Mark shrugged.

Walking through the narrow ways back to Downing Street, Blanche asked herself why she should want to threaten her marriage and her extraordinary life with Luke. Was she the first prime minister's wife to have such an intimate marriage with her husband and still, unexpectedly, find herself enjoying adultery?

Early that evening, Max Murphy dropped in on Jaspar in his office at Number Ten, making himself comfortable in an armchair. 'Re Blanche,' he said, 'something further has come up.'

Jaspar's face tightened as he waited.

'Two more people have spoken to me about seeing her with Fleetwood. Outside Whitehall Court. You will recall that's where he lives.'

'Who saw them?'

'Two more fucking Liberal MPs. They seem to spend most of their time using the back door to their club so they can take a good look at Whitehall Court.'

'Jesus. All we need is for one of them to mention it to Luke. Or to some rag. Have you got the dates?'

He wrote them down.

'What makes you sure Luke doesn't already know?' Max asked. 'If Blanche is defiant enough to have an affair with one of the enemy, she might be defiant enough to tell Luke.'

Jaspar swivelled his chair so his back was to Max for a minute or two. When he completed the circuit he said: 'It's out of character. She wouldn't be that unkind.'

'If you'd asked me six months ago, I would have said cuckolding her husband was out of character.'

'All that matters is keeping it quiet,' said Jaspar, his voice suddenly hoarse.

The two sat in silence until Max said: 'Maybe we'd better have a private chat with Blanche and put it to her straight.'

'That would just make her more defiant.'

'I didn't mean we try to dissuade her from fucking Fleetwood. I meant that we discuss with her how imperative it is to keep it quiet.'

'Too bad we don't know if she's in love with the bastard,' said Jaspar grimly. He got a whisky bottle from a cupboard and poured them each a drink.

'So much for my efforts not to smoke,' said Max, taking a pack from his pocket.

'What did you say to those Liberal cunts?'

'Something like: "Let me know when you see her with the Leader of the Conservative party. That might be mildly interesting."'

Jaspar's laugh was mirthless. 'When you think of the lies we've sold the media, you'd think we could get away with anything. But if this rumour grows legs, we're all in deep deep trouble.'

They lapsed into another silence.

'I wonder if we can count on Fleetwood to keep it quiet,' said Max. 'It could be very tempting for him to give little winks and nudges.'

'God, being unable to control a story is frustrating,' Jaspar replied angrily. 'We may end up having to tell Luke so he can be prepared to fend off questions.'

Max's groan was from the heart.

When Luke and Jaspar had their first meeting the next day in the Prime Minister's study, Jaspar came out with it almost at once. 'I'm the messenger of bad news,' he said.

Something in his voice frightened Luke.

'There have been two recent sightings of Blanche with Mark Fleetwood outside Whitehall Court where Fleetwood has a flat. Max told me yesterday that two separate Liberal backbenchers had mentioned it to him. Whitehall Court stands behind the National Liberal Club.'

Jaspar winced as he watched the colour drain from Luke's face. In the next moment, Luke leant forward with his elbows on his desk, fingers meeting in a tent shielding his face. For some minutes the two friends sat immobile and silent.

At last Luke sat back, his eyes meeting Jaspar's as he said: 'Do you remember the dates?'

'I made a note of them, but it's locked in my desk. I remember the first one was soon after Blanche returned from Richmond following her mother's death.'

A sound like a short moan came from Luke before he said: 'I thought you'd say that.'

Jaspar lit a cigarette and smoked quietly, watching the smoke, wondering if Luke would explain what he meant.

Luke was uncertain how to proceed. He didn't want to discuss his and Blanche's private life. Yet he couldn't bear for Jaspar to think that Blanche was wholly to blame.

'This job has its costs,' he said at last. 'The dying of her mother was excruciatingly painful for Blanche. The night she got back, she started to tell me about it. I reacted with utter insensitivity. And intolerance. The thing with Fleetwood must have begun soon after that.'

Again a groan.

'I had to steel myself to tell you,' said Jaspar. 'And of course it may be nothing much. But I thought you'd better be prepared if some snide question is put to you by one of the tabloids.'

They continued to sit together, saying nothing, the only sound the click of Jaspar's cigarette lighter. This was the first time that Jaspar found himself unable to come up with a way out. He was not only tigerishly loyal to Luke. He loved the man.

'Who can we trust besides Max?' Luke asked.

'In this sort of situation, nobody.'

They went on sitting together.

Chapter Twenty-five

THAT weekend both Daltons went to the constituency. Mayor's Sunday was a big local event. While Luke was dealing with his Saturday surgery, Blanche attended a school fair. In the evening they ate fish and chips in a cafe with Harry, the agent, who filled them in on local gossip. Then they went on to the Demo Labour Club.

By the time they got back to their small terrace home, Luke judged it too late to start on a desperately serious subject. Truth to tell, he was glad of an excuse to put it off a little longer. He dreaded it. In his mind he moved it to their agenda for Sunday. On the train.

'We can leave soon after the Mayor's lunch,' he told her. 'Let's aim for the 3:40. There's something we need to talk about.'

As usual, the bodyguards took seats well out of earshot, and the rhythm of the wheels rattling over the rail ties lent a soothing detachment as Luke began, almost as if he were confiding in a stranger, as people do on trains.

'I need to talk to you about Mark Fleetwood.'

Blanche had been gazing out of the window, and she turned her head slowly towards him and met his eyes for a moment before looking ahead into some middle distance in the carriage.

'I've been told that you are seeing him at Whitehall Court.'

Her first response was defiant. 'What's so unusual about calling on another journalist?'

Luke looked at her profile. He knew it so well, and the chin was slightly lifted. Glancing down he saw one hand clenched in her lap. He covered it with his own for a few moments.

'That is what I need to ask you,' he replied almost tenderly.

Kerchackity, kerchackity. Kerchackity, kerchackity.

This conversation can't be taking place, he thought, and at the same time knew that it was. As she didn't answer, he went on: 'Are you in love with him?'

It's a good question, she thought. 'Not that I'm aware of,' she answered. She had already decided not to deny the whole thing. She had too much regard for Luke to do that to him.

'Is it an infatuation?'

She turned to him as she answered: 'That's not the word I would use. I haven't seen him all that often, by the way.'

'If it's not for love, if it's not an infatuation, is it to hurt me that you have embarked on this dangerous path?'

'What is so dangerous about it?' she asked, her chin lifted again.

'We both know the answer.'

They realised that they were talking as if it were an accepted fact that she was having an affair with Fleetwood.

'Do you mean that my feelings for him might develop into something that would threaten our marriage?'

'I would have thought our marriage was already threatened by what you're doing,' he replied. 'But the danger I was referring to was that once this thing gets wider currency, you reduce me to a joke figure. A cuckolded prime minister is always ridiculous – like one of Hogarth's gross cartoons. It would have a detrimental effect on everything I'm trying to achieve, both nationally and internationally.'

Any tenderness in his voice had vanished.

'You're putting a lot at risk,' he continued. 'Why?'

'I guess I did want to hurt you,' she answered in a low voice. 'We both knew that your being Prime Minister would impose a new dimension on our marriage. But I wasn't prepared for the moral self-certainty that has grown in you.' Her voice tapered off. Now that she had told him this reason, it seemed to her inadequate for the hurt she had dealt him.

'Have you wondered whether the path you have chosen might be a new instance of your old self-destructiveness?' he asked.

'I don't know,' she answered.

Kerchackity, kerchackity.

'Would you despise me,' he said, 'if I asked you to give him up?'

'I wouldn't despise you. With all our ups and downs, I love you. But I'm not sure I am willing to give him up. He provides a ... an escape valve in my life.'

'And is that escape valve really worth the price we'll have to pay if you go on with it?'

She didn't answer directly. 'There are so many things I can and cannot do as the wife of the Prime Minister.'

'Do you think more restrictions are imposed on you than on me?'

'But you chose to be Prime Minister.'

'Is that fair?'

'Probably not,' she conceded.

'Will you at least think about what I have asked of you?'

'Yes.'

After some minutes he said: 'God, it will be nice to be back in the flat and have a drink together.'

She gave a small lopsided smile without looking at him. When he talked like that, it was hard to resist him. But she didn't want him to have his way.

*

'We can't go on meeting like this,' Blanche said, laughing, as she and the Chancellor nearly collided when Robert Oakes emerged from the connecting passage to Number Ten just as she came down the last stairs to the ground floor.

'I'm on my way up to your husband's study to discuss high finance,' he said with his crinkle-eyed grin. 'I hope you left him in a good mood.' He looked her up and down. 'Why don't we have a drink *a deux* soon at Number Eleven? Although I see as little as possible of my Cabinet colleagues, I still see more of them than I do of my next-door neighbour. My sons keep asking when you're coming to Dorneywood again.'

She had read in a gossip column a few days earlier that the Chancellor and Rebecca Knight were no longer 'an item'. Perhaps he wanted to talk about it. More likely, given his reticence, he was just lonely.

'Who's going to phone who?' she asked.

'I'll have my diary secretary ring you, and the two of you can settle on a date.' He waved a hand and made for the stairs. Blanche went out into Downing Street and set off for her newspaper office.

She had already e-mailed her column to the *Nation*, but she also needed to talk with the editor about one or two things. Normally when she went to see him, some journalists glanced up as she crossed the newsroom. A few carefully did not. One or two came up to chat with her before she reached the editor's door. Today when she entered the newsroom, she came at once on three reporters standing by the shelf where all the daily papers lay open. When they saw her, they broke off their animated conversation and strolled away in separate directions.

If there was something derogatory about her in one of the papers, she told herself, Jaspar would have alerted her. Wouldn't he? She was uneasy as she continued to the editor's office. His secretary was reading the early edition of the *Evening Mail,* and when she looked up and saw Blanche she quickly turned the page.

In his inner sanctum, she found Jules Barker was also reading the *Evening Mail*. He gave his wolfish leer, and her heart sank. Waving her to the sofa, he jabbed a splay finger on the open page. 'You can answer this in tomorrow's column. I see it as your middle item.'

'I e-mailed my column to you before I left home this morning.'

'I saw it. Change it. Save the middle item for next week and write about what everybody will soon know is uppermost in your mind.'

Blanche made every effort to keep her face expressionless. Her former editor had evidently put the knife in. 'I haven't the faintest idea what you're talking about,' she said.

'Take a look.'

His *Evening Mail* was folded back with the political gossip page on top. She saw that he had already drawn a red circle around the paragraphs printed alongside an informal picture of her with Luke. The caption read: 'The tolerant husband.' A separate picture was captioned: 'Lucky journalist Mark Fleetwood.' She picked up the paper, wondering if her face had paled, and read:

'Not every husband would be happy for his wife to lunch with his most vitriolic critic. But we already know that the Prime Minister is not like other men. Mrs Blanche Dalton has her own career as a columnist, and it would appear that she prefers the company of journalists to that of her husband's colleagues. She has been seen around London in the company of Mark Fleetwood, one of the Prime Minister's most derisive denigrators. What can he and Mrs Dalton find to talk about during their tête-à-têtes?'

'Tell me, Blanche,' said her editor with a chortle that made her want to run round his desk and swat him, 'if you could sue for libel, would you sue the *Evening Mail*? Or would your friend Thaddeus Spearman QC advise you that a court case would draw more attention to the story and you might not win?'

'The question is academic. This irritating piece has been written carefully to avoid libel.'

'What does the Prime Minister say about your friendship with Mr Fleetwood?' Again the leer.

'He finds it ironic.'

As she said it, she saw the crafty expression in her editor's eyes.

'Jules, this isn't an interview, is it?'

'You malign me, Blanche,' he replied genially, enjoying himself. 'But I want you to give Francis Artwell a comment that we can run in tomorrow's paper as a teaser for your column.' Artwell was the political team's parliamentary lobby correspondent.

'Wait a minute,' said Blanche. 'You don't expect me to write about a tabloid gossip snippet which doesn't really say anything anyhow.'

'If you think it says nothing scandalous about you, you're in denial, my dear.'

Blanche flushed at his archness. Everyone knew Jules Barker only used psycho-jargon sarcastically.

'I don't mean to sound bullying, Blanche,' he went on, 'but I wouldn't be an editor if I was prepared for one of my writers – even if she is the PM's wife – to skip aside when a story about her has just appeared in the press. It's now eleven-thirty. Postpone the middle item you've already written. Write a fresh one and send it to me by four. Once we see it, we can discuss your giving a comment to Artwell.'

Blanche looked at him steadily. She could simply quit, but then Jules's famous vindictiveness would be unleashed against both Daltons. She didn't want two editors gunning for them on personal grounds. She must keep unruffled.

'It's going to be very awkward to find the time at this short notice,' she said. 'I'll ring you at three and let you know what's happening.'

'You do that, Blanche.' His voice was not pleasant.

On the way back to Downing Street she brooded about Jaspar. She hated Jaspar, she told herself, yet she needed his help. Then she thought of Thaddeus, but soon her mind went back to Jaspar. If the bloody *Evening Mail* knew something about her friendship with Mark – that's what she called it now, friendship – word might have reached Jaspar before now. Could she go to him with her tail between her legs? This time she had her mobile with her. She pressed his number.

They met at the Downing Street flat. He didn't have long: he had to be with Luke at a lunch given by the editor of the *Times*.

'Have you seen that piece in the early edition of the *Evening Mail*?' she asked.

He nodded, his lips pressed together in a thin line.

'Jules Barker wants me to use part of tomorrow's column to answer it. I detest the idea. I'm to phone him at three and tell him my decision. If I do it, I have to send it in at four. I'd like to ask your advice.'

Jaspar gave a short harsh laugh. He was torn between rage at this bloody woman and the desire to lean over and kiss her cheek. That the day should come when she would recognise that she too needed him. Hesitantly, he kissed her cheek. Tears came into her eyes.

'Write as lighthearted a piece as you can,' he said, 'mocking yourself, mocking the *Evening Mail* without naming it. I can come back here soon after three, and we can go through it together. I'll tell Luke what we're doing. Meanwhile, let's hope no one at the *Times* has the balls to raise the matter. On our way there, I'll alert Luke. I've already thought what he could reply.'

'What?'

'You'll have to wait for my wife's column tomorrow.'

As he was leaving, she went up to him and kissed his cheek.

When she closed the door behind him, she felt humbled.

Even when working under stress, Blanche tried to eat something at lunchtime. Today she made a peanut butter and jelly sandwich and took it and a Coke over to her computer. She was convinced that Coca-Cola's sugar and caffeine made a good stimulant that didn't give her a stomach ache like too much coffee. She added an aspirin from the bathroom. Like all American school children, she used to believe she could get a high by dropping an aspirin in a Coke. She still did it, just in case, and watched the bubbles rise.

At three she phoned her editor and told him she would be filing at four. She'd hardly put down the phone when Jaspar returned. He pulled up a chair to sit beside her at her computer. She laid a print-out between them. He read through it rapidly, gave a grunt, lit a cigarette and started again, reading slowly. With his red pen he made a few deletions, re-jigged several sentences, inserted new phrases. She watched him in silence. When he had finished, he read it through once more.

'You and I should go to Hollywood,' he said, lighting another cigarette. 'We'd make a great team as scriptwriters. Black comedy our speciality.' He looked at his watch. 'It's almost time for my afternoon briefing of the press. Because the Prime Minister was a guest at the *Times*'s table, no one at lunch referred to the early edition of the *Evening Mail*. But it's bound to come up when the hacks are emboldened by the sheer numbers that attend briefings.'

'When you told Luke that I'd asked you for help, what did he say?'

'Not much.' He gave a nod and was gone.

She keyed in his changes, made a print-out and carried it to a chaise-longue. With her own red pen she made some minor stylistic changes, keyed them in and read down the screen a final time:

'When I was growing up in Richmond, Virginia, my grandmother told me: "Dear, New Yorkers like to see their names in the papers daily. But in Virginia, we expect to read about ourselves in the press only when we marry and when we die." With the natural curiosity of a child I asked her how I could read about myself if I was dead, but she brushed that aside. My grandmother was very autocratic. "If I can do it, you can do it," she said.

'Then I came to England and discovered that Londoners have something in common with those New Yorkers. As for politicians, we all know they are publicity mad.' That sentence was added by Jaspar.

'Living as I do in Downing Street, how do I feel when I read that from time to time I lunch with another journalist? Generally I feel nothing at all about it. Journalists may practise one of Britain's most despised trades (the others being secondhand car dealers and lawyers), yet we journalists do enjoy each other's company. However, when the innuendo is that I'm doing something naughty which would annoy my husband if he were normal, then I do feel piqued. Wouldn't you?

'For he does have normal feelings, and I often annoy him. Indeed he has been known to annoy me, though so far such moments remain uncommon. Does it irritate him when I have lunch with a member of my own trade instead of, say, a member of his? He has never said so. Nor would I expect him to. It would be a rum husband these days who tried to decree which persons his wife can sit down to lunch with.'

She didn't like the fact the sentence ended with a preposition, but no other way sounded natural. Returning to her computer, she pressed the e-mail button.

For some minutes she leaned back in her chair with her hands cupping her chin. Then she dialled the flat at Whitehall Court.

Chapter Twenty-six

Bᵧ luck she found Mark was at home writing his column. Her voice was glum. 'I suppose you've seen today's *Evening Mail.*'

'Half a dozen candid friends have been kind enough to draw my attention to it.'

'Jules Barker said I had to comment on it in tomorrow's column. He couldn't have me skipping aside from the buckshot, he said, even if I am the PM's wife. Jaspar helped me.'

'The master himself.'

'You're not going to comment on it in your own column, are you?'

'Do you want me to?'

'No.'

'That's what I thought.'

'I guess we'd better cancel our next meeting.'

A silence.

'Mark?'

'I was just thinking. It's tempting to take you to lunch at the Savoy Grill and let all those editors stare. But I expect that's childish.'

'I expect so.'

'Will you be in touch soon?' he asked.

'I expect so.'

'You sound a little bleak.'

'Yes. Well, see you somewhere some time.'

She moved around the flat listlessly. Luke was addressing some industrialists over dinner. This time no one's wife had just committed suicide, so it was unlikely to be cancelled. She fixed something to eat and thought how grateful she was to have a private telephone line. No journalist could get through to her to ask for a comment or, nearly as bad, to commiserate.

Lying in her bath, she found her unease deepening. Here was Luke trying to govern a country and all she could do was make mischief for him. After further brooding, she used plainer language to herself. She may not have consciously intended to land him in the shit, but her actions had made it possible for that bloody *Evening Mail* to throw rotten eggs at him. What could she say to him?

When she heard the front door close, she was near to panic. He stopped at the open door to the bedroom, red box in hand. Their eyes met, and she flinched at the sadness she saw in his. He nodded several times, as if to say: 'You were determined to mess things up and you've succeeded.' Unspeaking, he went to the drawing room and settled in the Eames chair.

She followed him. Without the confidence to sit down, she stood just inside the doorway. 'Did Jaspar tell you he helped me with tomorrow's column?' she asked in a subdued voice.

The red box was already open and lying on the ottoman in front of him. 'Yes,' he replied without glancing up. He took a file from the box. 'I've got to get through a lot of stuff before tomorrow's Cabinet. Don't wait up.'

She returned to the bedroom and almost at once switched out the light. When at last he came to bed, she was still awake.

He turned his back, and soon she heard the heavy breathing of someone in exhausted sleep.

Over their silent breakfast, they read the newspapers, Blanche turning first to her column in the *Nation*. After scanning it word for word – she never trusted the subs not to make some fiddly change – she said to Luke: 'Would you like to see it?'

'Not now,' he answered, keeping his eyes on the *Times*. 'Jaspar is coming to my study before Cabinet. He'll summarise everything in the morning papers that I need to know.'

His dismissiveness stung. She knew she deserved it.

Cabinet began as usual at ten. Upstairs in the flat, the private phone rang a few minutes later. When Blanche heard the voice at the other end, her face flushed with excited pleasure.

'Am I right to assume you're alone at this hour?' asked Mark. There was not a trace of sportiveness in his voice.

'Yes,' she replied warily.

'I must see you at once, Blanche. After you've heard what I have to tell you, you may not want to see me again – ever. I'm at home. How soon can you get here?'

Twenty minutes later, walking rapidly, she cast a hostile glance at the back of the National Liberal Club and then disappeared into Whitehall Court. When Mark closed his door behind her, she saw he was nervous. He gestured to the sofa and took a chair near it, stubbing out his cigarette and almost at once lighting another.

'I saw your column,' he said. 'You handled it well. Do you want some coffee?'

She shook her head.

He went straight into what he had to tell her.

'I have a foul story from Begova. There has been a gigantic cover-up. Bodies of more than a thousand Serbs, many of them mutilated, have been found in three mass graves. Mostly the old and the very young who lived in Begova and were unable to flee when the Albanian Muslims, with NATO backing, returned after the ceasefire. The Albanians massacred them. With British knowledge.'

'*What?*'

'The Albanians are our allies. Remember? They have been exacting a revenge on their Serbian neighbours every bit as pitiless as the savagery they suffered themselves. I suspect that the cover-up has gone all the way to Downing Street, which is pretending to consider evidence about whether or not British troops were involved in the massacre, but is in fact trying to keep the whole thing quiet. I'm going to write about it.'

He put out his cigarette. When Blanche, aghast, said nothing, he lit another.

'My sources,' Mark went on, 'have warned me there may be a risk in revealing it.'

'What do you mean when you say you suspect British troops were involved? You can't believe they actually joined in the massacre.'

'I think they stood by and did nothing. Remember how most NATO members refused to send their troops in on the ground, despite the British Prime Minister urging them to do so? They thought the peace would be much harder to manage than the war had been, and they wanted no part of it. Luke Dalton was determined to send in our troops so he would be seen as acting to keep the peace. How could a massacre of this magnitude have taken place without British troops knowing? Whatever the risk, obviously I must write about it.'

'Where do you think the risk is?'

For the first time his intense expression gave way to a wry half smile. 'Downing Street, I suppose,' he said.

Back at the flat, she picked up her copy of the Prime Minister's schedule for that day. After Cabinet, he had a succession of meetings with various people. Only one appointment, with an hour allowed for it, gave no indication of where it would take place or with whom. 'Meeting' was all it said.

Blanche could not sit still. Nor could she concentrate on a book. Nor could she draft ideas for next week's column. Luke had a dinner meeting which Jaspar had arranged with Abe Dixon, the *Washington Tribune*'s London correspondent, and four other bureau chiefs. Blanche supposed it wouldn't go on too late.

Soon after ten she heard the key in the door. She was still dressed, pretending to read in the drawing room.

'I thought I'd find you in bed,' Luke said.

'I must talk to you about something.'

'Let's leave it for now,' he said.

'About Begova.'

He looked at her sharply, then replied in an unconcerned voice: 'I think I'll pour myself a drink. Do you want one?'

'Yes. A whisky and soda, please.'

When she reached out to take it from him, they both saw the shaking of her hand. She sat back on the sofa, curling her legs under her, trying to relax her body lest it too tremble with tension. He sat forward in the Eames chair, intent.

'Yesterday I told Mark Fleetwood I didn't expect to see him again in any foreseeable future,' she said. 'He accepted that. Then today he rang and said it was important that he see me, even though I would probably never want to meet him after I'd heard what he had to tell me.'

Luke's tongue darted over his lips, his eyes fixed on her.

'It turned out,' Blanche went on, 'that he has been investigating a tip-off of a vast cover-up of a recent massacre in Begova. Many, many innocent Serb civilians were murdered by the returning Albanians and dumped in three huge graves.

British troops almost certainly stood by while all this took place.'

Luke gave a short, mirthless laugh. 'I find it hard to judge which of the two of you – you or your boyfriend – is the craziest.'

'That's the kind of line Jaspar uses when he's trying to throw someone off the scent.'

Luke shrugged. 'If your darling Mr Fleetwood wants to make a fool of himself, I'm surprised you don't try to make him see sanity. You're supposed to have his interests at heart.'

Blanche sipped her drink. Luke kept his eyes, like ice, fixed on her, as if trying to hypnotise her. She could have let the subject alone, let events unroll as they would. But his condescending arrogance angered her.

'You can't stop it. Mark is going to write about it,' she said, adding, though uncertain whether it would prove true, 'He has too big a reputation as an investigative journalist for anyone to block the story. His newspaper will stand behind him.'

Luke's face was chalky, with two spots of red on his cheekbones.

'Little Blanchie,' he said chillingly, a supercilious smile pulling his mouth up on one side, 'you know fuck all about geo-politics. Sometimes, little Blanchie, the means to an end is unattractive.'

'That's what Mark will write about,' she doggedly replied.

Luke's superiority vanished. 'He has no business investigating the matter,' he shouted. 'Anyone who reveals it is a traitor to Britain – and will be treated as a traitor. There are ways to stop him which are extreme but necessary. You had better use your wiles to stop him first.'

Looking at Luke, Blanche saw a stranger.

More calmly he said: 'If it comes out that I am directly involved, it will gravely threaten my work for international peace and harmony. Jaspar thinks I'd be certain to win the Nobel Prize.'

'I can't believe this is the man I married.'

She rose and left the room. That night she slept in the second bedroom.

Halfway through Friday morning, Mark telephoned the flat. 'I'm sorry to ring you, Blanche, when I'm not sure you are alone. Are you?'

'Yes.'

'I've been warned by MI6. I will be in extreme danger if I persist in publishing the exposé.'

After a silence, Blanche asked: 'What are you going to do?'

'What do you suppose?'

The question being rhetorical, she waited for him to go on.

'One odd thing is that I've also had a call this morning from Stanley Fox's private office. He's on his way to Chevening for the weekend.' Chevening was the Foreign Secretary's country house in Kent. 'He wants me to come there for an exclusive interview. At teatime today.'

Blanche did not need to be told that MI6 answers to the Foreign Secretary. 'His private secretary suggested that I drive myself there. "It would be more discreet," he said.'

'I don't like the sound of this.'

'I can hardly say no to the Foreign Secretary. And more pieces of the puzzle might fall into place. I'm sure,' Mark added drily, 'that they don't intend to dig a big hole in Chevening Park and put me in it.'

Because he detested driving in London, Mark kept his car garaged near a petrol station just before a dual-carriageway. He took a taxi there, collected his car and set off. Sometimes he stayed with a friend who lived in Kent, and he knew the way well – fortunately, for a violent storm had broken, blotting out all but what lay immediately before him. Cascades of rain bounced up from the road and were simultaneously flattened by the ceaseless downpour. As soon as he turned on to the dual-carriageway, he pressed down the accelerator, feeling confident enough to increase his speed.

A grey shape drew his eye to his right window, nearly obscured by the rain. 'Bloody fool,' he muttered as he realised a lorry was slowly overtaking him, raising blinding waves of dirty water as it lumbered past. Abruptly it cut in front of Mark's car, throwing up more filthy water which blacked out his windscreen. He jammed on his brakes. Nothing happened. At once he knew.

He could just make out that the gap between him and the lorry was closing. Evidently it was slowing down. With one hand blaring his horn, he jerked the steering wheel to the left, swerving towards the soft shoulder, missing the lorry's tailgate by inches. His car slewed out of control in a skid. He saw the concrete side-wall rushing towards him. He was helpless. Then the deafening crash of metal burst around him at the same instant that savage pain shot through one leg. He was only half aware that his broken car had turned over, flinging the top-side door open to hang from one of its hinges. In the sudden silence he heard a noise like a giant firecracker and in the confusion of heat and light knew he was about to be engulfed in flames. Some instinct pierced his semi-consciousness and he felt for his seatbelt to release it.

One should never underestimate human decency. A driver decelerated as sharply as he dared in the lethal torrents, turning on to the soft shoulder where he braked, his car not quite stationary when he jumped out. Without hesitation he raced back to the burning wreck, blessing the downpour for the moments it gave him before the whole thing blew up. Clambering on to the already blistering metal and reaching down through the open door, he dragged the injured man out. Another driver who had stopped came running up as the blaze spread. Together the two men carried Mark, groaning, along the soft shoulder. When the car exploded, the deadly spray of jagged metal stopped just short of them.

'Watch the other side of his face. It's badly burned,' one rescuer said to the other. They eased out his shattered leg from where it was twisted beneath him, fragments of bone jutting through the skin.

Chapter Twenty-seven

CLUTCHING her umbrella low over her head, Blanche made her way down the slippery front steps of the National Gallery. An exhibition of Piero di Lorenzo and his Florentine contemporaries was opening the following day, and she had gone to the preview to gather material for her next column. The heavens had opened when she mounted the stairs two hours earlier, and now the rain was torrential. Looking at the clock on St Martin-in-the-Fields, she thought of Mark driving to Chevening in this deluge. He and Stanley Fox might even now be sitting down to their tea and God knows what kind of interview. She could only guess as to the pressures the Foreign Secretary would employ to try and bully Mark into agreeing not to write about the cover-up. Denial that a massacre had occurred? Patriotism?

It would be impossible to find a cab in this Noah's Ark downpour. She might as well set off down Whitehall on foot. As she made her way round Trafalgar Square, her umbrella blew inside out, and she sheltered next to a newsagent's kiosk. Only when she had righted her umbrella did she notice the *Evening Mail*'s late edition placard: BLANCHE'S FRIEND IN BIG SMASH-UP.

Forgetting about her umbrella, she delved in her handbag for change, her hand trembling so much that she dropped some of the coins on the pavement. 'Better add some water to the whisky next time,' the newsagent remarked laconically.

Glancing at the photograph of Mark, she scarcely noticed a smaller picture of herself as she read across the text, the newspaper already sopping, to discover what had happened. The sentence which turned her stomach stood out as if printed in bold type: 'Surgeons do not yet know if they can save his leg.'

She broke into a jogger's trot as she made for Downing Street, her streaming hair and clothes clinging to her, the *Evening Mail* stuffed in her bag. Taxis went up and down Whitehall, but all were occupied. She was gasping when she reached the barrier, and her voice broke as she said to the police: 'Please help me. I have to get to a hospital in south London. I can't find a taxi.'

Ten minutes later she was on her way, a puddle gathering on the floor of the minicab. 'I want to hire you for the rest of the day and possibly this evening,' she told the driver.

Unfolding the sodden newspaper carefully so it didn't tear, she began the text at the beginning, reading every word with care in her effort to take in what had happened. Early in the account was a paragraph about herself: 'The Prime Minister's wife, Blanche Dalton, is a special friend of the injured man, and the two have been seen lunching together in out-of-the-way restaurants.' The *Evening Mail*'s piece earlier in the week had dismayed her generally, but this time her only distress was for Mark's injuries.

'How much longer do you think we'll be?' she asked the driver.

'Hard to say. Between the bleeding rain and Friday afternoon traffic, it's taking longer than it would normally.'

Amidst the thoughts that raced through her mind, some over

and over, it occurred to her that arriving at Mark's hospital bed was hardly discreet. For the first time she didn't care.

He was in a room off the ward, his fragmented leg fastened with splints and steel spikes driven through the flesh to hold sections of bone in place. For an instant she thought of the torture chamber in the London Dungeon. Little of his face could be seen through the gauze wrapping.

She stood unspeaking beside him, her eyes misted with tears, and digging a handkerchief from her bag she hastily wiped them.

'Hi,' she said.

He opened his uncovered eye, and after a moment or two it crinkled at the corner.

'I'm dopey from the general anaesthetic and morphine,' he said, 'but I know what I must do tomorrow. I need your help. The nurses found my keys among my ragged clothes. Will you reach in the side-table and get them? I don't yet feel like turning my head.'

Quietly Blanche did as she was asked.

'I want you to go to Whitehall Court. My notes are in my bedroom chest of drawers. Third drawer down. Under some shirts. I put them there before I left for Chevening. At the time I thought I was being a bit melodramatic.'

A short dry laugh followed, which made him cough.

When he got his breath, he went on: 'It's possible that MI6 are also looking for my notes. Once they start a "dirty war" with official connivance, there is a strong temptation to continue it. Listen carefully. I had already made photocopies of my notes. You never know. In the drawing room bookcase, about three-quarters of the way down, is a book with a bright red shiny cover, called *Dictionary of Espionage*. Take it out and you'll see two manila envelopes standing upright at the back of the shelf. If one set of notes is stolen, with any luck the other set will be undisturbed. With all its know-how, MI6 would hardly guess that a journalist could be so systematic.'

He began to cough again. When the spasm ended, Blanche asked: 'What happens if I find someone in your flat?'

'I'm sorry to ask you to take that chance. At the moment, there's no one else I trust. If you do disturb someone, keep calm. Say you're using the flat while I'm in hospital. Ask if you can help them in some way. MI6 may regard themselves as above the law, but they are hardly going to harm the Prime Minister's wife.'

'Goody,' said Blanche.

It was the first time that she had approached Whitehall Court by cab. 'I shouldn't be long,' she told the driver.

She found the light just inside Mark's door, and having fastened the safety chain she stood looking around, sniffing the air. There was nothing unusual in the faint smell of tobacco, but there was also a whiff of sweat, that feral smell of someone nervous. She was not afraid of anything specific that a stranger might do to her; she was afraid of the shock of being suddenly frightened. Glancing at the bookcase, she spotted the red jacket and was relieved that it appeared undisturbed amongst the unbroken line of books. She didn't stop to check behind *Dictionary of Espionage*. Her first concern was to turn on lights throughout the flat. If anyone jumped out behind her, she would have a heart attack, she was certain.

Going through to the bedroom, she stopped in the doorway to stare at the chest of drawers. It looked all right. She leant to open the third drawer. There were the shirts. Running a hand beneath them, she felt the hairs lift on her arm, for she touched only the bottom of the drawer. Quickly she moved the shirts on to the floor. Nothing remained beneath them. Tidily she put them back in the drawer and closed it, unthinkingly copying the neatness of the person who had taken the notes.

Fear was now focused on finding the photocopies gone. Rapidly crossing the drawing room, she heard her own heartbeat as she drew out *Dictionary of Espionage*. When she bent down she could see a patch of brown paper at the back, and when she pulled out six more books she found the two manila envelopes standing there. 'Oh thank God,' she cried, taking them out and kissing them.

Delving into a cupboard, she came upon a totebag. Perfect. She went to the drinks cupboard, took out a bottle of whisky and put it in the totebag with the two envelopes of notes. In the study she found paper and pens and some big writing pads. Just before she left the flat she returned to the drinks cupboard. From an open bottle she poured herself a whisky and drank it straight down.

Twilight had fallen when her cab pulled up at the hospital. The rain had stopped. Blanche glanced up at an indigo-blue sky; cloudless, it added to the sense of unreality.

Mark was propped up on pillows.

'My brain is working again,' he announced. 'I'm going to start writing now. Will you pour me a whisky and leave it where I can reach it? When I get tired, a drop of Scotch will be just the thing to keep me going.'

'As tomorrow is Saturday and the paper can't print it until Monday, does it matter if you don't get it finished before Sunday?'

'I will.'

When she got back to the Downing Street flat that night, Luke was not yet home. He came in late. Neither mentioned what had happened to Mark Fleetwood. They scarcely spoke. Again Blanche slept in the second bedroom. In the morning Luke left for Netherby before she was awake.

Mark was working on his piece when Blanche arrived at the hospital. 'I'll be in the visitors' room when you want me,' she said. 'I've brought a sandwich. And I have plenty to do. I want to draft a piece of my own.' Mark was so concentrated that he didn't take in her last remark.

A nurse came in to tell her Mr Fleetwood had finished his work and would like to see her.

'The editor isn't in the office today, but I've phoned him at home to alert him. He says to e-mail my piece to him there,' Mark said. His words were slightly slurred, like those of someone near the end of his strength. So little of his face was uncovered that she could barely glimpse his weariness and pain. She took his copy and e-mailed it and then read it through herself.

He began with the line: 'A funny thing happened on Friday on my way to interview Stanley Fox at Chevening, the Foreign Secretary's country house in Kent.'

Concealing little except his sources, he stated only what he knew about the Albanians: with NATO backing, they returned to Begova to slaughter Serb civilians who had remained there, mostly the old and the young who were unable to flee.

'I cannot yet prove that British soldiers stood by while it was happening, but I find it hard to believe that with the British Army on the spot, none of them witnessed the massacre or the dumping in three mass graves of what looked like more than a thousand bodies, many of them mutilated. I have reason to believe that the Prime Minister and the Foreign Secretary are directly involved in the cover-up.

'On Thursday evening, the Prime Minister was informed that I intended exposing this massive cover-up in my newspaper. On Friday morning I had a call from MI6 warning me that I was in grave danger if I persisted in going ahead with this. Shortly afterwards, I had a call from the Foreign Secretary's private office telling me that the Foreign Secretary was prepared to give me an exclusive interview in Chevening at teatime that same day. The private secretary advised me to drive myself there. "It would be more discreet," he said.

'As it is the Foreign Secretary to whom MI6 answers, I thought it prudent to conceal my notes in my flat before setting out to Chevening. In view of their importance to agents of the state, I had made photocopies of my material as I gathered it. These I concealed elsewhere in my flat. I then took a taxi to where I keep my car garaged near access to a dual-carriageway and set off for Chevening in a violent rainstorm.'

He described what then took place. He said nothing about his suspicion that the lorry had been hired by MI6, but readers would be bound to wonder about that themselves. By the same token he wrote: 'I understand that my car is too badly damaged for it to be confirmed that my brakes were tampered with.' Most readers would decide that confirmation was unnecessary.

'I am forever in debt to those two brave citizens who risked their lives to save mine. When I came around in a hospital bed after surgery on my crushed leg, I knew I must get hold of my Begova notes. I gave my keys to a friend who then went to my flat. There was no external evidence that my home had been burgled since I left it seven hours before, but my notes had been stolen from where they were hidden. Fortunately, as this article I am writing makes evident, the photocopies were not discovered by the intruder.'

He made no reference to his friendship with the Prime Minister's wife. He believed it irrelevant to what had been done to him. Outside MI6, who would ever know if he was right or wrong?

Late on Sunday morning, the paper's chief lawyer arrived at the hospital. Mark was asleep. Blanche was sitting in his room, writing on a big lined pad.

A shudder passed over the lawyer when he first saw Mark's condition. 'I'm afraid we'll have to wake him,' he said.

Blanche gave the lawyer her chair and perched herself at the foot of the bed. After an hour of legal arguments about inserting 'alleged' here and there, and so forth, Blanche, who had taken no part in the testy conversation, left the room to find a nurse. Two minutes later the nurse came in and said that Mr Fleetwood must be allowed to rest.

Luke returned from Netherby that evening. Blanche had prepared Sunday supper for them as if nothing had happened. She had no intention of telling anyone that Mark had managed to write his bombshell exposé from his hospital bed. Until Monday's paper actually appeared on the streets, she didn't trust Jaspar not to find a way to block it. Conversation with Luke was virtually non-existent.

Late on Sunday evening, the first edition of Monday's paper was packed in lorries for distribution. Mark's editor ran the story across the entire top half of Monday's front page. Jaspar Byatt appeared on Monday morning's *Today* programme.

'There is not a word of truth,' he said condescendingly, 'in Fleetwood's account of this so-called massacre. As for the suggestion that British troops might have witnessed such a thing, could anyone in his right mind imagine that British troops would stand by and do nothing if such a horror was taking place?

'Virtually everything that Fleetwood has written is rubbish. These are the paranoid hallucinations of a bitter journalist, twisted by the realisation that his accident in a rainstorm looks like ending his career.'

In answer to the persistent presenter asking if the Prime Minister could possibly be involved in a cover-up of a war crime of this magnitude, Jaspar replied dismissively: 'This is absurd. The story is fabricated.'

Then, with Jaspar cunning, he added: 'And I would point out to you that you are making yourself foolish by putting these questions to the Prime Minister's spokesman. I have no doubt that if you put them to the relevant minister, the Foreign Secretary, he would give you the same answer that I have.'

By midday, the media were pointing the finger at Stanley Fox.

Chapter Twenty-eight

By one o'clock, reporters and photographers were arriving in Mark's hospital room. The Sister had to go in to tell them he was too ill to give interviews.

'Take your photographs and then you must leave him,' she directed, remaining in the room to make certain they carried out her instructions. She then ordered her staff not to let anyone in without first consulting Mr Fleetwood. 'And he is not to be woken,' she added sternly.

In London, Blanche was on her way to the *Nation* to see her editor. In her bag was the article she had been writing since Saturday, when she had first read Mark's piece in the e-mail she sent to his editor. Her piece corroborated everything he had written. And more.

'Jules,' she began, 'I have a story for you that a week ago I could not have imagined I would ever write.'

'Let's see it.'

As he read it, Jules Barker's naturally florid face deepened to puce. When he finished, he tossed the pages contemptuously across his desk, almost spitting with anger as he said in a voice close to a shout:

'You must be insane to think the *Nation* would ever publish such a piece. It is treasonable. You as good as charge the Prime

Minister and the Foreign Secretary with attempted murder. Just because your boyfriend gave you a few good pokes in bed – no more of those now, I should think – you are prepared to assert that when you confronted your husband, he said that Fleetwood had to be stopped by whatever means, however extreme. You say your husband did not deny that British troops were present during the massacre. Why should he bother to deny anything so far-fetched? You say he did not conceal his involvement in the cover-up. Why should I believe you?

'I shall never be a party to indicting British soldiers for standing by while civilians were massacred. We don't even know if there *was* a massacre.'

Blanche's mounting rage was further heightened when she felt tears of fury prick her eyes. She snatched up her copy and left the room.

On the way back to Downing Street, she had time to think. Before reaching Whitehall, she had her cab drop her near an empty callbox. Using her phonecard, she dialled the *Nation* and asked for the office of the proprietor, Vincent Richmond.

'This is Mrs Blanche Dalton, the Prime Minister's wife. I urgently need to speak to Mr Richmond. Will you put me through, please, to his assistant?'

After a minute a woman's voice came on the line, identifying herself as Mr Richmond's personal assistant.

'It's Blanche Dalton. I hope that Mr Richmond is in London. I need to speak to him today. It's urgent.'

This time she waited several minutes before a harsh voice came on the line. 'It's Vincent Richmond. Nice to hear from you. What can I do for you, Mrs Dalton?'

'Can you see me today? Jules Barker has just turned down a story I have written implicating the Prime Minister in a massive cover-up in Begova. He says it is treasonable. I'd like you to see it and judge.'

After only a short pause Vincent Richmond said: 'Where shall we meet? Normally I would come to you, but under the circumstances I don't imagine Downing Street is a good idea. Nor should you come here.'

'Mark Fleetwood is, as you know, very ill in hospital. He lives in Whitehall Court, and he gave me his keys to collect his notes for his exposé. We could meet in his flat. Unfortunately his entrance to Whitehall Court is behind the National Liberal Club.'

'We'll have to risk that.'

'I'm in a callbox not far from Whitehall. I can be in Mark's flat in a quarter of an hour.'

They had met before, of course. Even so, when Blanche opened the door to Vincent Richmond, she hadn't expected his burliness to crowd the doorway. She gestured to an armchair. He declined coffee. At once she gave him her article and took another armchair while he read, his face impassive. When he had finished, he turned back to the first page and started again. This time when he reached the end, he laid it on the table beside him.

'You are quite sure you want this published?' he said. 'Not only Stanley Fox would have to resign. Your husband would have to resign as well.'

'Would he?' she answered in a toneless voice. 'I thought Jaspar Byatt would keep that from being necessary.'

'For once, even the demon magician would not be able to keep the lid on.'

Blanche put out a hand for her copy. Richmond gave it to her without hesitation, his eyes on her white face. She looked down at the pages as if they had nothing to do with her. When she looked up and met his intent eyes, she handed the pages back to him. He glanced at his watch.

'Do you think Mr Fleetwood would mind if I used his phone?'

He asked for the *Nation*'s deputy editor and was put through instantly.

'I'm not in my office, but I shall be soon. I want you to be there in twenty-five minutes,' Richmond said. He looked at his watch again. 'Do not discuss it with Jules Barker or anyone else. But have it in mind that you'll need to clear the top half of tomorrow's front page. We'll sling the proposed three leaders and have only one. After we meet, it will be clear to you what that should be.'

To Blanche he said: 'Where can you be reached this evening? The lawyers will want to talk with you.'

She looked at him blankly. 'I don't know. It's odd to think this may be our last night at Downing Street,' she said more to herself than to him. 'I don't think I have the gall to see Luke tonight, knowing what will unfold tomorrow. I'll go back to the hospital for a while, and then I will return to this flat for the night. For the first time,' she added.

She wrote down the telephone numbers. He received them with a little bow and with dignity took his leave.

Blanche returned to the hospital to tell Mark the die was cast.

'You told me your house in Lamont Road is let. Where will you live?' he asked.

'I know what you're thinking.'

'I'm going to be here for weeks,' he said, 'possibly months. You could use my flat as long as you liked.'

'I've already decided against it. It might suggest that I betrayed Luke because I wanted to be with you. That is not why I wrote what I did.'

They were quiet for a few minutes. Despite the tremendous rush of adrenaline which had enabled him to write his exposé, Mark remained extremely weak.

'When you come out of hospital,' Blanche said, resting her hand on his uninjured thigh, 'will you invite me around to

Whitehall Court? I feel sure that with a little imagination and enterprise on both our parts, your days as a Don Juan are not over. I've often wondered what it would be like to make love with a one-legged man. As the surgeons are optimistic, I'll probably never find out. But I'd also like to make love to a man with a limp. They've always been attractive to women. Think of Lord Byron.'

A nurse came in to say Blanche was wanted on the phone. It was the chief lawyer of the *Nation*. 'We need to meet to clarify one or two details. Vincent suggested that we do so at Whitehall Court. Can you return there now?'

While she gathered up her things, Mark asked: 'How do you feel about what's going to break loose when the first edition of the *Nation* appears?'

'Sort of numb. I could tell myself that I betrayed Luke because I was so horrified by his admission of what was going on, with his knowledge, in Begova. But I think what propelled me was when he and Stanley Fox tried to kill you. Certainly that's when I first knew consciously that I had to write the piece, whatever the consequences. I think I went into some kind of trance as I did it. In criminal law courts, wives are not compelled to testify against their husbands. And I did it voluntarily. I betrayed my husband voluntarily.' For a moment her voice broke. 'I wish Daddy was here.'

'Do you have the mobile with you that Jaspar Byatt gave you?'

'No.'

'Good. I'm deeply suspicious of anything that has passed through his hands. The mobile I had with me on the way to Chevening is a cinder, but I have a spare one at my flat. The charger's in the study. Use it to make any calls. But don't answer it. Some of my fellow hacks have the number. Downing Street has the number. God knows who else has the number. If I want you, I'll leave a message on the mobile and you can ring me back. The first edition of the *Nation* will come out by ten tonight. From then on, every newspaper and television studio in London will be trying to find you.'

On her way out of the hospital, Blanche used a payphone to ring her secretary. 'Sorry to bother you at home,' she said, 'but I need you to make a call to Downing Street for me. Please say I can't get back to London this evening. I'll phone Jaspar tomorrow.'

It was six when the *Nation*'s chief lawyer left Whitehall Court. Blanche had barely closed the door behind him when she felt so exhausted she had to lie down on the sofa. In a dream a phone was ringing. It stopped and then began again. At the same moment that she struggled out of sleep she realised that the ringing came from Mark's regular phone. She turned on the light to see the time. Ten past ten. The first edition was out. Then the mobile began to ring. Like an anarchic duet, she thought dourly. She got up to make coffee and then prowled around the flat, taking sips until it cooled.

Where should she go? What should she do? Should she telephone *Today* and propose to go on the programme tomorrow morning? Could she handle questions about what Luke had said to her? Perhaps she would only be asked how she could have set out to betray him. Maybe, like Jules Barker, no one would believe her. For unlike Mark, whose exposé had only speculated that British troops must have known the slaughter and mass burials were taking place, Blanche stated categorically in the *Nation* that the Prime Minister had not denied it and had threatened to do anything to keep it from coming out.

She turned off the ringer on the telephone and carried the radio to the kitchen while she made a sandwich, returning to the drawing room where she put on the television as well. At once a picture of herself and Luke filled the screen. With a conscious effort to detach herself, she watched the television and listened to the radio.

When Jaspar's face appeared, she turned down the radio. 'Naturally we have tried to protect Mrs Dalton's fragile health. Ever since a suicide in her family when she was a girl, she has been unstable, given to bouts of depression and destructiveness...'

Blanche switched it off. She saw how the story would be played: 'Unknown to the public until now, the Prime Minister's wife suffers from manic depression.' How often had Luke reminded her of her self-destructiveness after Jakie's suicide? Had it now surfaced again? Was destructiveness towards one long loved the opposite side of the coin?

She went to the drinks cupboard and poured herself a whisky, regretfully adding soda water, for she longed simply to knock herself out. Turning on the television again, she switched between channels, sipping her drink, regarding herself on the screen as if she were a stranger.

The mobile's bleeps remained unanswered, but she checked its messages and phoned back Mark.

'I wish we were together,' he said. 'You are being blackened now, which I suppose was inevitable, but I don't think Downing Street will get away with it this time. There are sleeping pills in the bathroom cabinet. Take two – no more – and try to get some rest at least. I wouldn't go on looking at TV any longer.'

Taking the radio with her to the bedroom, she put it beside the bed, turned low. Sometimes she caught the Dalton name, other times music, all of it indistinct enough to lull her into some kind of sleep. She came back to consciousness with the leaden sky of early morning showing where the curtains did not meet, and the leaden ache of loss. Six-thirty. Turning up the sound a little, she half-listened to the *Today* show, drowsing through the early interviews.

Suddenly she heard Jasper's voice:

'How could Downing Street lie about something of which we have no knowledge? Of course the Prime Minister is not going to resign. His wife's crisis has made him more determined than ever to keep a steady hand on the tiller. He is deeply saddened by what his wife has done, but he will not abandon her and he will not abandon the ship of state at this important time for Britain.'

Was it not curious, asked the presenter, that when two esteemed journalists risked so much to expose the alleged horrifying and disgraceful events in Begova, the Prime Minister's spokesman should proclaim one of them, Mark Fleetwood, to be an embittered liar, and the other, Blanche Dalton, to be mentally unstable? How could such a fact about them not have been observed before?

Ignoring the Fleetwood half of the question, Jaspar replied: 'It says much for the Prime Minister's protectiveness of his wife that until now her frailty remained a private sorrow.'

And if the Prime Minister had no intention of resigning, the presenter pursued, what about his Foreign Secretary? What was it he had to tell Mark Fleetwood so urgently which effectively lured Fleetwood into a car whose brakes, it had now been confirmed by engineering experts, had been tampered with?

'That is a question for the Foreign Secretary,' replied Jaspar haughtily.

'Will the Prime Minister and the Foreign Secretary be suing the *Nation* for libel?' went on the presenter relentlessly.

Blanche switched off the radio. Apart from the faint bleeps of the mobile, the flat was quiet. She wanted to get some coffee, but felt too sick at heart to move. What had she done? How could she possibly return to Downing Street? Where could she go? She couldn't imagine ever stepping out of this haven she was in. She should phone Mavis before the news reached her, but she had no energy. Anyhow, it was still night in Richmond. Time passed. At last she got up to make coffee and check her mobile messages. The *Times* and *Telegraph* editors. Several tabloid editors. Various television programmes. Vincent Richmond. Thaddeus

Spearman. Mark Fleetwood. She would like to speak to
Thaddeus. She had thought of phoning him. But she didn't have
the energy. She looked at her watch – twelve-fifteen – and
returned Mark's call.

'Is your radio or TV on?' he asked, excitement in the usually
detached voice.

'No.'

'Turn them on and leave them on. Stanley Fox has just
resigned.'

'Oh.'

She sounded more drained than stunned.

'BBC Television and Radio Four are on the way here to
interview me for their one o'clock programmes. You and I must
talk after that.'

'I probably won't come to the hospital today. I can't face
seeing anybody on my way to you.'

'You may be right. Just remember that you've been running on
adrenaline for the last few days, and now that you don't need it,
it's dropped into your shoes. You're bound to feel wiped out.'

She turned to the one o'clock news on television and radio so
she could see and hear Mark being interviewed. Both
programmes opened with the same announcement: 'The Prime
Minister has resigned.'

A short statement from his official spokesman said:

'In view of the doubts created by his wife, Luke Dalton feels
his personal integrity has been impinged upon. He has always put
his country before himself. With deep sadness he has decided it
is in Britain's interest that for the present he renounce the
premiership and the leadership of Democratic Labour.'

Chapter Twenty-nine

BLANCHE sat rooted to her chair. She would have no recollection of the next two hours when she was virtually unmoving, in a daze. All at once she became aware of a carriage clock nearby, ticking busily. It was already after three. With a fearful effort, she made herself ring Jaspar, only too aware that the last time she had seen him he had helped her with her difficult column about the *Evening Mail*'s first gossip item on Mark and herself. She and Jaspar had kissed each other's cheek for the first and now the last time.

'It's Blanche. How's Luke?'

'How do you suppose he is?' So constricted with anger was Jaspar's voice that he sounded choked.

'When do we have to leave Downing Street?'

'Tomorrow. Max is going upstairs to the flat shortly to collect a few essentials for Luke. He's leaving later today for Brussels. He wants to start laying the groundwork for his future. There will be plenty of opportunities open to him. He is hugely admired internationally – if not by you.'

'As we let our house in Lamont Road, I can't move our personal possessions back there.'

'That's your problem.' After a pause he added: 'You must be out of your mind.'

'Well, goodbye, Jaspar.'

She rang her secretary, who was still in her office.

'I need you to help me in the flat before the movers come tomorrow. Will you meet me there in an hour? We'll need to organise storage for most of the clothes and personal things like the Eames chair. Will you arrange for me to get in Number Ten's back door? I can imagine only too vividly what it's like outside the front door.'

She gazed blankly at Mark's telephone directories. After a while she took up one and focused on the London hotel section, choosing a residential hotel in Basil Street, where she arranged to stay for an unknown number of days. Soon after, she left Whitehall Court and a taxi took her to the back entrance of Number Ten.

Inevitably she met up with officials scurrying about. Any conversation was restrained on both sides, and brief. Her secretary was waiting in the flat with large empty cartons and labels.

Even though she was not cold, Blanche gave a slight shiver as she glanced around the drawing room.

'It feels as if someone has died,' she said. Her secretary made no response.

They got down to work. Two hours later, both of them done in, the secretary said: 'I think we've accomplished all we can until the movers come tomorrow. I'll be here with them. If there are any problems I'll leave a message at your hotel.'

A taxi was ordered to come to the back door. Soon afterwards, with three suitcases, Blanche departed Number Ten's flat, never, she assumed, to return.

In her room at the Basil Street hotel, she turned on the television with the volume off and collapsed on her bed, too tired even to order coffee. When she woke and glanced at the silent screen, she saw Robert Oakes coming out of the door of

Number Eleven. Jumping up, she turned on the volume:

'The Chancellor of the Exchequer, Robert Oakes, has been summoned to Buckingham Palace.'

Minutes later the black Jaguar turned through the front gates of the palace.

Blanche rang room service to order coffee and a chicken sandwich, and then lay down again, watching the screen and listening to the special news report. There were pictures of Robert's sons and his dead wife, Julie. Then Luke was shown boarding a plane for Brussels. A stab of pain shot through Blanche as she saw how diminished he looked.

'Come in,' she shouted impatiently to the knock on the door, now intent on following events on the screen without interruption. She felt detached about the changeover of power and simultaneously a little empty at finding herself an outsider.

She had just finished her sandwich when the camera zoomed in on a door swinging open at Buckingham Palace. Moments later, Robert Oakes emerged as Prime Minister.

Blanche was happy for Robert. He deserved the job and no one could be better prepared for it. As well as being intellectually the most formidable of her friends, he was possibly the nicest.

She thought of Thaddeus. The phone rang. It *was* Thaddeus.

'Dear girl. How lovely to hear your voice. Shall I tell you something about your friend Thaddeus?'

'*Anything*,' said Blanche. 'I can think of nothing better than to talk about you instead of the Daltons.'

'Ah. Well, I didn't promise that. On Monday morning, minutes after I'd read Mark Fleetwood's exposé, I heard Jaspar on *Today* rubbishing Fleetwood's report as the hallucinations of an embittered journalist. By this time I had guessed that you were the person who had informed Luke of the bombshell that lay ahead. When I listened to Jaspar blackening the man who had nearly been murdered for his enterprise, I said to myself. "This will tilt Blanche over the marital boundary. Luke and Jaspar had better look out." Your piece came out the next day.'

'Oh Thaddeus.'

'We should meet.'

'I didn't have the energy – or the guts – to phone you. How did you track me down so fast?'

'Ah. Call it secrets of a lawyer's trade.'

'May I ring you in a few days after I've caught my breath?'

'So long as you promise to make it sooner rather than later.'

Another knock came at her door. A bellboy handed her a letter delivered by courier. It was from Vincent Richmond: 'May I see you this evening? I could come to your hotel.' She wondered how he had tracked her down so quickly.

As she had a suite, she received him in her sitting room an hour later. He saw the dark circles beneath her eyes.

'I'm disturbing you because I have an offer to make to you,' he began at once. 'What with one thing and another, you may not know that I sacked Jules Barker last night. Would you be prepared to take his job? I'd like you to be the new editor of the *Nation*.'

Blanche's mouth dropped open in astonishment. After a time she said: 'I've never had an editorial job.'

'That's a good reason to start now. You are the woman in everyone's mind, and you will be offered plenty of jobs. No doubt publishers will be on the phone tomorrow offering you a small fortune to write a book on your experiences and disillusionment in Downing Street. I want you at the helm of the *Nation*.'

'May I give you an answer tomorrow?'

As soon as Richmond had left, she rang Mark's room. 'Is the media still mobbing your bed?'

'Things are quiet again.'

'Would it be too late if I came to see you tonight? I've had an offer of a job. I'd like to ask your advice.'

She was just slipping into her coat when the phone rang.

'The Prime Minister is calling Mrs Blanche Dalton.'

For a moment she thought it was Luke. Then Robert's voice came on the line:

'Events overtook our date to have a drink at Number Eleven. I'm still there and must decide whether to stay put and have the new Chancellor move into the flat you know so well at the top of Number Ten. When my sons are home for holidays, I need the extra space at Number Eleven. I wondered, Blanche, if you could come tomorrow for our drink. I'd like to ask your advice.'

No doubt he would. Did she really want to return to all that? Mark was waiting for her. As she thought about that, she felt a familiar thrill. Who could possibly know what the future held for her? She remembered that Whitehall Court, if she seriously considered moving there, was quite conveniently close to Downing Street.

'I'll see you at twelve tomorrow,' she said to Robert, and hung up.